WHISPER OF WAR AND STORMS

C. L. MECCA

B
Boldwood

First published in Great Britain in 2025 by Boldwood Books Ltd.

Copyright © C. L. Mecca, 2025

Cover Design by Jane Dixon-Smith

Cover Images: Shutterstock

A CIP catalogue record for this book is available from the British Library.

Paperback ISBN 978-1-83656-287-0

Large Print ISBN 978-1-83656-286-3

Hardback ISBN 978-1-83656-285-6

Ebook ISBN 978-1-83656-288-7

Kindle ISBN 978-1-83656-289-4

Audio CD ISBN 978-1-83656-280-1

MP3 CD ISBN 978-1-83656-281-8

Digital audio download ISBN 978-1-83656-284-9

This book is printed on certified sustainable paper. Boldwood Books is dedicated to putting sustainability at the heart of our business. For more information please visit https://www.boldwoodbooks.com/about-us/sustainability/

Boldwood Books Ltd, 23 Bowerdean Street, London, SW6 3TN

www.boldwoodbooks.com

To the strength in my storms and first whisper of resilience I ever knew. Thank you, Mom.

1

MEV

York, England

"I think I'm in love."

"Not again?" Clara asked. I could sense her eyes rolling even though I was too awe-struck by our surroundings to look at her.

As we walked from our hotel over the bridge into the city, I tried to take in everything at once. Remnants of the wall. The hustle and bustle of a swelling Saturday morning crowd, something we'd been warned about. Apparently lots of people were also in love with York.

"Can't help it," I half-heartedly defended myself. "Look at this place. It's like we stepped into a medieval village."

"Imagine that." My friend was almost never without her ever-present companion, sarcasm. When we first met in college, I could never tell when she was being serious, but after ten years of friendship, I knew her pretty well.

Clara opened the map the hotel concierge gave us. "York's medieval streets and buildings are beautifully preserved in the historic heart of the city. Strange it looks so"—she paused for dramatic effect—"medieval."

Laughing, I looked down at my hand for the millionth time since Mom gave me the unusual sapphire ring. "I still can't believe we're here," I mused out loud, nearly crashing into a passerby. "Sorry," I mumbled as Clara pulled the strap of my crossbody toward her, saving me from a swarm of bridesmaids.

"They don't just drive on the left," she said.

"Right. Of course." I turned back to see the bride in the center with white T-shirt and veil. "That driver wasn't kidding about the abundance of bachelorette parties... what did he call them?"

"Hen parties." Clara stopped on the corner. "I imagine it will only get worse as the day goes on. There's another one."

I followed her finger to another large group of ladies across the street. "This is where I want my bachelorette party." Despite the fact that we were only a few steps into the city, it felt as if I'd been here before. As if it were calling to me, welcoming me home. Maybe because York reminded me of Boston a bit. Or maybe because I'd been anticipating this trip more than any I'd ever taken. Either way, I was smitten.

"Right." Clara looked up and down from the map. Knowing I was crap at navigation, she attempted to get us around the city. "Maybe get engaged first," she said absent-mindedly, turning around to orient herself.

"I'd need a boyfriend for that." I peered into a place called Betty's Tea Rooms. "If we find it, maybe we can come back here for afternoon tea?"

"Do you have any idea how many pubs are in York? I'm pretty sure we won't be having tea today. Let's start this way."

Before we took off, I stopped her. "Wait." Clara turned

toward me. "I'm serious about us making time for tourist stuff too. And for work, of course. This isn't just about me."

The last thing I wanted was for Clara to spend the next five days helping me exclusively. It was enough that she agreed to hop on a plane across the Atlantic with less than two months' notice, and I was grateful for her company. But she had a job to do as well.

"Every second we're here, I'm working. Mentally cataloging. I'll get some pictures at some point, promise. But today is for you. So stop being silly and let's get started. This way to the Shambles."

Less than ten minutes later, we'd found the Ye Old Shambles Tavern and, despite the fact that it seemed to be a dead end, Clara and I stayed for lunch. We hadn't eaten yet, having flown overnight and arrived in York only an hour ago.

"I don't know how you can eat that with the skin on it."

In response, Clara took a huge bite of her fish, totally unrepentant. Sticking to my very safe steak pie, I looked around the place. "Two historians. You'd think we could have figured out this wasn't our place without having to ask the owner. I'm pretty sure he thought we were nuts."

"At least I have an excuse." Clara gestured to herself. "Not a practicing historian anymore."

"Technically not, but you still kicked my ass in Historian's Craft."

"This is true. And speaking of the ladies' room, I'll be right back."

"Loo," I called after her, accustomed to Clara's quick change of topics.

As I ate, my mind wandered to that class in our first semester at Boston U. Neither of us had a life plan at the time, and except for our mutual interest in history, Clara and I had no clue what we wanted to do with our lives. I somehow ended up as a museum curator specializing in ancient artifacts, and Clara, a travel writer and photographer. I loved aspects of my job, but I was sometimes wistful hearing about my friend's many adventures traveling the world while I worked in a dusty old office.

But who was I to complain?

I had a mother who adored me, a trustworthy circle of friends, and enough money in the bank to come here on a whim. I peered at my ring again.

Not a whim. A fool's errand.

"Mom? What's this?"

"Mevlida, where did you get that?"

Mom never used my full name unless it was serious. I picked up the small box that contained a silver ring with the brightest, most beautiful blue sapphire I'd ever seen and held it out to her. "I know I shouldn't have opened it. I found it looking for the silver purse you said I could borrow for next weekend's wedding."

My mother looked as if she'd seen a ghost. Taking the box, she opened it. I already knew what was inside. A single black and white photo of her standing in front of a pub, pregnant. Staring at the photo, she looked so sad that I regretted my intrusion even if I'd just been looking for answers.

Instead of putting the ring back and apologizing, though, I pressed her.

"I know you don't remember anything, but you must know where that is?" I asked, the nondescript buildings behind us giving no clues. "And you never told me there was a ring. Mom, please—"

"Take it," she said, handing the box back. "You can have them both."

"I don't want it. I want answers. Please, just tell me—"

"Mevlida." There it was again. I knew from her tone I would be

getting the same response as always. "I don't want to discuss it. As I've said many times, I simply don't remember what happened."

"I know that," I said. As unlikely as it seemed, my mother had traveled to York having been told it was the place to go for psychics wanting to perfect their craft. She remembered getting there, meeting a few people and then... nothing. According to my mother, she wandered from a darkened pub in the middle of the night onto the street with no memory of how she'd gotten there. And worse, as she discovered after making her way back home, with no memory of the man who had apparently gotten her pregnant. Obviously, she'd been drugged, but Mom always refused to talk about it. She had never gone back to York, looking for answers. "But you never told me there was a picture. And the ring?"

"Some questions—"

This time, I cut her off, already knowing the rest of that refrain. "Are better left unanswered."

"You're staring at it again." Clara sat back down.

"I can't help it." As I looked up, the same determination I'd felt the day I discovered the box flooded through me. Even if Mom couldn't remember, or simply refused to share, the name of the pub in the photo, I would find it. And answers about my past.

"It really is beautiful."

Thick like a class ring with strange symbols encircling the bright blue stone, its silver shone brighter than any other silver I'd ever seen. But its mysteries remained a secret, none of the symbols showing up in any database I'd come across.

Taking a sip of ale, I met Clara's eyes over the brim of my pint glass.

"I know that look," she teased. "We're going to figure this out."

"Yes," I said, as determined as ever. "Yes, we are."

2

KAEL

Gyorian Midlands, Elydor

"Again," I shouted, the warriors before me thinking they were nearly finished.

I knew better. They had just gotten started.

The sound of steel clanging mingled with flutters from a flock of glintwing finches. I hadn't heard the sound in many months. As I looked upward, shimmers of green and gold flew past. Many believed the glintwing finch to be a sign of hope and resilience, and though I didn't put stock in such signs, I understood why others believed as much. Their appearance meant spring was coming.

"Haven't you pushed them hard enough today?"

Though I heard my friend coming from behind, I didn't acknowledge his question. Adren knew the answer already.

"It was a freak accident. Their lack of training was not to blame."

"My father believes otherwise."

"Your father is a stubborn fool."

Sighing, I raised a fist into the air. Almost instantaneously, the sparring ceased. "Change partners," I called out, watching closely for any sign of complaint. Thankfully, there were none.

"You speak of the king," I reminded Adren, though my tone lacked the heat it should have, given it was my father I weakly defended.

"The king, and a man too consumed with hate to see clearly. But," he continued quickly before I could respond, "that's a discussion for another day."

I raised my brows, surprised Adren was giving up so easily. Though the warrior had centuries on me, he was still younger than my father. With his imposing height and muscular build, he could easily match the king in hand-to-hand combat. The latter, however, could easily take Adren down with magic. It was the reason Balthor had been king for many years. None could wield land magic as he could.

None could even come close.

"Spring is coming," I said, changing the subject. I had little desire to discuss the border skirmish that had left a Gyorian warrior dead. He'd fallen on a wooden spike that had pierced his heart, an "accident" as Adren said. But it had happened in battle, which meant the Aetherians were to blame.

"I was just with your brother who said the very same thing."

I wasn't surprised. Unlike me, Terran did believe in signs. To him, everything was a sign.

"Did he mention the Summit?"

Watching two particular men, I tried to discern why one continued to be disarmed. A skilled swordsman, he moved with grace and precision, his footwork impeccable and his strikes powerful. Yet, time and again, his opponent managed to knock the sword from his grip. As I observed more closely, I noticed a subtle tell—a slight tensing of his sword arm just before each disarming blow. His skill was betrayed by this unconscious signal, a weakness his opponent had instinctively learned to exploit.

Realizing Adren hadn't answered, I looked at him. Dressed in typical Gyorian fashion—a knee-length tunic and fitted trousers tucked into his leather boots—he didn't appear to be suited for training. Instead of asking about it, however, I continued to wait for his answer.

When it didn't come, I cursed. If Terran wasn't attending the Summit, that responsibility would fall on me. "Gods be damned."

"Terran claims to be needed here."

"For what?" I asked, not bothering to hide my irritation.

"He did not say."

Also typical of Terran. I loved my brother, but the air of mystery he created around himself, whether on purpose or by design—I could not discern which—frustrated me more with each passing day.

"If I go up there now, after what happened... Adren, you best not be smiling. This is not a jesting matter. Maybe you'd enjoy accompanying me on a journey north."

Adren pursed his lips together, no longer smiling at the prospect of me having to travel to Aetheria. Apparently my friend wanted to spar. I drew my sword from its sheath. "No magic."

This time, he didn't hide his smile. Adren unsheathed his sword. "No magic," he confirmed.

At the first strike, the sounds of the other men's swords diminished. At the second, they ceased altogether. All of the Gyorian warriors would be watching us, the prince and his right-hand man, two of the most celebrated swordsmen in our clan, if not all of Elydor. As I circled and struck, Adren easily blocking me, I wondered why we hadn't done this earlier as a way to ease my frustrations.

Since the attack, a rising sense of dread and anger had welled inside me. I was no longer to rule over Gyoria, nor did I want such a position. My brother was much better suited to the honor. But neither could I sit idly by while Father continued to turn his hate to the humans rather than the Aetherians who had killed one of my warriors. Had killed more Gyorians these past years than any humans since they first arrived in Elydor more than five hundred years ago. Yet the same man with no mercy for one kingdom preached temperance when it came to the other.

As cheers erupted around us, I blocked them out. Adren was one of my fiercest opponents and could easily outmatch me if I became complacent or lost focus.

"Prince Kael. Prince Kael." The chorus of cheers grew. "Adren. Ad-ren."

I was glad to hear my friend's name being chanted. He deserved every accolade, even as I laid him on the ground. It was a move my father had shown me many moons ago and one I'd never used on Adren, until now, which was what took him unawares. He'd expected a blow from my sword, not a sweep of my foot to his ankle.

Slaps on the back and my men cheering all around me improved my mood slightly. I held out my hand. Adren took it and bounded to his feet with a bow.

"As you are the victor, I do not deserve a boon, but I will ask for one anyway." He grinned. I knew before he spoke it what Adren would say. "Call an end to their training."

And this was why they adored him so. He pretended to be just another of my men when we all knew Adren held as esteemed a position in the Gyorian court as my closest advisor.

I sheathed my sword and considered how to respond. Spring was coming, which meant I should be able to...

With a wave of my hand, I covered the training field in flowers of every variety and color I could think of. Those who'd heard Adren's request had my answer, and those who hadn't soon learned the reason for the temporary bloom. As they fled the training yard, I watched as the flowers already began to wither. It was too soon for them to remain, the weather still not having broken completely just yet.

"A nice trick," Adren said, watching them fade with me.

"Those," I said, indicating the field before us, "or my move that gave you a view of the heavens."

"Both."

It wasn't long before all the flowers I'd summoned were gone.

"When do I leave?" I asked him finally, knowing his message was the reason he'd sought me out.

"Immediately." Adren tossed his hands in the air at my sharp look. "I am merely the messenger," he said. "I can come with you."

"No, you stay here with the men. One Gyorian subjected to Aetheria is enough."

I didn't blame Adren for his look of relief. Even when we were at relative peace, the journey was not a pleasant one. With few exceptions, Gyorians remained in Gyoria. Aetherians, in Aetheria. The humans in Estmere and the Thalassari in Thalassaria.

Peacekeeping summit, indeed. There could be no peace in Elydor. Not any longer.

Not after all that had happened.

3

MEV

"It's absolutely beautiful," Clara said as we walked away from the church.

I agreed wholeheartedly. But the feeling in the pit of my stomach distracted me from fully enjoying the beauty of York Minster. After two days of searching, we'd come up blank. Insisting on taking a break from our York pub crawl, we hit the Viking museum earlier and now the centerpiece of this amazing city. And it *was* beautiful, yet...

"Mev?"

I'd been staring at the ring again.

"Sorry," I said, meeting Clara's gaze. "I knew it was a long shot but..."

"But you were hopeful. We still have a few days. Don't lose hope just yet."

I wasn't usually one for pity parties and liked to think positively, but it was getting hard to keep my hopes up. Mom had always said everything from the time she went into the pub to leaving it in the middle of the night was a blank, but how could she not remember going there in the first place? I supposed it was a trauma response, though I was no psychologist. "We've been to the oldest pubs and every single building in the Shambles. I don't even know where to try next."

Clara pulled out the map from our hotel. I couldn't resist a smile. "Look at you, old school."

"I like this thing better than my phone." She lifted it up for me to see. "Look at the cute little pictures."

Clara was trying to cheer me up, and it was working. "I saw them. Very cute."

With her head back in the map, I thought about the strategy the museum director and I came up with. He was the one that identified the building in the photo as a tavern, courtesy of the few words we could make out on the glass window and my boss being an expert in European architecture. That's when I decided to come here, to find answers for myself.

I hated lying to her. Mom thought I was in Italy, accompanying Clara for work. Something told me that if I'd admitted we were coming to England, to York, she'd have tried to talk me out of it. And my mother could be very convincing... almost as convincing as I was determined to get to the bottom of her time in England.

"So maybe we grid it," I said, "starting from the bridge closest to the hotel."

"Or we go with cool names first. Look at this one. House of the Trembling Madness. Who wouldn't want to visit that place?"

At this point, with our best leads behind us, it didn't really matter to me. I was just grateful not to be doing this alone. "Cool names it is. Which way?"

As expected, House of the Trembling Madness was as cool as its name, the second-floor pub small but eclectic with high wooden beams and a cozy old-world atmosphere. Unfortunately, the bartenders had no idea where the picture was taken but were "pretty sure" it wasn't their place. Back on the street, and starting to get hungry, I was about to ask Clara if she wanted to find food when a sign across the street caught my eye.

Digging out the photo, I held it up.

"What are you thinking?" Clara asked, following my gaze.

"I don't know. There's something about that place but... I don't think it's the one."

She shrugged. "Maybe not, but The Crooked Key is a pretty cool name so, onward," she said, heading across the street without waiting for me.

A wooden sign with a key hung above an otherwise nondescript Tudor-style building. We walked into the front room, its wooden tables mostly full. Seeing the bar in a back room, I headed right to the bartender, our modus operandi firmly in place.

When it was our turn to be served, I asked the young woman, whose tattooed arms held very little uninked skin, if she recognized the building in the photo.

"We're pretty sure it's a pub, based on the windows and architecture."

She looked at the photo and, as everyone had done before her, shook her head. "Sorry, I'm not sure where that is. But it's definitely not this place."

My shoulders slumped. "We didn't think so, but maybe with renovations or something, you never know."

The bartender laughed. "This place hasn't been renovated, ever. Maybe a fresh coat of paint and some new wiring, but otherwise, the owner is pretty strict about keeping things as is. We're the oldest pub in York."

"My map says the Ye Olde Starre Inne is the oldest," Clara said beside me.

"Semantics. Their building dates back to the 1550s but it wasn't a pub until 1644. We're the oldest continuing running pub, even older than The Black Swan which was actually a pub before Starre Inne."

Semantics indeed. Seemed like being the "oldest pub in York" was a popular claim, which I understood given the marketing angle. "You mentioned the owner. Is he or she around by any chance? I'd love to have them take a look at this."

"Sorry, not at the moment." The bartender looked behind us to where a line had begun to form.

"Should we grab a bite here?" I asked Clara, my mouth watering as the smell of fish and chips wafted by me. I found the culprit immediately.

"Sure. Two orders of fish and chips and two pints of Beavertown Pale Ale, please," she ordered.

We sat at the only open table near the bar with our drinks. "I guess you saw me staring at the food?"

Clara laughed. "You weren't subtle."

As we waited for our meals, I took out my phone and logged the visit. The Crooked Key, no owner. If we had time before leaving York, I figured we could backtrack anywhere we hadn't been able to speak to the pubs' owners.

Putting down my phone, I glanced around the room. "Why is that guy sitting on a toilet?"

Clara turned to the table in question, one of the seats an old-fashioned toilet. "Um, no idea. That's the strangest seat I've ever seen."

"It is an odd place, isn't it?"

Nothing seemed to match. The Crooked Key was as

eclectic as it was old. In some ways, it was my favorite pub so far.

"That's interesting." Clara was pointing toward the bar behind me. I spun around in my seat. She wasn't pointing to the bar at all but a chalkboard beside it. I read the words aloud. "Welcome, travelers from afar. Within these walls lies the legacy of ancient journeys and hidden realms. Those who seek the truth of the mysteries beyond know history and magic intertwine here. Inquire within."

A chill ran up my spine as I finished reading. History and magic. I took a course in college exploring both and knew, at one time, that magic was believed to be the source of much unexplained phenomena.

"Cool." I thought Clara was talking about the chalkboard message until I turned back to see her staring at our meals. That was quick. "Thanks so much," she said to the waiter and then, "Cheers," to me.

Laughing at her liberal use of "cheers" since we'd stepped foot in England, I filled my stomach, unable to shake the chalkboard message from my head, even when Clara declared it was time to hit the next pub.

"Ready?"

Oddly, I wasn't. "Let me just check one thing first." Heading back to the bar, I asked one last question. "Do you know anything about that message?"

The bartender peered at the board. "Only that it's been the same message since I started. No one is allowed to touch it. Supposedly it's been there for years. Excuse me," she said, serving the man beside me.

It's been there for years.

Part of me wanted to head back to Clara and continue our search. But the curious part of me, the one that simply couldn't stop asking questions, won out. "Do you know who might have more insight about it?" I asked, nodding toward the board.

"The owner," she said, unceremoniously. I was definitely pushing my luck.

"Any idea when they might be available?"

"Can I help you?"

Somehow, I knew the voice at my back was the person we were discussing. Turning, a stout man, probably around fifty, looked at me as the bartender said, "Jon, she was asking about the chalkboard message."

I suddenly felt like a complete idiot. "I was just curious about it," I said, trying to catch Clara's attention. The picture was on our table.

"It's been up there for years," he confirmed, moving closer to the board. "No idea what it means."

"Why keep it up, then?"

If he was annoyed by my question, Jon didn't let on. "Not sure, to be honest. Superstition, I guess."

As he spoke, I re-read the words. And blinked.

Forgetting all about Jon and having Clara fetch the picture, I moved closer. It was too small to have noticed from our table, but just after the last word 'within' there was a tiny symbol. My heart raced.

I moved closer.

Staring back at me, a circle. Inside, a swirling pattern resembling wind with a small feather at its center.

My fingers fumbled to get the ring off my finger. Hands shaking, I turned it around, already knowing what I would find engraved inside. In the few months since discovering it, I'd dissected, researched, and memorized every facet of this ring.

"What is it?" Clara asked, now standing beside me. Turning to see The Crooked Key's owner watching me, I told them both. "That symbol is on my ring."

"Get out?" Clara moved closed to the board to have a look.

"Impossible." Jon said what I'd been thinking. As our eyes met, I noticed a suspicion there which hadn't been present a few seconds ago. "May I?" he asked, holding out his hand.

Reluctant to part with the ring, I reminded myself this was the very reason Clara and I had traveled across a damn ocean. For answers. I handed the ring to him, dropping it in his hand. Inspecting the stone and then turning it upside down, Jon looked between it and his chalkboard.

"Where did you get this?" he asked.

This time, there was no doubt. He was suspicious of me for some reason. Not caring for his tone, I asked for my ring back. "My mother gave it to me," I said defensively.

His eyes narrowed. "Your mother?"

Clara poked my side, shoving the photo into my hands. I showed it to him. "My mother," I said as he took it. "That's her, almost thirty years ago. I came here looking for answers because Mom doesn't remember a lot of what happened on that visit. And some of it is kind of important."

He didn't say a word.

Instead, Jon stared at the picture and then finally, after what felt like ages, he raised his head. Something was wrong. Very, very wrong.

"Are you okay?" I asked, forgetting that he'd all but accused me of stealing the ring. At least, that was how it had felt to me.

"What's your name?"

Again, no preamble. Blunt. To the point. But I supposed there was no harm in answering. "Mev."

Jon closed his eyes. Clara and I exchanged a glance. Everything about the encounter was strange and becoming stranger by the minute. Not to mention that symbol, which I'd not been able to find anywhere online, in any database, and which didn't seem to exist except on my ring.

And on that chalkboard.

Jon opened his eyes. "Short for Mevlida?"

"Holy shit," Clara muttered beside me.

I suddenly felt faint.

"Yes," Clara said when I didn't answer. "Mevlida Harper."

He took a deep breath. Exhaled. Looked me straight in the eyes. "Your mother was here."

And there it was. The confirmation I'd been waiting for since stepping onto the plane, hoping against hope one old picture could fill in some of my mother's blanks.

Before I could say anything, he added, "I'm sorry, I can't help you."

No. No, no, no. This was not happening. "Please don't do this. I've spent an entire lifetime not knowing about my mother's time here. What happened to her. Who got her pregnant. Why she doesn't remember anything. This picture, this ring, are the only things I have that tie me to her time here."

"Is your mother still alive?" he asked kindly, Jon's suspicions seemingly gone, if not his reluctance to help me.

"She is."

"I'm sorry—"

"Please," Clara begged. "Her mother doesn't remember even being with a man here. Nothing. When Mev found that photo and ring a few months ago, it was the first clue she's ever had to filling in the big gaping holes that have put my poor friend in therapy." Clara shot me a "sorry for revealing that, but we're desperate" look. "We visited nearly every pub in York looking for answers, and obviously you know something. Please."

People were looking at us now, the bartender included, but I didn't care. Wanting to simultaneously hug Clara and pound Jon on the chest, I did neither. It was like I couldn't move, or speak, my big moment of discovery followed quickly by the sort of frustration that had eaten me alive since I was old enough to ask about my dad.

"Please," I begged. "Please tell me what you know."

"You're not going to believe me," he said. Jon walked over to the bartender. "Basement key, please?"

The tattooed woman looked as surprised as Jon had been when I showed him my ring. I guessed the basement wasn't used much. Without a word, she reached under the bar and produced a very old-looking key.

"Come with me," he said, heading toward a door down two steps I'd spotted earlier on the other side of the bar. Clara ran back to the table to grab our stuff and re-joined us just as Jon opened it. Before heading through, he turned to look at me one last time.

"You're certain you want to know? Some questions are better left unanswered."

A refrain I'd heard from my mother a thousand times. One that only strengthened my resolve. Then, remembering the words on the board, I quoted them. "I seek the mysteries beyond and am officially enquiring within."

For the first time since seeing my ring, Jon smiled. "Right then. Let's crack on."

We followed him through the door.

4

KAEL

As thick forests gave way to open meadows, the chill that had begun to wear off in Gyoria returned more each day as I rode north. Stormbreaker navigated the trails easily, my horse having been trained in the mountains of Aetheria. Though the magic that coursed through every fiber of our world ran through its creatures too, making their lifespan longer than in the human realm, Elydor's animals were not immortal. So it was that Stormbreaker was nearly thirty years old and stronger than ever.

Ahead were the towering trees of Limina, their leaves shimmering with an ethereal glow as dusk settled. The border village was unique in many ways, the most striking being that its people welcomed me despite the fact that I was the son of their enemy. Though this route would add two days onto my journey to Aethralis for another useless peacekeeping summit, a hot meal and a bed would be a welcome respite from sleeping under the stars.

Slowing to a stop, I dismounted and knelt to the ground. Laying a hand over the grass, still green despite a harsh winter,

I felt the tell-tale vibrations and waited. Sure enough, a few moments later, two riders burst through the tall trees, only stopping when they were so close I could see their faces.

"Prince Kael," Caius, along with his partner beside him, greeted me as all Aetherian did, despite station, with a slight bow of his head.

"Caius. Laina." I greeted the pair in the Gyorian way, with a fist to my heart.

"You are on your way to the Summit?" Laina asked.

"I am."

I rode beside them, and we wove our way through the trees, deeper into Limina. Soon enough, cobblestone streets and ivory-covered cottages came into view.

"I trust you've been untouched by the recent skirmishes?" I asked.

"Skirmishes." Caius made a sound of clear displeasure. "An attack, as we were told."

"Nay," Laina added quickly, giving her partner a sharp look. "We were not touched."

Despite its position so close to the Gyoria/Aetheria border, Limina remained out of the fighting. Since I saved the life of the elder's daughter ten years ago, Limina declared they would no longer fight Gyorians which, of course, did not endear them to their fellow Aetherians. As the years passed, their neutrality became a beacon for travelers from both clans, and the animosity they received from Aetherians lessened. Now, it was simply accepted, Limina remaining one of the few places in Elydor that was a safe haven for all.

"Good," I said as we rode toward the sacred grove at the heart of Limina. All travelers were required to visit the spot, to give thanks for a safe arrival from wherever they originated, before seeking out their final destination. "I worried. The fighting was too close to your borders for my taste."

"That any Gyorian," Laina said, "would care for our safety, especially its prince, still surprises me, even after so many years."

"Kael is not any Gyorian," Caius argued. "He wishes for peace."

I raised my brows. "You do not believe most Gyorians wish for peace?"

His cleared throat was no answer. I looked at Laina who shrugged, apparently not wishing to jump into the conversation she herself had started.

"Caius?" I prompted as we arrived at the grove. The same shimmering leaves on the trees around us were found on the smaller ones at the center of the grove. No matter how many times I came here, the sight was one to behold. Some believed the lighted grove of Limina was one of the most beautiful sights in Elydor. That accolade I reserved for another place, but I could admit its beauty was mostly unparalleled.

"I would not disparage your father or those who think as he does," Caius said, dismounting.

"Yet you just did," I pointed out.

"Unintentionally."

"Mmmm." I let the matter drop. Arguing with him would serve no one. Besides, he was not entirely wrong. Though my father claimed he wished for peace as well as anyone, insisting on my representation of Gyoria at the Summit, his actions had certainly not endeared him or Gyoria to the Aetherians or the humans. Only a fool would argue otherwise.

Laina dismounted beside me. "I will tell my mother of your arrival."

"Thank you," I said, walking up to the grove and giving my

silent thanks. When I turned back, though Laina was gone, Caius remained. I'd known the man for many years and could sense something was on his mind.

"What is it?" I asked, leading Stormbreaker toward the stream that ran through the center of the village.

"These attacks... skirmishes... call them what you will, are becoming more and more frequent. And deadly."

"Indeed." I could not argue with him on that point, though my head had cooled significantly in the past few days. "We lost a good man, needlessly."

"Will you seek retribution?"

I watched as Stormbreaker leaned into the stream, the water level too low for him. With a wave of my hand, I moved a rock into place so that he could get closer. Even so, it was still a stretch for him. In response, Caius blew a wave of wind that propelled the water downstream, raising its level just enough for Stormbreaker to comfortably drink.

"Thank you," I said. "I am tempted to, aye. But know it will do little to temper the ever-increasing tensions at the border."

"Perhaps this Summit will prove to be more fruitful than the others."

"Doubtful."

Caius sighed. "If Gyoria and Aetheria can come to terms, the others will fall into place. We are proof such a thing is possible."

"We've had this discussion many times. You know as well as I, King Galfrid will never forgive my father, nor would he even accept such an offering. If they refuse to come to any peaceful terms, what chance does either clan have of doing the same?"

"You do not think peace possible?"

"No," I said, my answer immediate and final. "I do not."

Caius stared into the water as it rushed by. When Storm-breaker finished drinking, he waved his hand once more to stop the rush of wind he'd created. The stream's water level lowered once again.

"Why even attend, then?"

That Caius was frustrated, angry even, could not be helped. I'd not lie to a man who had shown me nothing but kindness throughout the years. "My father wills it. The one"— I could not resist a smile—"who does not wish for peace."

Caius didn't share my smile, but he did roll his eyes. I had no desire to fight him, or any in Limina. In a few days' time, I would be doing my share of fighting in the heart of our enemy's kingdom.

"I suppose you'll be wanting a hot meal and a bed?"

"In that order," I responded. "If it pleases you."

"It might please them even more." He waved a hand toward the gathering crowd, consisting mostly of women. Unpartnered women. Aetherian women who didn't seem to care that I was Gyorian. Or a Gyorian prince, for that matter.

One, in particular, caught my eye.

"If you can make that bed big enough for two, I would be grateful."

At that, Caius laughed, his good humor, it seemed, restored. For now.

5

MEV

As we walked into a small storage room, Clara gave me a "you realize this is creepy as fuck" look, and I couldn't disagree. But the fact was, as Jon pulled a string and illuminated the dusty old room, I had no choice but to explore this. The matching symbol. Jon's expression at seeing the underside of my ring. Those were real, even if it felt like a dream.

"Sorry for all the dust," he said. "Let me clear these off."

"I'm a museum curator," I told him as we helped wipe off old wooden crates and sat. Besides those and some boxes, the room was unremarkable if not thick with the scent of musky wood and faint herbs and spices. "I'm used to a little dust."

"A museum curator, huh?"

"Specializing in ancient artifacts," Clara tossed in, as if it mattered. It didn't. Nothing mattered except whatever Jon was about to tell us.

"Which is why," I said, the ring still in my hand, "this has been so frustrating. I should have been able to glean at least some information about it, but it proved to be a total dead end."

"Until now," he reminded me.

"Until now," I agreed, glad Jon had decided to finally help me. Willing him to get to his story, I didn't say anything more. I didn't want to talk about my job, and he seemed to sense my impatience.

"The reason you didn't find any clues is because..." He looked from me to Clara and then back again. If I didn't know any better, I'd think the pub owner was nervous. "That ring isn't from our world."

"Wait? What?" Clara screwed her face up, looking at Jon as if he were crazy.

"Excuse me?" I wasn't sure I'd heard him right either.

"This is going to sound bonkers, but please bear with me. Though I do think it's your mother's story to tell."

"She can't. My mother remembers nothing about her time here."

Jon seemed puzzled. "You meant that literally?"

"Quite literally. She remembers traveling to York, the apartment she rented, and her first few days here. But nothing else, except being in a pub, making her way out and into the streets in the middle of the night, and eventually finding her way back to the apartment and home to Boston."

"Hmm. He must have somehow erased her memory. I don't think that's common, but certainly possible," Jon muttered.

"Who's he? Do you know who drugged her?"

Looking up, as if seeing me clearly again, Jon shook his head. "Your mother wasn't drugged. We are not alone. There's another world out there. The portal to it, to Elydor, is behind me."

Clara stood up. "Mev, we really should—"

"I'm staying," I said, as firmly as I'd ever spoken to my friend. Sympathetic to her fear—Clara appeared decidedly pale all of a sudden—I nevertheless was going to hear him out. Even if it was clear Jon the pub owner was cuckoo for Cocoa Puffs.

"Then I'm staying too," she said, sitting back down. "No way I'm leaving you here alone."

If Jon was offended by Clara's insinuation, he didn't let on. In fact, he seemed more worried than anything. If anyone should be worried, it was Clara and me, sitting in an empty storage room with a mad man. At least the bartender knew we were in here.

"I'll start from the beginning. You can believe me, or not. But you asked, so here goes. This pub, once a tavern and inn, has been in my family for generations. It's original owner, Edwin Harrow, opened it up in the thirteenth century."

I thought quickly. York was a Roman city eventually settled by Angles, important to the Northumbrian kings. It went through a Viking period thanks to the "Great Heathen Army" and was later substantially damaged during William the Conqueror's time. But it thrived during the Middle Ages, the Shambles evidence of the fact with some of those streets still surviving to this day. So a tavern in the late thirteenth century was possible.

"It was his son, Richard Harrow, who was proprietor where our story begins."

"I really can't wait to hear this," Clara said, her disbelief evident.

Jon didn't even acknowledge her and kept going. "As the story goes, he was carrying a grain sack past that very door"— he motioned to the door we'd used to come into the storage room—"when your father came through."

"My father," I repeated, "came through a portal? From another world?"

Jon nodded. "Back then, the Elydorians didn't bother disguising their appearance, and apparently Richard was in for quite a shock. Imagine seeing an extremely tall man with long white hair wearing blue and silver robes with thread that appeared to glow, walk through a wall."

"Yeah, I can't," Clara said, her tone bordering on hostile now.

"King Galfrid was as surprised as anyone, too. He told me the story once. It's one of his favorites."

Now it was my turn to voice more than a little disbelief. "I'm sorry. Did you say, king?"

"Yes. Your father is one of the most powerful men in Elydor, the King of Aetheria."

Clara laughed. "I really do think we have to get going."

I gave her a look. "That symbol was on my ring," I reminded her.

"Sure," she said. "But I'm not sure if you heard the first part of the story. He's saying your father, the king of some strange-ass realm, walked through that wall"—her voice raised as she talked—"*and* lived in the thirteenth century. But is your father. Think about that."

I had, already, and didn't disagree with her. Turning back to Jon for an explanation, I raised my brows.

"He's immortal."

Clara laughed again, and this time I was tempted to join her. Except, any amusement I might have felt was tamped down by a crushing disappointment. I'd actually thought, for a second, we were onto something.

"Everyone in Elydor is immortal, though they can be killed. Anyway," he continued, as if telling us about the latest England football match, "after trying to open that portal for centuries, King Galfrid finally did it."

"This is insane."

"There's a lot more story to tell, but bottom line... the portal between Elydor and our world remained open for hundreds of years. The pub, and its secrets, were passed down from generation to generation of Harrows, though I'll be the last one to have seen it open. My kids know the story, but both were babies when it closed."

"Closed?" I asked, despite myself. Clearly this man had a few marbles loose, but I was invested in his tale, nonetheless.

"Your mother came through, after she married your father, and asked that I send a letter to the States, telling some relative she was safe but would not be returning. I didn't see her again after that, but from others that came through, I did learn she was pregnant with a baby girl, and that the new princess would be named Mevlida. I can only imagine how they knew the baby was a girl, even though you weren't born, but didn't ask. There were more pressing matters to talk about, namely rumors that the Gyorian king wanted to close the portal."

"Hold on. You're saying Mev's mother was married to a king? In this other realm?" Clara's incredulous expression was absolutely priceless. Yet she was asking questions anyway. I, for one, couldn't speak.

"She was. Your mother was the Queen of Aetheria. She came here, looking for the portal, and found it. The Crooked Key, back in the day, was a haven for those with any sort of intuitive abilities. Over the years, whispers of another realm brought curious visitors, some with actual abilities and others, not so much. Anyway, I had no idea she came back through before it was closed. I thought after she asked me to deliver that letter she returned, and remained, in Elydor. She loved her husband, and the life she'd built there." Jon wiped the sweat from his brow with the back of his shirtsleeve. It was hot in here, and getting hotter by the minute.

"Could we maybe finish this story out there?" Clara asked.

Jon shook his head. "Obviously, I knew you wouldn't believe me. So I wanted to show it to you."

"Wait a minute," I asked, my curiosity about the portal overshadowed by something. "You said someone wanted it closed. Who was he?"

"King Balthor."

"But I thought you said Mev's father was the king? What's his name?" At this point Clara was simply amusing herself, pretending to believe Jon's wild story.

"King Galfrid. There are four clans in Elydor. We'd call them kingdoms. Your father is the king of the Air Clan. Or at least, that's what we call it on this side. Balthor is the King of Gyoria. We call it the Earth Clan. Obviously they don't use that term because Elydor isn't on Earth."

"Obviously." Clara's eyes rolled so far back in her head, I thought they might get stuck there. I held back a giggle. This wasn't funny, not even remotely so. But Jon's story was so out there, and he seemed so very convinced it was true. I actually felt bad for him.

"Listen, I know how this sounds. Which is exactly why I didn't want to tell you. That and I took an oath. The same one I made my kids take, the same one my father gave me. But that"—he nodded toward my ring—"is an exception, to my way of thinking. You have a right to know."

He sounded so damn sure of himself. So I played along.

"Why did the Earth king close the portal, exactly?"

Realizing how ridiculous my question sounded out of my mouth, I wanted to take it back.

"I assume it was him. There weren't that many Elydorians

powerful enough. He hates humans. Always has, since they began to come through. He hated that your father gave them land, bordering his own, which made it worse. He hated the humans' brand of magic and how powerful they became, so quickly. But most of all, he hated them for bringing a disease to Elydor that killed his wife. His hatred of your father, and mother, was well-known. I would not be surprised to learn he was behind the portal's closing, or even behind your mother being forced back through by him. She would have never returned, and stayed here, willingly. Never."

"Killed his wife? I thought you said they're immortal?" Clara sneezed. The dust was getting to her, obviously.

"They are. But they can be killed. According to the tales, though Elydorians are immune to most natural diseases due to their magical essence, rare celestial events, like the one that created Elydor in the first place, can temporarily make them vulnerable."

One time, when I was in college, my English professor asked if I wanted to earn some extra cash. Though I was a history major, I was also really into writing and apparently BU got periodic calls from people asking for student editors. He put me in touch with a guy who wrote a book about being abducted by aliens. I finally met him in person the day I finished editing his manuscript. Clara worried about me meeting him, but I was too curious, wanting to see the guy who believed—100 per cent truly believed—he'd been abducted by little green men. No joke. His aliens were green, just like in the movies.

Jon, it seemed, fell into the same camp. And though I wanted it to be true, the whole story was just too much. I stood. "Thank you," I said, certain now that my mother must have gotten this ring from the same circle of people who believed in a place called Elydor. Or maybe my father was one of them, like a cult leader. "We really do appreciate your time."

Clara looked relieved to be leaving. She stood as well. "Yes, thank you for answering all of our questions."

"Before you go, at least take a look at the portal. That way, if you do talk to your mother about this, you can tell her the truth."

My mother. It hadn't occurred to me for a second, but Jon seemed to think my mother would know, and believe, all this nonsense. It was true, Mom's profession perfectly aligned with the idea of an immortal realm's existence. Even if I couldn't understand it, I never once doubted my mother's abilities as a psychic. Had she been wrapped up with these people during her time in England?

Before either of us could respond, Jon pulled back a dusty wall tapestry to reveal a hidden door at one end of the tiny storage room. The wood was darker and more polished than anything else in the room, as if it couldn't get dusty.

He opened it with a separate key chain from the one he'd used to bring us inside and didn't wait for Clara and me to follow. We exchanged a look, and even though I'd been prepared to leave, as darkness swallowed Jon, I couldn't resist. His tiny phone light bobbed down a narrow staircase. We followed, the air growing cooler and cooler with every step.

At the bottom of the staircase, a small chamber, otherwise nondescript except for an archway made of polished cream stone. Covered in intricate carvings of celestial symbols, its center looked much like the rest of the room, made of very earthly concrete. The archway though. It didn't look like it belonged here at all.

"I've never seen anything quite like this. Whoever did these carvings was a master of his or her trade."

"They're incredible," Clara said next to me, as enthralled as I was.

"That's it. The portal. Closed now for twenty-eight years."

Twenty-eight years. My age.

"Have you ever seen Elydor?" Clara's question was clearly lip service. She didn't believe Jon any more than I did, but he didn't seem to take offense at her tone. I'd have kicked us both out of my pub by now, even if his story was make-believe.

"No. Humans can't go through unless they already have some innate abilities already. Unfortunately, my family wasn't blessed with any. Just regular old pub owners."

Clara ran her hand along one of the carvings. "I'll give you this. It honestly does look like it's from another world."

"Because it is. King Galfrid made it himself."

King Galfrid. My father.

Ridiculous.

The urge to touch it, however, was strong. I gave in, as Clara had. Except, when I did, something happened. The cold stone came—and there was no other way to describe it—alive under my fingertips. I pulled my hand back.

Jon watched me carefully. "What is it?"

"I don't know," I said. "It's hard to explain. Does it feel," I asked Clara, "weird to you?"

"I'm not sure I'd use that word. It's cool, and smooth. But weird?"

I did it again. This time, there was no denying something strange was going on. Each of the carvings began to illuminate. Their outlines took on a slightly blue glow.

"Holy shit." I pulled my hand away, but the glow remained. For a second or two at least. And then it faded.

"That was really fucking strange," Clara said, echoing my sentiments exactly.

I looked at Jon. His expression was similar to when he'd first seen my ring.

"What?" I asked. "What is it?"

Jon opened his mouth, but didn't speak. He moved closer, touched one of the archway carvings, but nothing happened.

"Try it again," he asked me.

I didn't need any further prompting. It was as if the damn thing was calling to me. The urge to touch it was so strong that I was glad to comply. When I did, that same blue glow returned, and a humming filled my head. It was like being electrocuted, except not to such an extent. And it didn't hurt. But there was definitely an... energy... in the carvings.

"It's closed. That shouldn't be happening."

"Let me guess. That blue glow is what happens when the portal opens?" Clara's question wasn't laced with quite as much skepticism as before. Clearly, something was happening. Something unnatural.

"Yes. Exactly."

"So if Mev wanted to go through, what would she do? Just walk straight into the wall?"

I pulled my hand away.

"You can't go near it," he said. "We have to figure this out." He looked me up and down. "You said you're a museum curator. Do you have any intuitive abilities? Like your mother?"

He knew my mother was a psychic. Well, of course he did. If nothing else, we'd established the two knew each other. Which reminded me...

"Do you know who took that picture?"

"My father. Every human who's attempted to go through has been recorded. Though I'm not sure how she ended up with a copy, unless he took two. Or gave it to her for some reason."

Remembering his question, I answered, "I don't have any special abilities."

Jon started pacing the room, muttering to himself. "I need to get my dad. He's on holiday with my mum, but we have to get him back here. How long are you in York?"

Clara answered, their conversation muting into the background as the archway's hum murmured in my ears. I took a step toward it. And then another. It called to me, and no part of me wanted to resist. Obviously, there was no portal to another realm. So what harm would there be in taking a few more steps?

I did, and quickly too, before Jon could stop me. Putting my hand out in front of me to touch the wall, I was about to tell my companions the portal was indeed still closed when it went straight through. I heard yelling from behind me; both Jon and Clara were screaming. But it was too late to turn back. I had to keep going. Unbelievably, I was walking through the wall, my entire body filled with the same hum, the same energy, as when I'd touched the carvings.

Darkness enveloped me.

6

KAEL

"We've only just begun Kael."

I liked Lyra as much as any Aetherian, which meant I mostly tolerated her but did not trust her. I did respect the woman, though, so I stopped at the bottom of the gleaming white stone steps, turning back up to the noblewoman.

She descended the steps slowly with her head held high as always. The very definition of regal, Lyra also happened to be one of the most intelligent Elydorians I knew. When we served on the Council together, Lyra spent her days in the library, her nights reading ancient texts. Though a fine air-wielder, Lyra's greatest strength was her mind. One that seemed to be set on bringing me back.

"Two days is enough for me," I said, turning from the palace eastward. Even from here, I could see well beyond the borders of Aetheria. Built into the mountains, the northern clan enjoyed looking down on those around them, both literally and figuratively. It was that attitude of superiority that I'd had enough of for the day. Maybe forever.

There would be no peace between our clans. I was as

convinced of that this day as I had been before arriving in Aethralis. With its towers and spires reaching skyward, adorned with intricate carvings and symbols that told the storied history of Aetheria, along with fountains and streams crisscrossing the grounds, I had to admit... part of me missed the serene tranquility here. Often, I looked back to the years I'd spent in Aetheria, grateful the portal had closed, allowing me to go home. Being here, though, reminded me there had been some good times as well.

Unfortunately, I'd not include the last two days in such a manner.

"Tell me, how will we find any accord if you refuse to treat with the others? We can never be a united Elydor without representation from all four clans."

"Three," I reminded her. That the humans had been invited to sit around the table was one of the sources of our current discord.

Lyra calmly swept an errant strand of long silver hair behind her ear. She was an extraordinarily beautiful woman, unpartnered too, but not one for me. Too... Aetherian.

"That is your father speaking, not you."

"I am no parrot," I said, ironically evoking one of the breeds brought to Elydor by humans.

Lyra smiled, catching it. "And yet you acknowledge the humans in your speech. You acknowledge them when needed but discard their contributions when it does not suit you. The man I served with on the Council was more tolerant than that."

"Was he?" I challenged. "Or perhaps you only wished it so."

Lyra had often attempted to separate my politics from my father's and clan's tenants. And while it was true that I sometimes thought my father's ways were extreme, neither did I believe humans belonged in Elydor. And certainly they did not belong around that table. "There are three clans native to Elydor." I repeated my earlier words from the Summit.

"What does that matter? They've been here for hundreds of years, Kael. Seven Hundred."

"Not so long, for some of us."

"But longer than others in your clan, and mine, have been alive. Do the humans have less of a claim than the young ones? Or those who came before them, even?"

"I will not debate this again."

"And if we kick them out of the Summit?" she asked, pressing me as always. "Would that bring you back inside with the others?"

As I was the only Gyorian representative, my leaving had disrupted their precious Summit, a fact I cared not about since coming here was not my idea, nor did I believe it a worthwhile endeavor. I would fight, and die, for any and all Gyorians. Beyond that, Elydorian politics meant little to me.

"Farewell, Lyra," I said, finished with this conversation. I did not wish to argue with someone I respected, knowing we would never come to terms. "Until we meet again."

"May the winds guide you back to us," she said, with a slight bow of her head, as graciously as I'd expected. "Galfrid has disabled the Skyway enchantments so you may pass freely."

I laid my hand on my chest in parting, acknowledging her but saying nothing in return. I had no wish to come back to Aetheria anytime soon and therefore remaining silent was the preferable response.

I'd intended to leave the palace grounds immediately, but after fetching my mount and starting on the path south, down the Skyway and past its guards, a building in the distance caught my eye. A very familiar building. The one I'd spent more years inside than I cared to remember.

It had been so long.

Before thinking better of it, I veered westward. Even though it had been abandoned for many years, the grounds were kept meticulously, or so it seemed from a distance. The flowers that had withstood the winter were in need of a bit of life, and though I had no will to improve anything about my enemy's land, I made one exception. It seemed somehow... wrong. For there to be any state of disrepair in a place one held in such high regard.

With a sweep of my hand, I brought life back to the grounds and tied Stormbreaker to a tree, looking up at gleaming white stone steps, similar to the palace's. This building was not as large, and it had just one purpose. Climbing the steps, I expected to be locked out. The magic that King Galfrid had imbued us with was long gone, unneeded. Surprisingly, however, the doors were unlocked. Towering high above me, two glass doors lined, as the rest of the entrance was, in gold and white marble, easily pushed open.

I stepped inside.

Columns of marble. Floors of marble. The building gleamed as it had so many years ago. Likely the king kept it so, desperate as he was to open the Gate once again. My leather boots made no sound as I walked toward the door where so many had come through. Once, this had been a bustling place where humans seeking the magic of Elydor had been allowed entry and curious Elydorians had sought the human realm, most coming back almost as quickly as they passed through.

He'd been right to close it. They did not belong here.

Turning back, unsure what had made me come inside, I retraced my steps, suddenly anxious to leave this place. I was nearly at the doors when it happened.

I understood immediately what the tingling in my shoulders and down my back meant. Apparently, that magic was not gone at all but had only lain dormant. All members of the Council had been given the same ability to detect a human coming through the portal. It was our duty to decipher, sometimes easily and other times after days of disagreements, if the person, or persons, were to be allowed through.

Impossible, and yet, there was no other explanation.

If I'd felt it, the others would too.

Running back, I sped through the interior doors toward the antechamber. That every one was open to me verified that some of Galfrid's and his mage's magic still remained. All should have been locked, a Gyorian not welcome in any part of Aetheria unescorted, and certainly not in one of its most sacred spots.

If it were true, if the Aetherian Gate had been activated, I needed to get there before anyone else discovered it. Lyra was likely already coming this way, and she was not the only Council member at that Summit.

Unsure what to expect, I slammed open the antechamber doors, ones no human had been able to pass through for nearly thirty years.

7

MEV

The brief darkness was followed by a bright, almost blinding, light. After the darkness of the storage room, the scene before me was almost too much to take in all at once. A circular room, three plush couches with a table in the center of them. Ordinary, if not opulent, though I couldn't say the same for what lay beyond them.

The walls were covered in floor-to-ceiling windows, arched at the top, and the scene beyond them was one which didn't belong in our world. The earthly world. Snow-covered mountains, what I imagined the Swiss Alps to look like in real life, but more pointed. Higher and more magnificent than one could imagine.

Was it possible Jon had told the truth? From the humming that had filled my ears to traveling through the darkness—and now the scene before me, certainly not another storage room in a pub in York—evidence was everywhere.

Even as my brain attempted to catch up to the erratic beating of my heart and my hands began to tremble, I whipped round to see where I'd just come through. Instead of a white marble arch and cement wall, there stood a circular entranceway, roughly the same size, with celestial symbols etched all around. Ring after ring of symbols were lit by the same blue glow as the carvings I'd left behind.

I stood, frozen, unable to decide what to do. Most of me wanted to run back into that portal, throw my arms around Clara and not let go. Get back on a plane to the States, hide in my museum office, and forget this ever happened. But another part of me, the ever-curious one, wanted to stay. Explore.

At that thought, a peace settled inside my chest. How odd that a sense of belonging so suddenly replaced the terror that should have me tearing back through that portal.

Even so, the practical side won out. I needed to go back, tell Jon I believed him and, even if I could explore this... what had he called it... Elydor? I couldn't do it with so little information. I needed to talk to him first. Taking a deep breath, hoping it would work, I took a step toward the portal, its blue light becoming brighter.

"Not so fast."

A hand gripped my arm from behind. I hadn't heard anyone come inside the room, and when I spun around, I was fairly certain I might faint. A man stood before me, his chiseled jawline and piercing green eyes just two features almost too perfect to be real. He had dark brown hair that was neither short, nor long. He was tall and clearly muscular beneath clothes unlike anything I'd ever seen, similar to a medieval knight's armor if it were made out of fabric.

For all of that, he also appeared decidedly human. No alien green skin. Or elvish pointed ears. Just, human, but more perfect. Unfortunately, though, not very friendly. I pulled my arm away, or tried to, but he was much too strong.

"We don't have time for this." His voice was low and gruff

and decidedly irritated. About to ask what he meant by that, I didn't need to. The man lifted me up by the waist and carried me in the opposite direction of the portal.

Panic consumed me with every step he took away from it. "No," I yelled, pounding his back with my fist. "Please, no. I have to go back. I'm not meant to be here."

"No, you're not," he agreed, striding through the open doors I hadn't heard opening and into the foyer of all foyers. It was like the fanciest of hotels on steroids. Cream marble everywhere, like the arch in the pub. Pillar after pillar, gold chandeliers... didn't matter.

More fighting, less ogling, Mevlida.

"Put. Me. Down."

Unfortunately, the fact that my mother had enrolled me in Brazilian jiu-jitsu when I was young, and I not only held a black belt but had won several state and regional BJJ championships, meant nothing against this guy. Or whatever he was. As he descended a set of steps, also marble, of course, I was like a captive little child in his arms.

"Would you please stop?" he said, plopping me onto the most massive, but admittedly beautiful, brown horse I'd ever seen. My training kicked in full force then. A rule of thumb was, never let them take you to another location. That's where the murders always happened. No fucking way was I going anywhere with this handsome devil spawn.

"Sorry if I'm not making my abduction easy on you," I muttered, attempting to kick him away from me and hop down.

This couldn't be happening. I continued to kick, waiting to wake up in a hotel room in York. Surely I'd drunk one too many beers on our pub crawl and Clara would be urging me to rise and shine any second.

Unfortunately, not only had I not managed to escape, but the gorgeous brute was now mounted in front of me. He grabbed each of my arms, pulled them around his torso, and tied them together. The ropes were tight and itchy, my face smushed against his back.

Any delusions of this being a dream vanished as he spurred his horse forward. I bounced up and down, now as afraid to fall as I was to be abducted. It was more uncomfortable than a seven-hour flight in coach, not that I'd ever flown anything but. How people could sleep in tiny airline seats was beyond me.

Also beyond me? My current situation.

"Why are you doing this?" I shouted. If I weren't terrified— of being kidnapped, of stepping from a dusty pub storage room into this place, and discovering that it was actually real —I'd be able to appreciate the views around me. The only way to describe it was like being plopped into the elf world in *Lord of the Rings*. I was never a big fantasy girl, hadn't read the books, but my ex was obsessed, and we'd watched the trilogy at least three times. I liked the elves best, but honestly never thought I'd be visiting Rivendell in real life.

We were racing down a mountain, but above us, some of the buildings seemed to be on floating islands of clouds with waterfalls cascading onto more clouds below them. That same blue glow from the stones imbued everything, especially the waterfalls. The snow-capped mountains were the tallest I'd ever seen. Despite my dire situation, I couldn't help being mesmerized too.

Shouts from behind us interrupted my thoughts.

We were being followed.

"Help!" I screamed as loudly as possible. I didn't stop screaming, my throat raw with the plea. But my companion didn't seem fazed. I wondered if he even knew what was happening behind him. A few minutes later, I had my answer.

Miraculously, he slowed and spun in the direction my face was turned. I thought he would address me, but instead, he held up a hand, as if motioning "stop." I twisted to see what was happening. My eyes were surely playing tricks on me.

By now, I'd stopped screaming. Instead, I watched as he erected a barrier of dirt and grass between us and the other riders.

"No fucking way," I murmured.

"You can stop screaming," he said, urging us forward once again. Ironic, as I'd already stopped. There was no way to watch what had just happened, process it, and at the same time fight for your rescue. Clearly, the man was going to do whatever the hell he wanted with me. He'd just built an earth wall... with his hand.

"I already did," I pointed out, shifting in the saddle that was surely not made for two people and pulling away from his back as much as I was able.

"You've a better chance of survival with me than any of the people following us."

My God, his voice was deep. I thought on his words. Were they true? I tried to remember what Jon had told me about this world. Pretending, for a second, this wasn't a forced-drug-induced hallucination or the most vivid dream I'd ever had, I thought back to our conversation.

Humans can't go through unless they already have some innate abilities already.

False. I had no magical abilities, yet here we were.

There are four clans in Elydor. We'd call them kingdoms. Your father is the king of the Air Clan. Or at least, that's what we call it on this side. Balthor is the King of Gyoria. Or as we call it, the Earth Clan.

It didn't take a genius to figure out I'd landed smack dab in the middle of the Air Clan's kingdom. Even now, as we descended down a steep path, trees blocking any further view of our surroundings, it still felt as if we were among the clouds. There was a lightness all around us, a feeling of floating, even though I was firmly on this damn horse. And while there was a cool breeze, it wasn't cold. The weather was perfect, actually.

"If that's true, and you are not my enemy," I said, doubting him, "then release the binds on my hands. It's damned uncomfortable."

No response. At least immediately. And then, as quickly as he tied them, my wrists were unbound. As the ropes slipped away, and I gripped my abductor around the waist, not wanting to tumble to my death, I saw them fall to the ground.

Not ropes at all. Vines.

He'd tied my hands with vines. Constructed a wall of earth.

Balthor is the King of Gyoria. Or as we call it, the Earth Clan.

"Are you a king?" I blurted, immediately regretting it. The fact that my mouth worked before my brain was a joke among my co-workers and friends. Harmless, or so I thought. Never in a million years did I expect that particular flaw might get me killed. Maybe I should just announce my name and everything Jon had told Clara and me while I was at it.

He didn't respond. For a long time, my abductor said nothing. Apparently, his earth wall had worked. It had been a while since I'd heard any riders behind us. At this point, it was starting to get dark. Since we were still surrounded by woods, I couldn't see much. The trees seemed perfectly normal, as if the whole cloud city thing had never existed.

But it had, and evidence of the fact that this was not my normal world popped up periodically. A faint glow coming from certain plants, their leaves pulsing with light. Or the occasional glimpse of creatures darting between the trees— one looking like a cross between a squirrel and a butterfly, its furry body adorned with delicate, iridescent wings.

The air itself felt different, too. Clean and invigorating, the familiar scent of pine but mixed with something sweeter, almost like cotton candy.

Also familiar? My very real urge to pee.

"Hello?"

Nothing.

"Excuse me?"

Still nothing. The jerk didn't even turn around to acknowledge me. Damned inconsiderate kidnapper. I smiled at my own sort-of joke, one that would have made Clara laugh if she were with me. With any luck, Jon had stopped her from following me since there was a very good chance she'd at least tried.

I didn't dare let go, not at the speed we were riding. So I squeezed him, as hard as I could, instead.

"Did you just squeeze me?"

Finally.

"Yes. You weren't answering me."

"Perhaps because I'm busy saving you."

I didn't believe that for a second. "Can you save me from peeing my pants, then?"

Surprisingly, he slowed down. "Humans," he muttered, as if I'd committed some sort of capital offense.

Knowing I should hold my tongue, and preemptively

chastising myself for what was about to come out of my mouth, I let it loose.

"Apologies for being *human*. But maybe consider, for a second, I was in a pub in York with my best friend and accidentally stepped through—whatever I stepped through—and found myself in God knows where with squirrel butterflies and glowing plants and cities in the clouds. Not to mention that thing you did with your hands."

He'd slowed to a complete stop. By the end of my speech, he actually turned in the saddle to look down at me. I loosened my grip.

The corners of his lips raised.

Dear lord. There were a lot of things I was sure were deadly about this guy, and that smile was certainly one of them.

"I can do a lot more than that with my hands."

My mouth fell open. Was my kidnapper... flirting with me?

"Can you produce a restroom? Sorry," I said, remembering I was in England. "Loo?" Wait, not in England. "Or whatever you call it here?"

He looked as if he were trying not to laugh. Turning back around, he spurred the massive horse on once again. So apparently, I had to pee in my pants. Fabulous.

"I'll take you to a stream," he said.

What the hell did that mean? A stream? Seemed like an odd place to pee, but beggars couldn't be choosers, I supposed. Alive was alive, and so I wouldn't complain. For now.

"And no," he added.

"No, what?"

"I am not a king."

Good to know. So not the Earth King, or whatever. That was something.

A few minutes later, as promised, a stream came into view. But it wasn't an ordinary stream. Its water was a clear crystal blue, a beautiful blue that was anything but earthly.

He dismounted and lifted me off the horse as if I weighed as much as a pack of Post-it notes.

"Prince Kael," he said in a confident tone that bordered on cockiness, looking straight into my eyes. I'd do well to remember, despite those green eyes and perfect jaw, that this man was my literal kidnapper.

"Princess," I tossed out in response to his high and mighty tone. Then realizing giving him my actual name might not be a good idea, I added, "Mia." If only Clara was here to hear that one. She was a huge *Princess Diaries* fan.

Ignoring his raised brows, I thought about his response. Was he actually a prince? If so, did that mean the king Jon mentioned was his father? Questions for another time. For now, unable to hold it much longer, I blurted, "I really do have to—"

He pointed to some nearby shrubs. Without another word, I sprinted toward them, his words following me. "If you run, I will feel it."

What an odd thing to say. He would feel it?

I had questions.

Lots and lots of questions.

8

KAEL

I watched the thicket, the strange human disappearing behind it. Leading Stormbreaker to the stream, I knelt down and laid both hands on the grass below me. Closing my eyes, I felt the ground, the water running in the stream beside us, the human's movements, and smaller ones as well. Animals of the forests of Aetheria, some similar to our own and others unique to this region... and then, nothing. I had no doubt those pursuing us would have been able to knock down the wall I'd constructed. But the hoof prints I'd laid in the fork just beyond that wall, heading east when we'd taken a western path, seemed to have worked.

Even so, until we crossed the border into Gyoria, I would not feel safe. I had to get this human to my father, to the elders and mages who, with luck, would be able to determine how she'd come through a closed Aetherian Gate.

That human woman emerged.

Surprisingly strong, she was a whirlwind of contradictions. Her long, dark blonde hair framed a beautiful face that seemed perpetually caught between curiosity and defiance.

Like her personality, the human's eyes couldn't seem to choose one path; brown and blue mixed together in a hazel color that was rare among Elydorians but more common among humans.

Yet, there was little common about this one. I sensed it, wishing I had the human capability of foresight to determine what role, if any, she would play here. Unfortunately, my father had ensured no human in Elydor would ever willingly ally with a Gyorian long enough to assess the woman. It was one of many arguments we'd had over the years over our strict policies against any interactions with them.

Content we were safe for the moment, I relieved myself, hearing the human return as I did so. Her shoulders slumped when I emerged.

"Am still here. Sorry to disappoint you, princess." Of course, I was not sorry in the least. Only glad I had been at the Gate when she'd come through; a stroke of luck or, some would say, something more fortuitous.

Before she could respond, I went to work.

It was as good a spot as any. If we were to make it to Gyoria, she would need to eat and rest, at least for a spell. Waving my hands toward the clearing, I gathered rock sticks and other materials, quickly fashioning a small hut complete with two pallets of moonleaves. I built and started a fire and then, most importantly, blended it seamlessly with the landscape, making it impossible to see. Next, I constructed another shield for Stormbreaker, and a post to tie him to beside our temporary lodgings. Imbuing both with as much copper as could be found in this soil, a defense against erosive air magic, I finished by taking out a bit of quartz from my leather satchel and used it to conceal the energy that had been created fashioning both structures.

"You really just did that."

She stood at my side now, that curiosity of hers having returned, replacing the anger, at least for now. This human was a fiery one.

Sighing, my suspicion confirmed, I said, "You know nothing of Elydor."

She was an Uninitiated.

Knowing its smoke was our best chance at discovery, I added smokeshade to the fire. Thankfully we were far enough south that the plant was readily available. Next, I moved two large rocks toward the fire.

"Your throne, princess."

Without waiting to see if she would sit, I returned to Stormbreaker to retrieve a bow. By the time I'd caught and skinned a rabbit, darkness had fallen. I didn't have to wait long for her reaction to our meal. Hundreds of years ago, it would have been different. But as the human world innovated, those who came through knew less and less about living with the land, neither theirs nor ours. Their technologies were useless here, thankfully, and in many ways our world remained a much simpler one.

"What is that?" she asked as I prepared our meager meal.

"Rabbit."

"How were you able to do"—she waved a hand at our surroundings—"this?"

It would be a long night. And despite my dislike of humans, even ones as comely as this one, I'd also taken her for a reason— to discover how she'd gotten through the closed Aetherian Gate.

"How did you come to be here?" I asked, leaning forward to roast our meal over the fire.

"I believe I asked a question first."

"You're no longer afraid of me?" Or more like, she did not wish to be. But the fear was there, behind her mask of bravado and indignation.

"Should I be?"

If she'd have asked any other human on Elydor the same question about me, they'd not hesitate to say "aye." And though it was true I bore no love for humans, neither did I kill indiscriminately as some would have her believe.

Did I mean her harm? Nay. But that did not mean my father would take kindly to her presence. Since I did not wish to lie, even to her, I offered the truth. "Perhaps."

It had been many years since I'd been forced to explain Elydor to a human. Even when the Gate had been open, that task had fallen to those who had wanted them here. Never me.

"You would call it magic, a term used here too thanks to your kind. Your turn. How did you come to be here?"

She stared first at me, and then into the fire. "This is really happening, isn't it? I'm not dreaming or hallucinating?"

Aye, very much an Uninitiated.

"I am as real as you are, princess."

She looked up, as if just noticing me. Acceptance was happening more quickly than usual. They were rare, the Uninitiated. But unmistakable when it happened. The wide-eyed shock. Fear. Curiosity. Eventually, acceptance.

"How?" I prompted once more.

She blinked. "I... we were with Jon in the pub and..."

My eyes narrowed. The human lied. If she were with Jon Harrow, she knew of Elydor. The pub owner's son would have told Mia everything before sending her through.

"He told us of the portal. Of Elydor. But said it was closed and had been for many years. When I touched it, the stone... glowed. And then it started to hum, like a buzzing in my ears. I stepped through without a word, without warning him. Without realizing what was happening."

I watched her closely. So not completely Uninitiated, but clearly she knew very little of Elydor if she had no knowledge of our magic.

"You have abilities of your own?" I asked, knowing they would only intensify the longer she remained here. "What are they?"

"I have none. Jon did mention only those who possessed some sort of intuitive abilities could pass through, which is why I didn't think much of getting too close. I have none," she repeated.

Staring at the woman, I pulled the roasted rabbit from the fire, pulled off a piece of meat, and handed it to her. Expecting her to decline by the way she looked at it, Mia surprised me by taking it.

I ate, attempting to make sense of her story. "If you have no magic, then how did you know of The Crooked Key?" Knowledge of Elydor typically was passed through a particular community of people, one she claimed not to be a part of. "And why did Jon allow you to pass?"

Something did not make sense.

"I accompanied my friend on a work trip to York when we stumbled into the pub, and I read a chalkboard message that intrigued me. When I asked the owner, Jon, he told us of the legend and took us to the basement to show us the portal. He didn't tell us much before I touched the carvings and ended up"—she waved an arm around our makeshift camp—"here."

I took a bite of rabbit, handing her another. "Why do you lie to me?" I asked her bluntly.

Taken aback, she was either genuinely surprised or pretended to be as much.

"Lie? What do you mean?"

I could tell her Jon and his family had taken a sacred vow, one that had been passed through his family for centuries, not to reveal the portal, as they called it in the human world, to anyone who could not come through. And even if so many years had passed that he assumed the vow no longer held, Elydor relegated to legend, he'd never have let her attempt it.

So I said as much. "Jon would not have allowed it."

Her chin raised. "Well, he did. I'm here, am I not?"

Indeed, she was here. But something about her story did not make sense. "He did not try to stop you?"

"It all happened so quickly. Why does it matter? Why would he not have allowed it?"

Still not believing her, but wanting to see how much she knew, I watched her carefully. "Because if you truly have no magical abilities of your own—to foretell the future, to look into the past—and you tried to come through that Gate..." I thought of the last time one had done so. It had not been a pretty scene.

"What? What would happen?" she demanded.

So I told her.

"You might have died."

9

MEV

Clara.

Oh my God, please be okay. Please don't have tried to follow me.

The soreness of my backside, the smell of smoke… it was all too real to be a dream. Somehow, Jon's crazy story of an immortal realm, and a portal to it in his understated York pub, was true. The proof surrounded me.

And then there was Prince Kael.

Every time I caught myself staring at his handsome face, I cursed under my breath. If it wasn't bad enough that the man had literally kidnapped me, he was also as arrogant as they came and much too brusque for my taste.

"He didn't share that particular bit of information?" he asked, skeptical. Not that Kael didn't have a right to be. Half of my story was true, but the other half, not so much. Whether or not this guy's father was the same man who had likely forced my mother from Elydor, before closing the portal, it still seemed unwise to tell him everything I knew. Which, to be fair, wasn't much.

Only problem?

I was a terrible liar. Couldn't play poker for the life of me.

"No," I said finally, remembering his question. "I'm sure he meant to. It just... didn't come up."

"Seems like an important piece of information." He handed me another piece of meat. I took it, trying to push away the fact that it was the same animal he'd carried to the fire earlier. I shuddered. "Either way, the fact that you're alive means, know it or not, you have some sort of intuitive abilities within you."

My mother had always said as much. For years she tried to train me, coax glimpses of the future from me. But nope. Nothing.

"I doubt it."

Looking up for what seemed like the millionth time, I took in the sight above us. In some ways, it was the same kind of sky I was used to, though the kind you'd see on a very clear night in the country. But with more stars, all brighter, and some more blue or green than white or yellow. It felt as if we sat among them, the sky closer to the ground than it was back home.

Home. Earth.

Fucking hell.

"Will you take me back?" I asked, already knowing the answer. If he intended for me to turn right around and go back the way I came, we wouldn't have ridden so far away from the Gate for so long.

"No," he confirmed. "Not yet. There will be people looking for you. It's best, for now, that I take you with me."

"Why will people be looking for me? What is this place? And why do you speak my language? And, for that matter, look like a human?" I'd thought of a thousand questions throughout the day, and he seemed to be inclined to answer very few of them.

Dispensing with the remainder of our meal, Kael leaned forward, elbows resting on his knees. "I don't look like a human."

Of all the questions to answer, he chose that one?

"Yes you do," I argued. "Two arms, two legs. Non-pointed ears and all that. Human."

"Elydor," he said in a tone that didn't even attempt to hide how little he wished to tell me this story, "is older, much older, than your realm. The human theory of Earth's creation—"

"The big bang theory?"

"Yes. That's not far off from our own. A celestial event that imbued this land, and those who live in it, with an energy you don't have in your world. In the beginning, all Elydorians were one, but eventually their abilities began to manifest differently. Those who could manipulate water migrated to the south; those like me, who were able to manipulate the land, to the midlands; and the air-wielders, to the north."

"That's where I came through? In the north?"

"Aetheria, aye." He didn't bother to hide his contempt.

"You don't like them?"

"We don't like anyone."

Your mother was the Queen of Aetheria. There were more pressing matters to talk about, namely rumors that the Gyorian king wanted to close the portal.

Holy shit. There was so much to unpack there, I couldn't even attempt it. But one thing was blatantly clear. It was a good thing I hadn't told him everything.

"Who's 'we'?" I asked, knowing the answer already.

"Gyorians."

"Earth-wielders." I thought about all I'd seen him do today, and didn't need him to acknowledge it.

"This isn't Earth," he said, irritated.

"I stand corrected. Apologies if it's taking me a minute to adjust to that fact. It's not every day I travel to immortal realms." Then it hit me. "Jon said you were immortal. Does that mean... how old are you?"

"Old. Very old. To answer your earlier question, when you came through the Gate, the magic that lives in everything here balanced your essence with ours."

I had no idea what that meant. What question was he even answering? "Huh?"

"With some exceptions, like that word you just uttered, everything we say to each other is able to be understood."

"You're saying..." This was getting more and more bonkers by the second. "We are speaking different languages right now? But it sounds like English to me? And I sound... Elydo-rian to you?"

Another sigh. I wanted to kick dirt in this dickhead's face, but he'd probably wave his hand and make it come flying back right to me.

"That's one way of putting it."

Like I said. Dickhead. At least, maybe, he wasn't a murderer, though I wasn't a huge fan of his "perhaps" when I'd asked if I should be afraid of him—which I was. Terrified, actually. I'd decided not to let him see it. Prince Kael, very likely the son of the same man who banished us, was like a shark. If I ran around dripping blood, it would only give him a reason to circle.

"So why will people be looking for me?" I asked as inno-cently as possible.

"The Aetherian Gate has been closed, as Jon undoubtedly told you, for nearly thirty years."

Twenty-eight, to be precise.

"And?"

"And the Council will want to know how it happened. Everyone, actually, will want to know how. But the Council especially."

I waited, but he didn't seem inclined to tell me more. "The Council?"

"Representatives from each clan who guarded the Gate and determined who was allowed to pass through it."

"Clans. Like kingdoms?"

"Sure."

Ugh. He was so smug. "And there are three?"

"Aye, three. Aetheria. Gyoria. Thalassaria."

"You mentioned humans, though. Where are they? How long have they been here? Did they all go back? Don't they have a clan?"

I was certain Jon mentioned its name; that was who I needed to get to. Other humans. My people.

"The Gate was opened over seven hundred years ago. The humans that came through live in Estmere, to the east."

"So four clans then."

"Three," he corrected me.

"But you just said—"

He stood. "Enough questions. Rest. We leave before dawn."

I'd have asked more questions anyway, but the dickhead stood up and walked toward his horse. If I was less afraid than I had been earlier, that was one of the reasons. A man, or Elydorian, or whatever, couldn't be that kind to his horse but also be a total monster. Could he?

I stood, my backside needing a break anyway.

With so many questions still swirling through my brain, I walked into the hut he'd built. With a wave of his hand. It was so incredible, and impossible, that I pushed the memory away. I wanted to forget all of it. Just go to sleep, and wake up, realizing this was all a big dream.

Or nightmare.

But something that I couldn't explain, a *feeling* not unlike the pull that had drawn me to the portal in the first place, told me this wasn't a dream at all. It also told me there was a familiarity here that made no sense. Nothing about it was familiar. I shouldn't feel liked I belonged in this place at all. And yet...

A bed of leaves awaited me. I'd never even camped before, never mind slept on the ground like this before. But as I sat, it was surprisingly comfortable. I picked up some leaves and found an interwoven vine "mattress" beneath it.

How had he done it, exactly? Did all Gyorians have that same ability? More importantly, the only question that really mattered... was his father their king?

If Jon was right, and if my mother had actually lived here, marrying the Air king, that made this entire situation eminently more dangerous.

Rolling onto my side and closing my eyes, I decided to give them just a little rest while I waited for Kael to return.

10

KAEL

She was a threat to my people.

As I watched Mia, who'd just turned toward me in her sleep, I had to remind myself of the fact. Not only was she human but somehow she'd managed to come through the closed Gate. She'd also lied, though exactly how I couldn't be certain.

She was a threat, even if she had the face of a goddess, and the body of one too.

Her eyelids fluttered open, even though the sun hadn't yet risen. Stars shone more brightly here than in her realm, casting a soft glow into the openings of our shelter. Enough to see her, to sense her fear.

Hardening myself against her, remembering tales of a mother I never knew courtesy of a human, like her, I stood. "Come. We leave at once."

We didn't speak while I readied Stormbreaker, Mia heading wordlessly to the same thicket she had when we'd arrived. I'd put the fire out long ago. Summoning a tremor that rattled our shelter to the ground, I covered all evidence of our presence with a fresh growth of grass, the small mound blending seamlessly into its surroundings.

"How can you do all those things?" Mia asked, riding behind me as she had the day before, though this time without her wrists bound.

"Are you going to question me all day?"

Able to envision the face she made even without turning in my saddle, I was tempted to smile. The woman had very little ability to hide her emotions.

"Is that a problem? I'd think it was the least you could do, kidnapping me and all."

There was no help hiding the fact that I was, indeed, taking her against her will. Mia had made it clear she wished to return to the Gate. And I had every intention of sending her back home, but not until we learned how she'd gotten through and why, and ensured no one could do it again.

"As for the kidnapping—"

The rest of what I'd been about to say was cut short by a scream. Specifically, her scream. If our pursuers were anywhere nearby, particularly of the Aetherian variety, we would be easily discovered.

"What. Was. That?"

I looked up, having hardly noticed the shadowwing flying low above us. With a wingspan of over six feet and feathers that absorb the light around them, it often appeared as if it were a moving shadow.

"A shadowwing. It will not harm you."

"Maybe you can tell me about some of the other creatures here? Specifically, which ones are deadly."

I didn't answer. Instead, I put all of my focus into feeling beneath Stormbreaker's hooves. I closed my eyes, allowing him to lead. Feeling the ground beneath us.

Nothing.

"In my world," she said as I opened my eyes once again, "it's considered rude not to answer someone when they talk to you. And to kidnap people against their will, too."

This time, I did smile.

"Shall we play a game?" I asked, debating our path forward. If I'd convinced our pursuers that we'd headed southwest, they would not realize their folly until reaching the gorge. Already having decided I could not take her immediately home, as that was exactly where the others would be heading, I also had to consider those following us may have split up.

If we continued on this path, it would take us due south, but I could not be certain we weren't being followed. Which left one option none would expect me to take. East. To Estmere.

"Is the game you don't talk to me and I try to read your mind instead?"

An intriguing idea. "I thought you had no intuitive abilities?"

"Ugh. You are positively maddening. If I'd met you back home..."

I waited, but Mia didn't continue. Turning just enough in my saddle to catch her expression, one I could not read, I prompted, "Aye?"

"Never mind."

If I didn't dislike humans so much, I might have found myself admiring this one's spirit. Turning back to the road, knowing it would get trickier as we headed on a downward path, I continued.

"A question for a question. I'll begin. If you'd met me back home...?"

She went quiet.

Truth was, this was not my game. The very person we were going to ask for refuge, one of the few humans I trusted, had taught me the game.

"If I'd met you back home—"

I interrupted her response as inspiration struck. It was wrong of me, but...

"If you lie, I will know and the game will be over." It had been so long since I'd met an Uninitiated, I nearly forgot how easy they were to manipulate.

"How will you know?" she asked, taking the bait.

"Just as I know you lied, at least in part, about how you came to be here." It was a calculated risk, but the reward was worth the potential payoff.

I'd turn back to see her expression but did not wish to give myself away. No doubt those full pink lips of hers were turned down in a pout. Her perfectly arched eyebrows would be furrowed together, her hazel eyes a storm of indecision.

"How is lie detection earth magic?"

"It is not... earth magic," I reminded her. "We are in Elydor. Is that your question? Do you agree to the rules?"

"Fine. Yes, that's my question."

She was as disgruntled as ever, but thankfully was not kicking me or attempting to flee. "There are enhancements to our magic. Like when I used a bit of quartz to conceal our lodgings last eve. One of many of the minerals Gyoria mines."

A partial truth.

"Including lie detection?" she asked, rightfully skeptical.

"Ahh, but you forgot the rules already. A question for a question."

"Holy shit."

Because we'd just turned a corner, uncovering a small

clearing, I knew her rather colorful phrase had not to do with me but the view. Closer to the borders, misty forests and towering trees with silvery bark began to give way to small rocky outcrops, hinting at a sturdier terrain. With the same pristine rivers as up north, this region's rolling hills, its tall grass swaying softly in the breeze, would appear even more spectacular as the weather warmed. I tried to remember the budding spring of her world, but had forgotten much of it. The human realm offered nothing to me which was why I'd visited so rarely when the Gate had been open.

"Why do you not tell me the full truth of your journey here?" I asked her.

"I cannot say."

She believed my claim. Otherwise, Mia would not have just admitted shielding the truth from me earlier.

"Cannot? Or will not?"

"My turn. How quickly you forgot your own game."

Quick-witted too. "What is your question?"

"You introduced yourself as Prince Kael. What does that mean? There is a king? Or queen? In each realm?"

"Four questions, so I will be generous and answer two. Aye, there is a king or queen of each clan."

"Seriously?"

Ignoring that, I slowed Stormbreaker, sensing a movement in the land ahead. Listening, waiting, I prepared for us to ride hard, though I'd no desire to turn around. Likely it was not another Council member but... ahh, yes. Riding to the side of the white graveled road, we stopped. A few moments later, a herd of deer bounded toward us. One by one they filed past.

"Silver-winged deer," I said. Without waiting for her to ask about their delicate wings, I added, "And yes, they can fly. But only very short distances."

Content with the knowledge there was more to her tale than she'd first claimed, I backed off on that line of questioning.

For now.

"If you'd met me back home?" I asked, for the third time, more curious than I should be.

"I can't believe this," she muttered. "If I'd met you back home," she said, obviously convinced she had no alternative but the truth, or to end the game, "I'd want to hate you but would probably end up dating you instead, the red-flag magnet that I am."

Date. I knew the word, akin to courting. "Red flag?" That was new to me.

"Boy, you are really bad at this. Try again next time. My turn. So, does prince mean the same thing here as it does for me? In other words, are you the son of the Gyorian king?"

"Most Uninitiated ask about our magic. Our immortality. Yet you seem more interested in my standing, why?"

Silence. I was on to something, it seemed. "Ah yes, an answer first. Yes, it means the same thing in your world as it does in mine."

"So you are the son of the Gyorian king?"

I didn't answer. In response, I got a shove to the back.

"Aye, the King of Gyoria is my father."

"What is a red flag?"

"It's like... a sign that someone, a man in this case, is trouble. Something that should warn you off, but doesn't."

Interesting. "You'd wish to date me, in your realm? Even knowing I was trouble, as you say?"

I'd been trained to detect the smallest of movements, from long distances away, in the land beneath us. Mia's slight stiffening at my question did not go unnoticed. I turned once again. As expected, she was upset. My eyes narrowed.

"It's a sensitive topic," she blurted. "The reason why I date the absolute worst guys. Walking red flags. We'd need an entire afternoon on that one."

Sensitive topic. Hmm.

We rode in silence, the terrain requiring my attention, even though Stormbreaker was well-trained. Sometime later, when the land once again flattened, she broke the silence.

"Am I truly in an immortal realm called Elydor with clans who wield elemental magic?"

Her complete acceptance came quicker than most. "You are," I said, waiting for her to continue. But she never did. I knew Mia had more questions. They always did. But she asked none.

I should have pressed her for answers. Attempted to learn why she was so curious about my standing. Taken advantage of her belief of my lie-detecting abilities. Instead, I wondered why she dated "walking red flags." Why it was a sensitive topic. Was she dating one now? Was she married? I'd not noticed a ring, as the humans wore.

Fortunately, I had no time to dwell on answers to those nonsensical questions. There'd been a shift in the ground below us. We were being followed. And whoever it was, though they were some distance behind us, were coming more quickly now than before.

"Hold on," I yelled, just before spurring Stormbreaker forward. The chase, it seemed, was on once again.

11

MEV

I was going to die.

He was the son of the person responsible for separating my family. For closing the portal. Me thinking the absolute worst of my father. And if I was being particularly uncharitable and avoiding responsibility, the reason I was attracted, rather than repelled, by red-flag men.

Of all the rotten luck. Why him? He hated humans. And Aetherians. So what the hell was he doing there when I'd come through? It would be my next question, if I survived the day. My eyes had been squeezed shut, my ass bouncing up and down and my arms wrapped tightly around Kael's waist for what felt like hours.

Finally, we slowed down. But then, without even fully stopping, Kael leaped from his horse, slapping the great beast on the rump and yelling, "Grab the reins," and, "Stay." I assumed the first command was for me, and the second, for his horse.

Where the hell was he going?

I was about to ask that very question when his hands began to twist and turn, dirt and leaves and grass forming a wall on the road, just like the first time. I grabbed the reins, but never once having ridden a horse, I had no idea what to do.

Was there any chance I could escape?

Unlikely. And I'd probably break my own neck trying.

I watched in fascination as Kael constructed a wall clear across the road. As much as I hated him, there was a part of me that had to admit the sight of him like this was... well, incredible. Otherworldly. Like I was watching a movie.

Suddenly, after he'd finished, the wall came crashing down. Kael moved away just in time, and there on the road, on the other side, was another sight to behold. A woman, and a beautiful one at that, atop a stately white horse. Her own hands waving furiously.

Kael knelt down to the road and slammed his fist to the ground. It tremored beneath us all, but affected her more. Riding backward, she nearly collapsed into what appeared to be a break in the road.

Had he just... created a mini earthquake?

"Don't make me do this, Lyra," he shouted as she narrowly avoided certain death. If she'd been caught in that chasm...

"She isn't yours." The woman looked directly at me then. Her hair was so beautiful, long and flowing, a silver shade that almost glowed, not unlike the carvings in The Crooked Key. "We all wish to know what happened."

With a wave of her hand, the woman named Lyra dismounted.

Aetheria. Air magic. Back and forth the two alternately summoned nature, one from the ground, the other from the sky. With a twirl of her fingers, Lyra created a funnel of wind, sending it directly toward Kael.

No sooner did he escape that wind funnel than he hurled a

rock that came from God knew where toward her. I screamed, not wanting to witness the woman being smushed to bits in front of me.

She just flew.

More accurately, levitated briefly. Lyra's feet had left the ground as she effortlessly avoided the rock, but she didn't go far into the air.

I watched, mesmerized, not just by Kael's ability and strength but the grace and calming beauty of Lyra's skills. Just like in the pub, a stirring inside me made me wish to go toward the gust of wind she'd produced, attempting to knock Kael off his feet.

He didn't fall. Instead, Kael jumped into the air, landed, and simultaneously pounded his hands on the ground once again. This time, there was no doubt what he'd done. The man created a damned earthquake and the chasm that opened, while it didn't swallow her, was certainly too wide to cross.

As quickly as it began, the fight was over. Kael ran toward me and mounted. As we rode away, I turned back, the woman growing smaller and smaller as we sped from the scene. This time, we didn't stop. I begged Kael to do so, well after the encounter, but he didn't.

After what felt like forever, we finally slowed, the reason for it becoming apparent as a castle in the distance came into view.

"Hold on," he said. "I realize you are human. We're almost there."

So my kidnapper had a thoughtful side, realizing my very human needs might need attending to. Sure enough, that castle seemed to be our destination. I knew something about castles. This one was of the motte and bailey variety. If it were anywhere but in Elydor, I'd have thought the structure a magnificent example of eleventh-century architecture. But compared to all that I'd seen so far, the most striking thing about it was how... ordinary it was.

Kael didn't let up, not even as we approached the gate-house. I expected the guards stationed above us to make inquiries, but before we were even upon them, the portcullis opened, its metal hinges creaking alongside the klop, klop of horse's hooves on wood. Crossing the motte, the only out-of-place feature the bright blue water beneath us, Kael called out, "A privy, if you please?"

"There, my lord," a man surrounded by very normal-looking animals—chicken and hens among them—said. Kael raced toward the turret when the man pointed, and by the time we dismounted, it felt as if I'd burst at any moment.

"Quickly." Kael grabbed my arm. "This way."

For a man who had to ask for the privy, he seemed to know where he was going. Or at least know his way around the castle. An arched entranceway led to a door. Whipping it open, Kael confirmed we'd found our mark. I rushed inside, hardly even caring if he closed the door of the garderobe behind me.

So much for counting ABCs while I washed my hands. There wasn't much inside the small room except a hole and, surprisingly, some form of toilet paper on a wooden stand. Briefly considering grabbing a few extra pieces—the stuff was softer than anything I've ever used—I decided against it.

Pulling open the door, I found Kael leaning against a stone wall.

Furious, I was about to lay into him, not caring about the power he'd unleashed against that Lyra, when he said, "My apologies, Mia. It was not my intention to cause you pain or discomfort."

Well, that was wholly unexpected.

"You did wish both, and worse, upon that poor woman. She could have died."

He laughed, the arrogant ass. Literally laughed, as if a woman's life meant nothing.

I crossed my arms.

"She was not in mortal danger."

My jaw dropped. "Not in mortal danger? You threw a boulder at her."

"Lyra can handle a little rock."

"Kael. That wasn't a little rock." Oh my God, he was ridiculous.

Out of nowhere, the hairs on the back of my neck stood up straight. It was the same sort of feeling one got when finding themselves in a dark, empty parking garage and someone walked toward you.

I was in danger.

"What is it?" Kael asked.

No sooner did the thought pass through my mind than I shrugged it off. This place was getting to me. Holding my bladder for too long had done something to my brain. Not to mention getting so little sleep, or food. I'd been in therapy before and knew trauma. This whole escapade was going to cost an arm and a leg to untangle, if I made it out of Elydor alive.

"I don't know," I said, that strange sense not going away.

"So it's true?"

The voice at my back was like a sledgehammer between my shoulder blades. Kael looked at me strangely just before standing up straight and addressing the newcomer.

"Draven."

I spun around.

This one didn't have shining silver hair or Kael's unearthly good looks, or anything that made him appear... Elydorian.

We were in the human kingdom.

Had to be. But Kael hated humans? Or at least, his father did.

"I was told you came racing in here."

Kael cleared his throat, nodding toward the privy. "Some discretion, if you please?"

I'd kill him. How embarrassing.

Draven's eyes narrowed on me. That strange feeling hadn't completely gone away. I didn't like this guy, even more than I didn't like Kael. But I plastered a smile on my face anyway.

"Pleased to make your acquaintance," I said, trying to sound as formal as possible. "I'm Mia."

"And a human." He tried to act gracious. Charming even, since that smile meant to disarm. But I didn't buy it. "Where do you live? I've not seen you before."

Kael stepped between us. "I'm here to see Issa."

"Lady Isolde, to you." This Draven's tone was night and day from how he'd spoken to me.

Without a word, Kael pushed past him, grabbed a hold of my elbow, and walked away without a response.

"It's good to know I'm not the only one you ignore."

Kael looked at me as if I'd said something untrue. "I don't ignore you."

I actually snorted. "You do," I verified as Kael released my elbow. "We're in the human clan, aren't we?"

"They're not a clan," he said, striding toward the keep. Where was Stormbreaker?

"When I say kingdom, you correct me."

"Kingdom is your word. Clan is ours. But Estmere is not a clan."

He was so frustrating. "Then what is it?"

"A nuisance," he said, as more than one woman stopped to stare at him. Apparently I wasn't the only one that noticed his good looks. I wondered if they knew he was a walking red flag too.

"Then why are we here if you hate humans so much?"

He didn't respond.

"See, you just did it. Completely ignored me."

Kael stopped, just before the doors of the main keep, and stared down at me. "I've spoken more words to you in the past day than I have to anyone in a week."

"Yay for me. Still doesn't negate the fact that you ignored my question."

"Prince Kael."

As the man who opened one of the large wooden doors of the keep greeted Kael, I turned to find Draven but didn't see him anywhere. Good riddance. The guy gave me the creeps.

"Come inside. Lady Isolde knows you are here and will receive you in the solar chamber. Supper has been cleared, but I will bring a tray for you and your guest."

"Thank you," Kael said as we were escorted inside.

I'd been to a handful of castles before but never one that looked like this. Even the more medieval castles, one of which I'd stayed at for two nights on a research trip to Scotland, had touches of modernity. This was like truly stepping back in time. No lights, except from wall sconces we passed. The floors were lined with rushes instead of carpet. And the servants looked like, well, servants.

"My lord," the man said as we arrived at the end of a corridor where an ornate wooden door stood open. Inside, a comfortable chamber filled with tapestries on every wall. A lit fireplace made it quite cozy. There were half a dozen wooden chairs lined with velvet cushions and a long table along one wall. A trunk sat in the middle; on it, more than a half-dozen candles. Seemed like a fire hazard to me, but what did I know?

"Do make yourself comfortable," he said as a maid scurried into the room with a tray. On it, three pewter goblets and a pitcher of, if I were lucky, wine. If I ever needed a drink, it was today.

The maid brought each of us a goblet. I looked to Kael who nodded. Taking a sip, I nearly cried. It was as good a red wine as I'd ever had. I knew very well medieval drinks did not taste like the ones we drank today.

"Why is everything here so... medieval? Like you carrying a sword. How do you not know about guns?"

As Kael took a sip of wine, I couldn't help but notice his lips. The way he looked back at me wasn't helping either.

"We know of human modernizations but have no need of them."

"Not true. You have toilet paper."

Kael actually rolled his eyes. "We do not have toilet paper."

"I beg to differ. Back at the gatehouse they had some." I left out the fact that it was the best toilet paper I'd ever used in my life.

"It's silkspore, not toilet paper. Your question is one humans have grappled with since they arrived. And one of the reasons they don't belong here. Elydor requires balance. Foreign materials, guns, electronics... we've no need of them nor would Elydor allow for it."

He spoke of Elydor as if it were a living thing.

Kael stood, so I did too.

If this were a medieval castle, the woman that just joined us was its lady if her bearing told me anything. Except, she wasn't dressed like the lady of the castle. Judging by the others

I'd seen in the courtyard we passed, I'd expected a gown with flowing sleeves, maybe a kirtle and overcoat. Definitely not breeches and a cream tunic. Small strands of dark brown hair, braided, framed a face as beautiful as the Aetherian woman, Lyra. But darker, as if she'd spent much more time in the sun than the other woman.

She looked ready for battle. Beautiful. Fierce. And in Kael's arms. As if I gave a wit about that. But the same man who'd hauled me over his shoulder without a thought and only answered me half the time had his arms wrapped around this woman as if they were lovers.

"Issa," he said, releasing her. "You really need to get rid of Lord Draven."

She arched a brow. "I haven't seen you for, how long? Years? And that is the first thing you say to me?"

"It has not been years, and aye, I do not like the man."

I couldn't disagree with Kael on that.

Issa... Lady Isolde... looked at me. She couldn't be much older than I was, maybe even younger. But it was hard to tell; the wisdom in her eyes aged her well beyond a twenty-some-thing-year-old. I'd never seen such full lips on a woman before either, or at least not without some filler. And her light brown eyes were fascinating, the way she held my gaze.

"I'm Isolde," she said, sticking out her hand. Not only was she human, she was a modern one, despite her clothing and surroundings. I offered my hand back.

"No doubt Kael would have introduced us if he had manners," I said, surprised by my own bravado. And rudeness. I wasn't usually so sour, but extraordinary times and all... "Mia," I added, remembering I hadn't offered my name. "Your man called you Lady Isolde, yet you offer your given name to me?"

She glanced at Kael, smiling. "I like her."

"Makes one of us."

I made a face at my captor but then offered Isolde a smile back.

"Any friend of Kael's is a friend of mine," she said. "I've no need for formalities. Sit. Tell me, what brings you both to Hawthorne Manor?"

Manor? Although a manor house could be as large as this castle, it typically was not a defensive holding, and from everything I'd seen, this place was built for defense.

"Can we remain here for a few days?" Kael asked.

Isolde waited for more, but Kael wasn't forthcoming with any additional information. So he wouldn't tell her about me? Was he worried I would reveal myself? Ask for her aid? If she was human, this was the ally I needed.

On the other hand, the two were obviously very close. She might not side with a stranger over her friend. I looked between them, but said nothing. For now.

"You will tell me no more?" she asked finally.

"Only that I would appreciate any who are pursuing us to be turned away."

Isolde sighed. "Kael, I've no desire to be embroiled in your war."

"*My* war?" He laughed. "Surely you jest. You know as well as anyone I've attempted to avoid bloodshed whenever possible these past years."

Isolde frowned.

"Two days is all I ask."

"Of course," she said tightly, turning to me. "And your friend?"

"We are not friends," I said, earning a sharp glance from Kael. Something held me back from saying more, at least in front of Kael. But if what Jon had told us was true, this man was the son of my father's enemy, which made him my enemy too. I needed more information, and it sounded like we'd be here long enough to get it and ask Isolde for help.

"As Kael has few human friends, I am not surprised to hear as much. Why then, do you accompany him?"

"I cannot tell you Issa." That from Kael. "And I wish to share her chamber. Mia is in danger, but that is all I'm able to tell you."

Share his chamber? Hell no. "Kael, I hardly think—"

A knock at the door was followed by the steward's arrival with a tray of food. I was hungry, tired, sore, and confused. For the moment, hunger got top billing. But after a meal and some sleep, it was time to plan my escape. I'd just have to figure out who to trust with the information swirling around in my head.

I'd come through the portal, the Aetherian Gate as Kael called it, despite the fact that it was closed. The son of the man responsible for separating my parents and for my awful thoughts about my father had kidnapped me.

It was time to face the truth. Despite a recurring sense of peace, even while being held against my will, this was no dream but a nightmare. And one I fully intended to wake up from.

12

KAEL

There was every possibility Mia would tell Issa what had happened. It was a chance I had to take. Lyra was following us, and others looking for her may realize I had diverted this way as well. Though a human, I had no doubt Issa would remain loyal to me, but this situation would certainly test our bond of friendship.

After sleeping for a short time on a pallet in the spacious bedchamber Issa had given us, I awoke well before dawn. A quick walk around the battlements, confirming our position, for now, was safe, I returned to find Mia still asleep.

A knock at the door helped me decide if I should wake her.

"My lord," a maid said, her arms filled with clothing. "Lady Isolde sent these for your companion." I took them, as she continued. "There is a gown, or if she prefers, breeches and a tunic, as our lady wears."

I thanked the young maid who promised to return with a bowl of scented water and invited us belowstairs to break our fast. I asked instead for a tray to be brought here.

"Why can't we eat breakfast in the hall?"

She was awake.

I'd watched Mia sleep, attempting to stir the anger that typically came when I was around humans, Issa an exception. Instead of anger, I found myself wondering what she lied about. And more importantly, how she'd come through a closed Gate.

I unfortunately also found myself admiring her beauty. Her long hair, tied back in a ponytail, as her people called it. Mia's unusual clothing did little to reveal a comely shape, her breasts pressed against my back as we rode telling me all I needed to know about what was beneath.

"Why are you looking at me that way?"

I stepped closer. There were few windows in this chamber, only arrow slits, as Hawthorne Manor was built for defense. Issa's parents, now both dead, had seen to its construction themselves. Its position along the Gyorian border meant both Issa and her parents, nobles in high esteem with the human king, saw little peace.

Especially these last thirty years.

"Your hair," I said, the little light that did shine through hitting the top of her head at just the right angle. "It seems... lighter, almost."

It was an offhanded comment, but the look on her face made me wonder if there was something more to it. Her eyes widened temporarily, before Mia schooled her features back to sleepiness. She yawned.

"That's odd." Kicking off the coverlet, she hopped from the bed.

"Issa sent some clothing." I put the pile where she'd been sitting. "Your choice of gown or breeches."

Mia looked at the pile, frowning. "And if I do not wish to wear either?"

The response I'd expected. "You are much too conspicuous in that. It draws attention."

She laughed. "Only here would a pair of jeans, tee, and a hoodie draw attention. By the way, why wasn't I cold on the trail? There still seemed to be snow on the mountains where we came from—"

"Aetheria."

"Sure. And last night Isolde said something about spring coming, which means it's winter? So you have the same seasons as we do?"

"Uninitiated." I sighed. "Put those on, and I will answer your questions."

"What does that mean? Uninitiated? You've used that word before."

Another knock at the door. That would be the maid. Rather than having her speak with Mia, I took the bowl and clothes and sent the girl away.

"Rosewater to cleanse yourself," I explained. "I will give you privacy to get dressed and answer any questions you have."

With that, I left the chamber and waited outside. It took less than two minutes, or what a human might mark as such. We kept less rigid time in Elydor, or had, until the humans influenced that too.

"Oh," she said, opening the door and seeing me.

"Going somewhere?"

"No." Her sensuous lips pursed together. "Just wondering if I'm a prisoner."

This had to stop. Though none were in the corridor, neither did I want anyone to overhear. Stepping back into the chamber, I closed the door behind us.

Before Mia moved away from me, we were almost toe to

toe. If she were any other woman, and not a human, I'd have acknowledged my body's reaction to her.

"I told you of the Gate Council. Every one of its members, representatives from all clans—"

"Except human."

"Irregardless. Each were imbued with magic to alert them when someone came through the Gate. It was our duty to be present when that happened, determine if that person, or persons, would be allowed through. I'd assumed after so many years that the spell had dissipated, but it had not. I knew the moment you came through, which means every person on the Council did too. They will be looking for you."

"Like Lyra?"

"Aye. Like Lyra."

"And I am safer with you than them? Is that what you're saying?"

"Aye."

"Bullshit."

"You do not believe me?"

"No. I do not."

Smart woman, though that fact meant I had to be more vigilant. "Get dressed, Mia. We've much to discuss."

As I turned from her, I heard her mutter, "Wonder if the term high-handed means anything here?"

Leaning against the stone wall, I waited for as long as I supposed it might take, attempting to sort through the past few days' events to keep my mind from what was happening behind me.

The skirmish. Another dead Gyorian. Mia coming through. Imagining my father's reaction. In truth, I worried about that last one. While it was true that I fully intended to get Mia safely into Gyorian territory, my father did not necessarily share my desire to avoid any unnecessary bloodshed. He believed my brother and I "too moderate" when it came to humans, but we both also felt his beliefs bordered on fanatical.

"My lord?"

The maid had returned. I took the tray from her. "Thank you. I will bring this inside."

"Lady Isolde inquires, if you will not be coming to the hall, if she might visit you both in your chamber?"

There was no avoiding her. Issa had told me as much last eve before we retired. We could shelter here, but she'd require more answers than I'd thus far provided.

"Of course," I said, bringing the tray of warm bread and fruit inside. Since the humans traded freely with Aetheria, and to a lesser extent, with Thalassari, their crops benefited from a hybrid between their cuisine and our own.

I was wholly unprepared for this version of Mia.

"Don't you dare laugh. I figured I could wear this until we had to leave. I've always wanted to try on one of these medieval gowns."

Why would I laugh?

Her hair was down, the gown Issa lent her a vibrant green with gold thread lining its sleeves and neckline. That neckline... I could not tear my gaze away.

"Yeah, I know. I don't usually show this much boob."

She was outrageous. "You look beautiful."

The words came out of my mouth before I could stop them, because they were true. Shaking my head to clear it, I put the tray of food on a table as Mia attempted to sit. It took her multiple attempts to smooth the gown beneath her.

"This is all so confusing," she said, reaching for a glass. "No modern plumbing, but coconut oil for my hair. And orange juice. Where do you get oranges from? Yet no windows. It's like I stepped back in time to medieval England but with some modern touches, and not necessarily the ones I'd choose. Though I'll admit your version of toilet paper is pretty sweet."

She began to eat.

I sat back, watching her as Mia popped a strawberry into her mouth. She quickly picked up a handkerchief as the juice ran down her lips. By the stones, this was going to be a long journey.

"It would be less confusing if the humans had never arrived."

"No?" she asked between bites. "You carry an iron sword, and yet can wield magic. Your buildings are made of marble and glass, but surely such materials are inferior to what you could contrive with your"—she waved her hands in the air—"magic."

"We use materials native to Elydor. I cannot contrive something from nothing, but I can manipulate any element found here already. As can each of the clans."

Finally, she finished the damn strawberries. I thought back to her earlier questions.

"Uninitiated are humans who come through the Gate with no prior knowledge of Elydor. Seasons here are different, in part because the land responds more to the magic of each region than to solar patterns. While we've adopted human names for seasons, Elydor doesn't experience the same extremes as Earth. The weather is temperate year-round, though we do mark time similarly to you, and certain flora and fauna appear only during specific times. In Aetheria, for example, you'll see snow during winter—and on the mountain peaks, even in summer—but without the intense cold you might expect. It's more an effect of air magic binding the snow to the landscape."

As expected, my explanations did little to ease her curiosity. "Snow, but it is not cold? How is such a thing possible?"

I closed my fist. It was easier standing on the ground, but I was not an infant Elydorian. Turning my hand, I opened it. Mia gasped.

"That is"—she leaned forward—"one of the most beautiful flowers I've ever seen. It looks like a Hawaiian hibiscus. How did you do that?"

"Watch," I said, waiting for another gasp. It wasn't long in coming. The flower, though it had materialized, faded quickly.

"Where did it go?"

"The sea blossom is native to Thalassari, our southernmost clan. But since I'm neither in Thalassari, nor is that flower in season, it does not remain."

Her perfectly formed mouth opened and then closed.

"But... you just said you can't produce something not in existence. So how did you do that?"

"I can temporarily create objects that exist naturally within Elydor, but they cannot be permanently maintained if the conditions aren't suitable." And then, remembering the speech I used to give, I continued. "One time, we all had the same... what you would call it, magic. But as the years passed, some migrated south, to Gyoria. Others, further south, to the sand and tides of a tropical Thalassaria. Some of the elders remember those times, when Aetherians could initiate tremors in the land, or when Thalassari could wield air. Eventually, the longer each remained in their region, the more their magic evolved to what it is today."

I took a bite of bread.

"And you are immortal?"

"Aye."

"But can be killed?"

"Correct."

"But you age, clearly. You are not a child."

Neither was I having child-like thoughts of Mia at the moment.

"I am not. We age, as you might, but more slowly."

"Forever?"

"As far as we know. Some elders are over three thousand years old."

"Holy shit. What do they look like?"

Usually, I was annoyed by Uninitiated human questions. But Mia learning about Elydor, while filling her stomach, meant she forgot to be wary, and angry. I liked this Mia more than I should.

"The same as all vaelith."

"Vaelith?"

"Those who have lived for more than one thousand years. They are revered for their wisdom and authority in all clans."

"Are you vaelith?"

"No. I am haranya, those who have seen more than one hundred years. My father is thaloran, as are all those who reach five hundred years."

"I'm still confused."

"I've heard humans say haranya appear as if they have lived thirty years in the human world. Thaloran, maybe forty-five or fifty years, and vaelith as if they are sixty or seventy years."

"That's... ideal. I'm surprised humans who know about this place haven't tried to figure out how to replicate it in our world. It's basically the fountain of youth."

"They have. Your example, the fountain of youth, for

instance, is a legend that stemmed from encounters with Elydorian magic. Explorers like Juan Ponce de León believed they could find a source of eternal youth but misunderstood our natural longevity as a physical fountain."

"So the fountain of youth—"

"Was an attempt to capture the essence of vaelith's longevity by those who've visited our realm. But without true knowledge, their expeditions led only to peril and failure. Typically human."

"Hey," she said, the indignant Mia returning. "You forget, I'm human."

"I haven't forgotten." Nor could I, even for a moment.

Mia waved a hand as if to dismiss me.

I sat up straighter.

Unless I was mistaken, when she did so, the slightest bit of air wafted toward me.

"Mia," I said, more sharply than I'd intended. "What was that?"

"What was what?"

Had I been imagining things?

"When you waved your hand..." I stopped, realizing how nonsensical I was being.

"I really do hate that tone. Do you guys have the word 'bully' here?"

"No. We don't."

I dismissed the thought as another knock at the door interrupted us. I opened it to find Issa on the other side, but I could sense immediately that this was not simply a good-morning visit.

"Kael. You have to leave."

13

MEV

The woman, Isolde, pushed right past Kael, no easy feat given his size. She closed the door behind her after telling Kael he had to leave.

But weren't we supposed to be staying another day? I had to find an ally. Escape Kael's clutches. I couldn't leave yet.

"I know," Kael said when Isolde put her hand on his arm. It was a touch of familiarity.

"Draven has not kept her presence quiet. I told him to do so but—"

"Let me guess? He undermines you, as usual."

She pulled her hand away. "He was my father's closest friend."

"Your father's, Isolde, not yours. I do not understand why you trust the man."

"We have little time to debate this now. He hates you, Kael, as well you know. And seems inclined to uncover your purpose here." She nodded to me. "And hers."

"Collect your belongings," Kael said to me, in his typical gruff manner.

I assume it was him. There weren't that many Elydorians powerful enough. He hates humans. He hated that your father gave them land, bordering his own, which made it worse. He hated the humans' brand of magic and how powerful they became, so quickly. But most of all, he hated them for bringing in a disease that killed his wife.

Jiminy Christmas. How could I have forgotten it all so quickly? More importantly, what the hell had happened when I'd waved my hand? As Kael suspected, something *had* happened. That same feeling, as when I came through... but this time, in my hands.

I had to think this through.

Kael's father had potentially sent my mother and me through the Aetherian Gate and closed it, and that's who Kael was taking me to.

Before he could stop me, I blurted, "I came through the portal." Shit. "Aetherian Gate. He was the one to find me, and now he's taking me to Gyoria against my will."

Wanting to squeeze my eyes closed to avoid the look of murder Kael was now giving me, I stood my ground. Held my chin high, like my mother had done all these years. I would not be cowed by him. Despite the fact that he could toss boulders like pebbles and create an earthquake to swallow me whole.

"Is this true?"

Thankfully, Isolde turned her ire on him instead of questioning me.

Yep, he was definitely going to kill me if he had the chance. Despite the fact that he was staring hard at my cleavage earlier. Worse, my traitorous body had forgotten, momentarily, that he was the enemy.

Before he could answer, I added, "I wish you had his abilities so you would know definitively that I am not lying. I am what he calls an Uninitiated and—"

"Abilities? Not lying?" She looked more than a little skeptical, her questions aimed at Kael.

In response, he shrugged, as if he didn't have a care in the world.

Oh. M. Gee.

What a giant asshole. "That isn't one of your abilities, is it?"

"Lie detection?" Isolde looked as if she'd burst into laughter any second. Instead, she stared at me. "No, it isn't one of his abilities. Mia, how did you get through the Aetherian Gate? It's closed."

He could glare at me all he wanted, but Kael had tricked me.

"Apparently, it isn't," he said. "Neither is my ability to detect its dormant passage. I was at the Summit when she came through. Lyra and likely every past Council member are now following us."

"Splendid." Isolde let out a huge sigh, as if she wasn't the only one in this chamber wanting to murder another of its occupants. Kael was still really pissed, too. "I assume you intend to take her to your father?"

"I do."

"And you expect me to allow you to simply walk out of here with the poor woman held captive? I love you, Kael, but there are limits. Even for me."

She loved him? That wasn't good, but at least she was willing to help anyway. Also, who could love such a man? Granted, he was hot as hell, and every place I'd touched him was as solid as that rock he'd tossed, but I knew as well as anyone, physical attraction only got you so far. He was also high-handed, reticent, a deceiver and... did I mention high-handed?

"We don't have time for this, Issa. I am not leaving her. And surely you know I'd not allow an innocent woman to come to harm."

I watched Isolde closely. She did the same to me, the woman's indecision clear in her expression. Her shoulders rose and then fell as she let out a deep breath. This beautiful noblewoman, dressed like a warrior, held my fate in her hands. Before she spoke, I guessed how she would respond based on the look of sympathy she now gave me.

"I will not be the only one with a keen interest in her well-being. If I learn of any mistreatment by your father—"

"You will not. You have my word."

"Please," I begged her, knowing it was useless. Clearly these two had a long history. "Do not let him take me."

I couldn't tell her the real reason why I was desperate not to be brought to Gyoria to meet the man who'd likely ruined my mother's life. Not without Kael learning my true identity.

"I am so sorry, Mia. We have an accord, Kael and I." The look she gave him was, and this could not be more shocking, one of adoration.

"Come," he said. "Issa's word here is law, as Lady of Hawthorne. None here will help you if she does not will it. And as I said, you will not come to any harm under my care, Mia."

Yeah, I wouldn't be so sure of that.

But fighting them both was futile, obviously. I'd have to find another ally, another way to escape and get back north. But not in this gown.

"My clothes," I said, looking down at the very impractical attire.

"Take it, and the breeches and tunic too. You may need them."

I looked around the chamber. "My own clothes? The ones I came in?"

"Are gone." That from the lying kidnapper. "They are out of place here and will draw too much attention."

Great. I loved that college hoodie. It reminded me of some good times, ones when I'd felt less unsettled, more sure of my life's purpose. When things were carefree and simple.

And so I found myself tossed onto Stormbreaker in a freaking gown (no time to change, apparently) waving goodbye to my would-be savior and leaving Hawthorne Manor. As we sped away, Kael not speaking to me, I thought back to that weird tingling which had happened three times. When I'd come through the portal, when I'd met Lord Draven and when I'd waved my hand around. Though there was a similar quality to them, the first had been obviously the strongest, affecting my entire body and every nerve ending. The others were more localized, but nonetheless distinct. The time with Draven, more negative than positive, but still similar.

Do you have any intuitive abilities? Like your mother?

I don't have any special abilities.

I'd told Jon the truth. My mother said, even as a young child, she could sense things. She described it like subtle déjà vu, as if fragments of the future overlayed the present, making reality slightly surreal. She tried many times to help me evoke her sense of clarity, moments where patterns and outcomes became visible in a way they hadn't before. But I'd never experienced a rush of adrenaline or a calm knowing as she described. After Mom had been trained by a woman in Boston, she'd been able to turn those moments of clarity into predictions of the future. Me? I couldn't so much as guess what I would eat for dinner, even if I went grocery shopping myself. I was a mood eater, so even if I bought grilled chicken and lettuce, I'd find myself down the street at our local bar for a cheeseburger, salad be damned.

Tossing everything I'd learned so far around my head, thankful I didn't need to hold on for dear life since we were riding at a more reasonable pace, the only logical conclusion I could come to was that nothing made sense.

Most especially, given all of the confusion and uncertainty of this world, the pervading sense of peace that periodically settled over me. How could I belong here when everything felt so confusing and uncertain? Yet every time I had that thought —one urging me to escape, to find a way home—another pull, nearly as strong, told me to stay.

I hated silence. It made me uncomfortable. "Were you two lovers?"

Mevlida! Seriously?

I'd relegated that particular thought to the bottom of my list of questions, so of all the things to pop out of my mouth, that was not the most pressing matter at hand. Not by a long shot.

Kael seemed to think it was a strange question too. He turned sideways, so I could see his profile. Although most of me had no desire to step foot in Gyoria, I was also really curious to see if the others looked like him. Or was Kael a prime Gyorian specimen? Not that it mattered.

"We were not... lovers. Though I find it intriguing, given your current situation and our visit to Hawthorne Manor, that is the first question you would ask."

Yeah, join the club, buddy. Time for some major spin on the situation. "I only asked because it surprised me that she sided with you over a fellow human, especially given your distaste for my people." I tried to sound nonchalant. "I figured you must have been together, in that way."

And then it occurred to me...

"Wait. Do Elydorians have sex? You seem mostly human-like but..."

At that, Kael laughed. Actually laughed, the sound surprisingly pleasant.

"Yes," he finally answered. "We have sex. Would you like to see how it compares?"

Was Kael actually teasing me?

"No thank you," I said, even if that wasn't 100 per cent true. I obviously would not act on it, but pretending I wasn't attracted to him was just silly, despite the fact that Kael and his kidnapping put the red in red flag.

"So why did she help you?"

"Issa's father was a powerful nobleman. Unlike the other clans in Elydor, the humans are divided, each noble holding sway over their own territory with no single ruler to unify them. Nearly ten years ago, a sickness plagued the humans, one as fierce as any that had torn through Elydor. Her father fell ill first, and then her mother. Issa herself came to my father, begging for his aid."

"Why would she do that, knowing your father hates humans?"

"Because she was desperate to save her parents. The human physicians could not find a cure and advised her that the only hope was use of Gyorian aevumite, a stone known for its healing properties if used correctly. My father denied her request."

Bastard. Of course he did.

"I'd been the one to escort her to my father. And though

she was a human, because of the callousness of his rejection and Issa's courage in coming to him in the first place"—Kael sighed—"I secured a bit of aevumite and followed her toward Hawthorne Manor."

To say I was in shock was an understatement. "You tried to save a powerful noble family? Against your father's wishes?"

"I did. Though it obviously did not work. Issa was named as her father's successor, and her status in Estmere as keeper of the border in this region was secured. As you saw, she is as much a warrior as those who serve her, a necessity in these parts. Issa prefers not to leave her fate to others. I've trained with her, and admire her as much now as I did when we first met."

So many questions.

"What did your father say when you did that?"

"He named my brother as successor, despite being the second-born son."

Holy shitballs. "He disinherited you?"

Kael was quiet then. Obviously this was a sensitive topic, with good reason.

"He did."

"Yet you still serve him?"

"I serve Gyoria and must respect the will of its king."

I didn't know if I should admire Kael or be appalled at his loyalty to a man who clearly did not deserve it. That kind of blind devotion could be dangerous, and yet, it was strangely admirable too.

New topic.

"So the two of you stayed friends? Seems strange, given your history. And her beauty."

There, I said it.

"Issa is very beautiful," he said. "But the son of a Gyorian king could never partner with a human noblewoman. Bedding a woman like Issa, without any intention of partnering, would be a dishonor to her."

Well then. I guess one-night stands weren't a thing here. Or at least, not with a noblewoman. It was all very... medieval.

"Is partnering like marrying?"

"It is."

I'd have asked more questions, but we stopped suddenly. Kael put up a fist, which, I supposed, was his caveman way of telling me to be quiet. I didn't see or hear anything. After passing through the same open meadow as yesterday, Kael turned in the direction of a forest, the path we rode a narrow one. No strange animals, yet. Just really pretty trees, and lots of them.

"They move away from us, heading north."

"They?"

"Riders, far ahead."

"And you can hear them, so far away?"

"No," he said. "An Aetherian could, as they are able to manipulate sound waves. But I can feel them in the ground below us."

I assumed we would begin to ride since the riders were headed away from us, but instead Kael turned to me once again. He looked at my hair. I'd put it in a low braid—a pony seemed somehow at odds with my attire.

Kael slowed us to a stop.

"What? Why are you looking at me like that?"

Kael's eyes lowered to my own.

"I thought maybe I was imagining things, but in the sunlight... your hair definitely looks lighter today."

I pulled my braid forward. Sure enough, it looked almost as if my natural color was coming through. When I was little,

I'd looked like a normal girl, except—and there was no good way to describe it—my hair was a pearly white. Teased for as far back as I could remember, I'd always hated it. When I was old enough, my mother allowed me to dye it blonde, as I'd been doing ever since. It usually took a good four weeks to start peeking through and I got it colored just before we left for York.

Lyra.

Her hair had been shades of silver and white, tinged with blue, a striking feature that was hard to forget. Air clan. White hair. It made sense.

Holy. Shit.

Act cool, Mev. Do not let him see your panic.

"My hair usually does this in the summer, turns really blonde. Strange it would happen now. Maybe your sun is stronger than ours." I tried to sound nonchalant, despite the fact that I could hear my own heartbeat in my ears. If my natural white came through anywhere, it was at the roots. This definitely wasn't normal. But then again, this Dorothy wasn't in Kansas anymore.

He continued to stare at me.

"Don't we need to be somewhere?"

I was tempted to smile at the utterly droll look he gave me, but at least Kael did spur us forward once again.

For some time I watched the landscape, dreaming of how I might escape. Trying to ignore the fact that Kael must work out an awful lot, from the feel of him.

But mostly, I really didn't want to die.

Hating to ask, knowing he'd pay me lip service, I finally did anyway.

"Kael? Will you promise not to let your father hurt me, like you said to Isolde?"

I didn't plan to be around when I met his father, but just in case, I'd get any assurances I could at this point.

"You have my word, Mia," he said, without turning back. "And a Gyorian never goes back on his word."

"Even to a human?"

"Even to a human."

I'd take it. As if I had any other choice.

14

KAEL

It was as good a place as any to rest Stormbreaker and break our fast. Mia would need a respite after riding all morning, and though Elydorians could go for longer periods without eating or drinking, we did have similar bodily functions to humans.

I had survived for many years with less tormented thoughts than on this morning's ride. Aside from ensuring we weren't being followed, and avoiding the areas of conflict which were in abundance along both the Gyorian and human border, other questions remained.

How did she come through the Gate? Would others be following? Was it, after all this time, reopened? Or was Mia an anomaly? What was she holding back from me?

Almost as importantly, how was it possible that a human could affect me the way she did? It was as if the pull she'd mentioned that had taken her through the Gate was drawing me to her as well. Try as I might not to smile at her outrageous comments, I found myself doing so more and more often.

And then there was that vow.

I hadn't hesitated. Not that I would wish any innocent to come to harm, but in promising not to allow my father to hurt her, I'd positioned myself between the two. His methods for gaining information—as he had from King Galfrid's mage who finally revealed the secret to opening and closing the Gate—could be extreme.

"This is the most beautiful lake I've ever seen."

Her words brought me to the present.

It was small, but with a dense area of trees we could use for camouflage, which made the spot ideal. But I supposed, with its bright green color, courtesy of Elydorian lumina moss, it was a beautiful location as well. Even if we were on human land.

Dismounting, I reached up to aid Mia, lifting her down to the ground.

"How the hell did women deal with these things?" she asked, shoving her gown to one side. "First order of business is changing. I hope Isolde's other outfit fits since *someone* got rid of mine."

She untied one of the saddlebags where I'd stored the additional clothing, and I watched as Mia stormed off toward a thicket between two trees. For a woman who'd been plucked from her realm—one with so little magic that most did not even believe in those who possessed it—and subsequently taken against her will, she was managing remarkably well. Still, I had no doubt she would attempt to escape, but Mia would not get far. Gyorians were expert trackers, especially on land. I should probably explain that fact to her.

By the time she emerged from the trees, I'd set up a makeshift camp. There was no fire this time, as we would not be staying, nor a shelter, but I'd hidden Stormbreaker and provided us with stone seats.

"This outfit barely fits," she muttered, folding the gown as best she could and shoving it into my bag.

I disagreed.

Issa's breeches fit perfectly, if slightly snug around the hips highlighting every bit of Mia's curves. The short tunic fell just beneath her waist and unfortunately covered most of her breasts, though it was more fitted than the clothing she'd arrived in. Since the humans' fashion drew both from their own, as well as the Elydorian clans, their clothing sometimes served to denote nobility. Other clothing, like what she wore now, were more functional. In short, she looked like a cross between a human and Elydorian warrior. Leather boots laced up and over the tight breeches, her hair still pulled back in a braid. It was damned inconvenient to find myself attracted to my charge. One I was supposed to hate.

"What?" she asked, hands on her hips.

It was easier when Mia was afraid of me. She'd taken my vow to heart, it seemed, and now held nothing back. I could not imagine this woman in my bed. What it would be like to attempt to tame her there.

Not that I'd want her to be tamed. Not truly.

On the other hand...

"You should know, Gyorians are expert trackers, given their tie to the land."

She froze.

"What does that mean, exactly?"

"It means I can hear you walking, if I so choose. It means, there is no escaping from me."

She had the good sense to appear shocked. "Escape? Me?"

"Nor should you wish to," I clarified. "If you wish to survive in Elydor."

That did not please her, but I had not been aiming to do

so. I'd made the vow, unthinkingly, and therefore had to make our roles clear.

Mia crossed her arms angrily.

"I wonder which is the real Mia? The one I've traveled with thus far or the one that attempted to get Issa to rescue her. The one who stomps around our camp like a wild trexan."

"A what, now?"

"Trexans are found mostly in Gyoria but venture across the borders, especially when humans hunt them. You might think it was a boar in your world. Known for their strength and stubbornness, we consider the trexan a symbol of tenacity and resilience."

She seemed surprised. "That sounds suspiciously like a compliment."

"It's not. Their tusks are sharp and their bullish temperament is not unlike yours, hence the comparison."

"Thanks."

I held back a smile. "You are a strange one, princess."

The nickname, ironically, fit her. I knew the world Mia had come from, one which did not include riding all day or nibbling on roasted rabbit and stale bread, yet she never once complained. Not about that, at least.

"Here." I held out a piece of bread. "It is all we have today. We'll ride until I reach the Gyorian border, likely well past nightfall."

"Sounds like fun." She took the bread, her fingers brushing mine as she did.

Sitting, Mia ate in silence. I handed her a water skin which she took, but did not drink from. "It's dangerous as a human, to not drink for too long a period."

"It's also dangerous to be kidnapped by your... by you."

What had she been about to say?

Despite her protests, Mia drank anyway. I took the skin back and sat, peering out into the lake and seeing it from her eyes. It had been so long since I'd been to the human world, but I remembered the dull color of the first river I'd seen after passing through.

"What did you do? In your realm?"

"Like, my job?"

"Yes. Like your job," I repeated.

"I am a museum curator specializing in ancient artifacts. I guess you don't have them here?"

"Ancient artifacts?" I asked.

Mia rolled her eyes. She did that a lot, at least with me.

"Museums."

"Not really. We have places where ancient artifacts, as you call them, are kept. Aetherians are especially obsessed with cataloging Elydorian history."

"You don't think it's important? To remember your history?"

"To the extent they do? No. I leave that to the mages."

"Then they have all the power. Speaking of power, I've been wondering. Who are the most powerful here? And don't just say Gyorians because you're biased."

Finished with her bread, Mia wiped her hands clean of any crumbs and leaned back, lifting her face to the sun and closing her eyes as if she didn't care whether or not I answered her question. I watched her, taking in everything at once. The curve of her hips. The swell of her breasts. Mia's smooth cheeks and full lips. Her hair that I was certain appeared a different shade now than when she'd come through the Gate.

"Well?" she asked, Mia's eyes whipping open, the moment of serenity over.

"You told me not to say Gyorians."

"Seriously? You are so predictable."

I wasn't. And would like to show her how very unpredictable I could be. "What did you want me to say? The humans?"

"No. I mean... whatever. The truth would be nice."

"The truth is, it's complicated. Ask four people, and you'd get four different answers. Our magic is very different from each other. And even the humans have... strengths."

"Such as?"

"Their innate abilities, when arriving in Elydor, are enhanced. If someone can see the future on Earth, they can do so more easily here. Those skills can be useful, in certain situations, but not so much in combat. The future doesn't matter much if a tree-sized boulder is being hurled at your head."

"What about between the clans?"

"Also complicated. Age matters. Training too. But so does inherent magical ability. In theory, the king or queen of each clan is the strongest in their clan."

"In theory?"

"There have been exceptions."

"And their offspring? Are you the second most powerful Gyorian?"

"Yes," I said. "Though my brother might disagree. But offspring do usually inherit their parents' abilities. As I said, though, training matters. But again, there are exceptions. Thalassaria once had a queen, and a notoriously lazy son who cared more about fucking than training, yet he became one of the most powerful their clan had ever seen."

"It's weird to hear you say 'fucking.'"

"It is originally a human word," I admitted. "Though I can do more than simply say the word."

Her unabashed expression was precisely what I'd imagined it would be. Teasing her was enjoyable.

"What happened to him?"

"He drowned. Ship capsized."

"How does the most powerful Thalassari drown? Don't they use water magic?"

At this point, Mia was sitting up, leaning forward, eagerly listening to every word. I normally became impatient having to break down every detail of our world to an Uninitiated, but with her? I quite liked Mia's enthusiasm to learn our ways.

"They do. And can even breathe underwater, for a spell. It's a long story but, as I said, Elydorians can be killed. Especially if you lack any semblance of humility."

Mia turned her head toward the lake, thoughtful. As she did, the sun's light hit the back of her head. Jumping up from my spot on the rock, I made my way toward her.

"What are you doing?" she asked as I stood behind her.

Before responding, knowing she wouldn't allow it, I reached up for the tie that bound her braid together.

"Kael?" She swatted my hand away. "What the hell are you doing?"

I grabbed her wrist. "Stop," I said, my tone sharper than intended. With my other hand, I continued. Pulling off the tie, I threaded my fingers through the braid, loosening it. The fact that Mia didn't try to stop me with her other hand, or attempt to twist away, was almost as telling as the silken strands that unraveled.

Dropping her wrist, I used both hands now, trying not to think of how smooth the loosened hair felt beneath my fingertips. Completely unbound, I no longer had a reason to touch it but could not pull away.

"Kael..." Her voice cracked.

Closing my eyes, as if doing so might make me forget what I was seeing, I thought back to that morning when she'd waved her hand and the slightest bit of air had wafted toward me.

I thought I'd been imagining it. That I'd had too little sleep.

But I wasn't imagining the fact that Mia's hair, once blonde, was currently a muted shade of white, more obvious now than it had been that morning, and even more so unbraided.

She shifted toward me, and I let her hair drop from my hands. Opening my eyes, I stared into hers, cursing myself for a fool. If I'd stopped staring at her breasts, I might also have noticed the blue I once saw there, mixed with brown and green, was brighter than most humans with similarly colored eyes.

I hated the fear in them.

But she had cause to be afraid if my suspicions were accurate.

"I was once on a Council," I said, my voice measured as I wrestled to remain calm. "Responsible for deciding if humans were allowed entry into Elydor. That same Council was tasked also with controlling Elydorian travel into the human world. Which is how I know there was only one from Elydor in your realm when my father closed the Gate. The queen's unborn daughter."

"So he did close it," she muttered. "Kael. I did not know my identity until moments before I fell through, when Jon told my friend Clara and me the story. An immortal realm? How could I possibly believe anything he said was true? But then I touched the portal, and it seemed to... come alive. To call to me."

Of course it did. Elydor rebelled against any loss of its magic which was why so few of us stayed long in the human realm. The longer we remained there, the more our magic began to dwindle. The opposite of what was happening to Mia.

Nay. Not Mia.

"Mevlida," I said. "Your name is Mevlida. When the humans foresaw the queen was with child, and predicted that babe was a girl, she told them her name would be Mevlida."

Tears pooled in her eyes. "Kael, please—"

My hands balled into fists at my sides. Not human. Half human. The other half, Aetherian.

"Though your full name is Princess Mevlida of Aetheria, daughter of King Galfrid."

"I... I guess. Yes."

Princess.

It felt right because it was right.

She began to cry.

15

MEV

Of all the times I should have run, Kael unbraiding my hair made the top of the list. One second, he'd been talking to me as if we weren't opposite sides of a coin that, once tossed into the air, could not have two winners. The next, he'd been right behind me.

The second I realized what he intended, *I knew*.

Knew in the same way I knew I had no choice in The Crooked Key's basement but to touch that portal.

Knew in the same way, from the second I met Lord Draven, that he was dangerous.

It was as if some invisible force inside me pulled me toward the answer. As to the question of, "What is Kael doing?" that force told me, "Discovering the truth."

It happened much more quickly than I expected. Too quick to properly formulate a plan, as if one could be formulated when the guy who'd kidnapped you could hear vibrations in the ground. Could kill a person as easily as I could tell the difference between a whisper and a shout.

Sitting here, huddled inside myself, knees pulled to my

chest, getting Isolde's too-snug outfit wet with my tears, was not the kind of plan I had in mind. When he touched me, I flinched. Lifting my head, finding Kael seated next to me, I waited for the hand on my back to move toward restraining my wrists again.

Incredibly, that never happened.

Instead, Kael pulled me toward him. His other hand laid my head half on his shoulder and half buried it into his chest. The unexpected gesture, after what he just discovered, made me cry even more. I held on as if this wasn't my enemy but a friend. Someone who might feel badly that I'd gotten plucked from the world I knew into one I hadn't known existed. Someone who was tired and hungry and scared.

So fucking scared.

Even now, wrapped in his arms, as Kael whispered, "Shhh," and "All will be well," I wondered if it was some kind of ploy to break me down before he delivered the killing blow. But at this very second, I didn't care.

"We are enemies," I sobbed, thinking maybe he'd figured out the rest of it, but not that part.

"I know."

Now Kael stroked my head. That he was capable of such a gesture surprised me most.

"He told me," I added. "Just before I stepped through, Jon told me about... about your father. When I realized who you were..."

Kael never answered. Eventually, the pain in my chest became a dull ache, the realization that he wasn't going to kill me—at least not yet—sunk into my brain. Of course Kael wouldn't kill me before he took me to his father so they could interrogate me first.

"That was smart."

Sniffling, I lifted my head. Wiping my cheeks with the back of my hands, I brought my gaze to his.

"It was smart, not to tell me your name."

I thought that was what he'd said. "Do bitter enemies usually compliment each other in your world?"

"Not usually."

He didn't deny the fact that we were bitter enemies, though.

"Do they usually let them cry into their shoulders?"

Now that I'd stopped, the fact that we sat so close our legs still touched, that his hand was still on my back, was difficult to ignore.

"We *are* bitter enemies, right?"

"We are, indeed."

Loquacious, as usual.

"Then why haven't you bound my wrists, thrown me onto Stormbreaker's back, and rode toward your father with me yet?"

Kael looked at my face as if he were memorizing my features.

"Because if I bind your wrists and throw you anywhere, it will be onto my bed."

As if he didn't just say *that*, Kael jumped up as quickly as he'd joined me in the first place.

"We will camp here tonight."

He seemed almost to say it for himself and not for me. I only heard him because I'd been staring at his lips. Kael had very kissable lips.

As if in a trance, I watched him prepare a camp, as he had the first time. Maybe it wasn't my place to mention it, since he'd kept me alive and all, but curiosity got the better of me.

"You don't seem to be blending the shelter as well as last time."

Not surprisingly, that earned me a look, but not much else.

Because if I bind your wrists and throw you anywhere, it will be onto my bed.

Not once had Kael hinted that he thought of me as anything more than a captive, a puzzle that had to be solved. Not seriously, at least. Between his gentle treatment of me and that comment, I honestly didn't know what to think.

I watched him care for Stormbreaker, as gently as he had cared for me.

"Kael?"

No answer. That was really annoying.

"Kael?"

He'd started making a fire.

I jumped up, walked to him, and stood close enough that he could not ignore me.

"Prince Kael."

He turned. "Yes, princess?"

I forgot my question. He looked down at me, jaw set, eyes narrowed, and frankly? The guy was terrifying. But also mesmerizing in a "he could kill me with one swipe of his hand" sort of way.

"One of my BJJ professors told me that if someone disrespected me, the question wasn't, 'How should I respond?' but instead, 'What environment did I create that made that person think disrespect was okay?'"

If he understood my meaning, Kael wasn't letting on.

"In other words, I must have given you the impression it's acceptable not to respond to me." Thinking harder on this, I was pretty sure the advice didn't apply to situations where you'd been kidnapped by someone with magic. But still... I was going with it. "In case you were wondering, it's not. I seem to remember we had this discussion already, too."

"Yes," he acknowledged, "we did."

"And?"

"And you need a bath." Stalking past me, he added, "We both do."

We'd ridden like bats out of hell and now he wanted to make camp, in the light of day... and take a bath?

"Wait a second." I began to follow him to the lake's edge. Surely he didn't mean to do what I thought...? Kael leaned down and began to remove one of his boots. "Aren't there people chasing us? I tell you who I am and your response is to make camp and—"

My words were cut short as Kael moved from his boots to his leather gambeson. At least, that was what it looked like to me, though I'd admit battle armor was not really my forte. I didn't need to guess if he intended to disrobe in broad daylight, in front of me.

Though his back was to me, the second he removed his shirt, I no longer had to wonder if he was as muscled as I'd imagined. Swallowing at the sight of him, I gathered my wits with just enough time to turn away. A few minutes later, after hearing a splash, I turned back around. Sure enough, his trousers were sitting in a heap on top of the rest of his clothing.

"Are you naked in there?"

Dumb question.

"Do you bathe with your clothes on?" he asked.

So many responses to that...

"Well, I don't usually bathe in a lake, first of all."

Without acknowledging my comment, he disappeared under the water. When Kael came back up, he slicked his wet hair back. I was about to move closer when I remembered how clear the water was. I'd be able to see everything.

"Second of all?"

"Oh, so you did hear me?"

"I always do. You haven't given me permission to disrespect you, Mevlida. As I said before, I'm not a man of many words."

I nearly blurted "Why?" but that felt too intrusive. Too personal. Instead, I said, "Second of all, I don't like cold water."

"It's not cold."

Even at this time of year? I supposed it made sense, since the air was more like an early summer's day than one at the start of spring, at least where I lived.

"Third of all, you are naked."

He actually smiled. "As we've established. I forgot how prudish humans could be."

Did he just call me a prude? "I am not a prude."

"But you find offense with the naked form?"

I found the opposite with Kael's naked form, from what I saw, but that wasn't the point.

"So Elydorians just run around naked with strangers?"

"We're not running, nor are we strangers."

"Now you're pretending not to understand my figures of speech?"

Kael looked as if he wanted to throttle me.

If I bind your wrists and throw you anywhere, it will be onto my bed.

I turned away before he could read my expression. Looking at him, at Kael's naked chest, and thinking of what he'd said... nope. No can do.

"First of all," I heard him say, repeating my words. "I didn't camouflage or shield our shelter because I don't want to hide our whereabouts. Second, I know you humans wash yourselves often, as we do, and this might be the last lake we come across for days. Third of all, I am getting out now so you can come in, but you might not want to turn around."

"Why don't we want to hide our whereabouts?" I asked as water splashed behind me. Willing myself not to move even an inch, I stood as still as a statue.

No peeking. He would be even more incorrigible if I did.

"I'll explain after your swim. We have much to discuss before we're discovered, Mevlida."

It was weird to hear him call me that. No one used my full name but my mom. Oddly, from him, I didn't mind it. Usually I hated my real name. It was so... different.

"Mev," I said. "My friends call me Mev."

"So not Mia, but Mev." His voice was directly behind me.

I spun around before my brain could register that he couldn't have possibly gotten dressed that quickly. And he hadn't. Kael wore only his tight trousers that were more like leggings than pants. I was intimately familiar with them, their backside especially. And now the rest of him was bare and glistening with droplets of water.

He was magnificent.

"No, not Mia," I squeaked out.

"Princess." His eyes dropped to my lips. "Mev."

16

KAEL

Focusing on preparing a meal, I tried not to imagine Mev in the lake behind me. It was difficult, periodic splashes of water reminding me I was not alone.

Mev. Not Mia.

Not some random woman who'd stumbled through a Gate that had been closed for nearly thirty years. How had I not pieced it together the moment she waved her hand this morning? I'd dismissed my instincts, something I'd been trained never to do. I could blame the woman herself, one who had unsettled me from the start, but the cause hardly mattered. That her true identity had never occurred to me, despite her age, despite her magic manifesting, was testament to Mev's ability to keep such a thing secret as much as it was an indictment of my wavering focus.

She was getting out of the water.

The urge to look back was as strong as the one to comfort her had been. Despite her identity. Despite the fact that if my father knew I'd shown her even a hint of kindness, he would have my hide.

I comforted her and would do it again.

"That moonleaf sap worked perfect. It was just like soap."

She stepped into my line of vision. Hair wet. Barefoot. Issa's breeches hugging her hips in all the right places. I quickly looked away, back to the fire.

Remembering her dislike of being ignored, I made a sound that could be interpreted as "good." The fact was, speaking too freely had done me more harm than it was worth throughout my life. My father did not take kindly to dissension, and the two of us rarely saw eye to eye.

My brother, Terran, was much better at talking.

Thankfully, I had other skills.

"What's so funny?"

I looked up from the rabbit. "Pretty sure you wouldn't want to know. Sit with me."

Scrambling on the rock beside mine, Mev hugged her legs to her chest. I was struck with how vulnerable she looked. And beautiful too. But with a fire inside whose source was no longer a mystery.

"Your father is very powerful, Mev. Now that you're here, your own power will begin quickly to manifest, as it has already."

She reached out a hand and waved it. "I've already tried, but there's nothing there. Just that one fluke this morning."

"Oh, there's something there. Trust me."

She blinked. "I really wish I could."

And there was the heart of our problem. My only path forward was honesty. It had always served me well, and I would trust in it again. Even if that honesty was a betrayal of my father.

"When I realized your true identity, my first thought was that my father might kill you."

Mev's eyes widened in fear. I quickly reassured her. "I will not be taking you to him."

That fear turned to disbelief. "You won't?"

"No, I won't. His hatred for humans runs deep. He blames your father most, and I cannot trust his actions were I to bring you to him. I would like to believe he would be merciful, but pleas of your innocence will, I fear, go unheard. To him, you will be nothing more than King Galfrid's daughter and a grave threat to our people."

"I am no threat. My father." She paused. "It's odd, you know, to say those words. I thought ill of my father for so long, thinking he took advantage of my mother. That he drugged her and got her pregnant."

As I'd done the first time, taking our meal from the fire, I allowed it to cool. "Why did you believe such a thing? She told you nothing?"

"She remembers nothing of this place. My mother can remember traveling to York, and attending a meeting, but little else except for stumbling into the dead of night from what we now know is The Crooked Key, and finding her way home. Pregnant. She assumed the worst, of course, and when I was old enough to know the truth, I did too. It was only when I found this"—she held up a ring she took from her pocket— "and a picture of my mother in York that I was determined to come solve the mystery that she just wanted to leave behind. I traveled to York with my best friend, Clara, and we found the pub where the photo was taken. When Jon realized who I was, he began to tell us about Elydor, but honestly? We thought he was crazy."

"You never knew," I said, my mind racing. "He must have found a way to erase her memory."

"That's what Jon said."

Jon. He was not crazy at all. His family had a long history of keeping Elydor a secret, one my father, frankly, never thought they could keep. But the Harrows had proven both loyal and resourceful throughout the years.

"Your parents were very much in love. I would imagine it was difficult for her, believing she had been drugged, as you say, and taken advantage of in the worst possible way."

"In love," she murmured, looking up toward the sky.

I never really knew the queen but could easily see how the Aetherian king had fallen for her, if she was anything like the daughter. I grabbed the rabbit meat, tearing off a piece. Making my way to Mev's rock, one large enough for us both, I handed it to her.

We ate in silence.

"If you're not taking me to your father," Mev said finally. "What do you plan to do with me?"

I didn't mean to look at her in *that* way, but neither could I help the errant thoughts that ran through my mind. Ones I had to dismiss. My father would not be pleased when he learned of Mev, which he would. But he would be even more displeased if I developed an affinity toward the daughter of his most bitter enemy.

"Kael..."

"We will learn how you came through so it does not happen again. In the meantime, you must be trained. Coming into your magic without knowing how to wield it could be dangerous. For you. For me. For anyone you come in contact with."

That surprised her. "You're going to train me?"

"No." I waved a hand around our camp. "I did not conceal us, fully expecting we will be followed by Lyra."

"The woman you tried to kill?"

"She was never in any danger."

"Didn't seem like that to me."

I stifled a smile.

"Why do you want her to find us after going through such extreme lengths to run from her?"

I cocked my head to the side, sure Mev could work that one out.

"I hate when you look at me like that."

"Like what?"

"Like I'm an idiot. Just because I don't know your ways, or how to use magic, or anything about Elydor... I'm actually pretty smart."

"Are you now?"

"Yes." Her chin lifted. "I am."

I never doubted it for a moment. "Only an Aetherian can train you properly," I said as she ate. "Lyra and I served on the Council together. She is also smart." I received a glare for that one. "She comes from a noble family and is highly skilled in air magic. Most importantly, I trust her. As much as I can trust any Aetherian. I'd have preferred to bring you to my father, but that is now out of the question. This, it seems to me, is the next best alternative."

I took a bite of rabbit, wishing I'd not sat so close to Mev. The urge to touch her was stronger than I cared for, but she would likely take offense if I moved away now.

"I want to go home."

She said it so softly, I wondered if the words were meant for me or herself. Mev could not go home, not until we learned why she'd come through in the first place. Otherwise, we could not be certain it might not happen again. The fact was, we were still enemies. And I needed something from her as much now as ever.

There was one person who might persuade her to stay without being coaxed into it.

Her father.

Knowing it would be unavoidable once Lyra became involved, and also knowing my father would have my head for it, I considered one last time if this plan was the best course of action. Unfortunately, I had little choice.

"Do you not wish to meet your father?" I asked.

She'd been staring at the fire, but at that, Mev's head whipped up, her eyes more blue than green now. Her hair, becoming whiter with each passing moment. How could I possibly have missed it, even concealed?

"At first," she said, refusing more meat, "I just wanted to go home. Clara will be worried. And if I am gone too long, my mother will find out and lose her mind. I thought if I could escape you—"

"You could not."

She frowned. "I know that now."

Mev could escape me, though, once her magic was fully formed. Asking Lyra to train her, to work with me, would be risky.

"Anyway... I just... of course I wish to meet him."

She was scared. "He will be very glad to see you, Mev. Your father has been searching for a way to reopen the Gate since the moment your mother left."

"You mean, since the moment she was kidnapped and sent through? Jon suspected my mother did not return freely, so I assume he was right? It was your father's doing?"

I winced. "Aye, he was. And we have been battling with Aetheria since that very day."

Her eyes widened. "You have?"

"I'll spare you Elydorian politics and the whispers of war

which began well before you and your mother left. For now, I need to tell you what to expect in the coming days." She pushed a strand of still-wet hair behind her ear. "Why did you color your hair?"

Mev pulled the strand out to look at it herself. "I don't know if my mother was more weary of explaining the unusual color away or if I was tired of being teased about it. I was still in elementary school when I'd convinced her to allow me to dye it blonde, and it's been that way ever since."

"I prefer this color. Even though it marks you as Aetherian."

"It does?"

"Many have similarly colored hair, or silver hair like Lyra's, and blue eyes. Just as the majority of Gyorians' eyes and hair are darker, like the land whose magic we wield."

"And the Thalassari?"

"The sun has tanned their skin, and their eyes are the colors of the sea, but no one shade of hair color predominates the water clan. It's their lack of clothing, more than anything, that gives them away."

"Lack of clothing?"

I shrugged. "They have an affinity for using very little of it."

"What can they do? With their magic?"

"Manipulate water. Hold their breath for extended periods underwater. Create storms, though you can do that as well."

Her eyes widened. "I can?"

"If you're here long enough, aye. Aetherians can manipulate air which means they are able to wield storms and sound waves."

"Meaning?"

She no longer hugged her knees. Mev had turned toward me and now sat with her legs crossed, waiting for my response.

There should be no reason for my hesitation. If Lyra found us, Mev wouldn't just know about her magic, she'd be using it before long. But it wasn't lost on me that giving this woman such power meant she'd be less controllable.

"Meaning, they can project whispers over long distances. Some more skilled or powerful Aetherians can levitate for short periods."

"I saw Lyra do that. Can they fly?"

"Not exactly. More like keep themselves in the air for extended periods."

"You said, more skilled or powerful. As if those are two different things?"

I doubted Mev realized she twirled a section of her hair. Watching her, I imagined using it as leverage to pull her into me and taste those lips of hers.

By the stones, the woman was much too enticing.

"Please don't go caveman on me now."

I understood her meaning, knowing more than I cared to about human history. "Some Elydorians are born with more natural abilities than others. Some train harder and become more skilled. Others, like your father, and mine, do both."

"Who is more powerful?"

I hesitated, knowing the weight of my words. "It's impossible to say for certain. Both are immensely powerful in their own right. Your father can command the very air we breathe. My father wields the land itself. Their magic is... different."

"But who would win in a fight?" she pressed.

I sighed. "They've been enemies for many centuries, more

so these past years, and their clashes have been devastating at times. In a direct confrontation, it would depend on many factors, including the terrain. In open air, your father might have the advantage. Underground or in rocky regions, my father would likely prevail. Their powers are so different that a direct comparison is almost meaningless."

"So, it's a stalemate?"

"In many ways, yes. That's why their feud has dragged on for so long. Neither can gain a definitive upper hand, so the balance of power remains tenuous at best."

"You are obviously very powerful too?"

"I am."

"So why don't you end the feud? Wouldn't it be better if everyone got along?"

I didn't blame Mev's naiveté, knowing so little about Elydor. "That will never be possible."

"How do you... Kael? What's wrong?"

I jumped from our makeshift seat and bent one knee on the ground. Closing my eyes, I laid both hands on the grass and felt down to Elydor's core.

Lyra hadn't been the only one alerted to Mev's presence when the Gate opened for her, but she had been the one tracking me. In case it was one of the others, I stood.

"Get inside," I said to Mev. "Do not come out until I call for you."

Mev didn't move. Actually, that wasn't entirely true. She hesitated and then jumped down, hands on her hips, and froze in place.

"Mev," I said, a warning in my voice that she didn't heed.

"Princess Mevlida," I tried again, in a less commanding tone. "Please."

"I liked just 'princess' better. But since you asked nicely that time..." She went inside the hut.

Whoever was coming was still far enough away that we could have run. Instead, I checked on Stormbreaker, tossed the remains of our meal into the fire, and waited.

Thankfully, I didn't have to wait long.

17

MEV

I could hear voices which meant no one was dead. Yet.

Sitting on my makeshift bed, I ran a finger along the blanket. Kael had called it silken fern. Apparently weaving leaves into blankets at will was another one of his talents.

They can project whispers over long distances. Can levitate for short periods.

The idea that I could do those things was ridiculous. How often had my mother attempted to teach me her ways? Meditation, visualizing exercises, journaling... nothing had worked. I just wasn't psychic. I'd always been amazed by my mother's abilities, and that whole time, my father was an immortal who could wield air magic.

Wait a minute. Did that mean...

Can you hear me?

What in the ever-living hell was that?

It was as if the voice was just beside my ear, but at the same time, nowhere.

Mevlida?

I wasn't imagining things. Someone had just whispered my

name. Without thinking, I stumbled out into the waning daylight.

I halted immediately at the sight of Kael and his beautiful companion. And then I realized he wasn't frowning. Or snapping at me to get back inside. Or fighting with Lyra. In fact, he was actually smiling at me.

"You heard me?" Lyra's voice, the same one in my ear, was soft. Melodic.

"That was you?"

"Indeed."

I'd heard her. How was that possible? It was as if she'd been standing next to me in that hut. Not only that, it was as if hearing that voice was the most natural thing in the world, as if she'd always been meant to communicate this way.

Once, for Halloween, my mother's seamstress friend made me a beautiful belly dancer's costume. The pants were lavender chiffon, and I remember wearing that outfit for weeks. That's what Lyra's clothing reminded me of, though hers were pale blue. The pants were so thin I could almost, but not quite, see through them. Her top was silk, the scooped neck lined in delicate silver embroidery. She wore a lightweight, flowing cape fastened with a silver clasp, and her head was adorned with a delicate circlet of silver and crystal. Her soft leather sandals made no sound as she moved gracefully toward me.

The overall effect was ethereal, like she was part of the sky itself.

Reaching me, Lyra inclined her head as if in reverence. I glanced at Kael who watched us closely. I wanted to ask him what she was doing, but no words came out of my mouth.

"Princess Mevlida. It is an honor to make your acquaintance."

Her head lifted.

What was I supposed to say to that?

"Um." Not a good start. I'd pretend I was at one of those fancy Boston museum dinners. "The pleasure is mine. It's Lyra?"

Her eyes were pale blue. And kind. Although she looked maybe thirty, if she were a human, faint lines appeared when she smiled. I wondered how old she really was.

"Indeed."

"How did you do that? Talk to me in the hut?"

"I will show you."

"Lyra has agreed to train you," Kael said. "We've come to a tentative agreement."

"Tentative only," Lyra said, looking at Kael as if he were a wayward child. I could attest to the fact that he was anything but, sitting behind him on Stormbreaker these past few days. "Because you are—"

"Lyra," he warned. I knew the tone well.

"I will say it until my dying breath, Kael."

"Say what?" I asked her pointedly, ignoring Kael's scowl.

"That his stance on keeping the Gate closed is wrong. His hatred of humans, wrong. Kael only believes such things because—"

"Because I have no mother, courtesy of them," he ground out.

I had a feeling Lyra was going to say something different. I raised my hand, as if in class. "Excuse me? Them? Maybe say that to me directly?"

Kael glared at me and promptly stalked off.

"I'd ask if he's always like this, but I already know the answer. Apparently, there's an even worse version of him. I saw him try to kill you."

"Kael would never kill me. Though he did delay me. I'll admit he hid you well."

I watched him head toward his horse, unsure if Kael planned to offer Stormbreaker comfort, or the opposite. Their bond was obviously very strong.

When I turned back to Lyra, she was studying me. Heading toward the fire, Lyra seemed to move as if she were almost floating. I'd never met someone so elegant before. I'd seen her fight, though. She was more than just a beautiful woman in an outfit that would win every costume award at a Halloween party.

And yet... this wasn't Halloween. And certainly no party.

With a waft of her hand, similar to Kael but slower and more graceful, she stoked the fire.

"Wind?" I asked, assuming that was how she'd done it.

"Aye. Come," she said, indicating I should stand next to her. "You clearly have the ability to wield air, and I suspect you'll be quite powerful given your lineage. And that you could hear me, without training..." Lyra pointed to my hand. "Lift it and close your eyes."

I did as she asked.

"Take a deep breath. In and out. Calm your breathing and your mind. Listen to the sounds around you. Feel the breeze. Note where it originates and which direction it is heading."

This was something I could do well. In BJJ, managing energy and maintaining composure during rolls and competitions were crucial. I would think identifying wind patterns to be similar to understanding an opponent's movements to anticipate their moves.

"Consider the air. Is it a gentle breeze? A gust? Or is it still? Feel it, fill your lungs with it. Then slowly move your hand and attempt to push it toward me."

I did as Lyra said and tried to move the slight breeze toward her. It was faint, but that electricity I'd felt the other times was there, as if it simmered beneath the surface rather than coursed through me.

"Good. Do it again. Keep your eyes closed. Concentrate on the air and your steady breathing."

I did it again. And again. Twenty or thirty times more, and finally Lyra asked me to open my eyes.

"Look at the fire. Imagine putting it out with air."

"I hate to put bad ju-ju out there, but isn't there a big difference between my little wisps and putting out the fire?" Since she'd stoked it, our little campfire had grown and was now spitting and crackling and... no way I could put it out.

"Not really. Just in the amount of energy you use. Everything you need to do it, and more, is already inside you. Just keep breathing, feel the air around you, but this time, instead of moving your fingers and hand, reach behind you as if gathering all of the air there and send it forward. Visualize putting it out."

I reminded myself I already knew how to harness energy and move with purpose. And tried to lean into the... *rightness* of it all. When I felt ready, I reached behind me and directed the flow of air which seemed to respond to my command. I could feel the "electric" current, the subtle shift as it moved forward. It wasn't about the force I used but aligning my intention with the element, just as I had learned to align my movements with my opponent's energy.

Where there had just been a fire, none existed. The gust was not only strong enough to put it out, but I also swept up every leaf in its path, sending them swirling into the air. If there had been anything else between me and the fire, it wouldn't be there anymore.

"You will learn to control it better, but that is an excellent start, princess."

"Mev," I corrected her, not wanting us to be so formal.

"Guess I'm the only one you like calling you princess, huh?"

I hadn't seen him approach, but at the sound of Kael's voice, I spun around, wanting to see his expression. Wanting, dammit, his approval. Clara would be appalled that my red-flag tendencies toward men translated to immortals too.

Which reminded me...

"Kael," I asked him, realizing I could have asked Lyra too, "am I immortal here?"

"I'm surprised you didn't ask that already."

I waved my hands in the air. "Was a little busy meeting my air-magic instructor and, you know, putting out fires." I still couldn't believe I'd done that.

"Of sorts."

It was Lyra, and not Kael, who answered. Because, you know, he hated giving straight answers. I hadn't worked out the reason just yet, but I assumed it had something to do with him maintaining his "man of mystery" mystique.

Unfortunately, it worked. Was damned irritating though.

"What does that mean?" I asked her, watching as Kael moved toward our hut, constructing—with his hands—a second structure.

"It means that some human children have no magic at all and age normally. Others do have magic, like you, and their aging slows down in direct proportion to their abilities. Judging by the fact that you put out that fire, a skill that can takes years for some Aetherians to develop, after essentially just learning you even had the ability... I would say you are demi-immortal. That you will live for many centuries."

I was going to faint.

Only once in my whole life had I ever fainted, and I didn't even remember that. My mother said I'd been sick, and the two of us were arguing, and I went down like a sack of potatoes.

So I had no idea if I was actually going to faint. I only knew that everything seemed to be spinning suddenly. My vision blurred, and I felt as if I would throw up. I put out my hands to catch me, heard a deep voice in my ear and then... nothing.

18

KAEL

"I've never seen you like this," Lyra said.

Mev hadn't woken yet. She lay on her bedroll beside us. Even now, an uneasiness that her state was temporary, as I first assumed, grew with each passing second.

"Do not make more of it than it is. I hardly even like the woman."

"Then why are you staring at her as if you'll lose your supper?"

Ignoring her, I felt Mev's head. It was cool. No sign of fever. Nothing to indicate illness, and given the topic we'd been discussing, I had every reason to believe she'd simply fainted. But why wasn't she opening her eyes? Humans rarely remained this way for long.

"If you vomit on me, I'll kill you."

The fact that Mev said that before even opening her eyes made me wonder how long ago she'd come around.

"Are you alright?"

Her eyes fluttered open. "What does it matter to you?"

I blinked.

"You said a few seconds ago you hardly like her," Lyra reminded me.

"He hasn't suddenly become effusive while I was out?" she asked Lyra who looked as if she'd start laughing at any moment.

"Fortunately, not. Do you really want him to talk more? Spout his anti-human sentiments? Or—"

"That's enough, Lyra."

Lyra made a sound which indicated she clearly disagreed. "I'm not one of your subjects to be ordered about."

"I can't believe you have subjects." Mev moved to sit up. "Poor things."

I pushed her back down. "Don't get up too quickly."

She rolled her eyes and didn't listen. Of course.

"I'm fine." Mev stood and Lyra followed.

"I can assist you to our shelter," she said to Mev.

It was not happening. I stood as well. "She stays here, with me."

"Perhaps you should let her decide? Or is she your captive still?" Lyra shot back.

"Good question," Mev added.

Although there was no chance Mev was sleeping anywhere but beside me, I took a risk and asked, "Where would you like to stay? It is your choice. But I did construct this shelter for two and Lyra's for just one person."

She looked from me to Lyra, clearly torn.

If Mev thought to escape during the night, I could feel her vibrations. Lyra knew that, and her expression said as much. There was no good reason to want to keep her with me except that... I wanted her with me.

"I guess since we're already set up for two, I can stay here."

"It would take Kael very little for him to rectify that. Are you certain?" Lyra asked.

"I'm sure."

Seemingly satisfied, Lyra turned to leave. "If you need me, just whisper my name into the wind."

"Will that work?" Mev asked.

"It shouldn't, but based on what you did today, it likely will." Then to Kael, "See it doesn't become necessary for her to do so. King Galfrid will be as pleased if his daughter is harmed as he was when she was taken."

Knowing as much already, I said nothing but waited for Lyra to leave.

"That was rude. You can be a real asshole sometimes, Kael."

"You have quite a mouth on you, princess."

At that, she turned that mouth into a pout, one I couldn't stop staring at.

She cocked her head to the side. "Most of the time, I think you hate me. Except for when you look at me that way."

"I don't hate you, Mev," I said, my voice barely a whisper and foreign to my own ears. Softer. More gentle. As if she'd be convinced of something that should be true.

I should hate her. I'd been taught to hate her.

And yet, I didn't.

Mev looked directly into my eyes. There was no sign of the woman who had fainted upon learning she was likely, if she remained in Elydor, demi-immortal. This was the woman who had rightfully hidden her identity from me. The one who'd taken her chance with Issa, telling her everything and attempting to escape me. Who defied me, even when she'd been scared.

"Prove it."

I needed no further encouragement.

Closing the distance between us, I reached for the back of her head, wanting to feel Mev's hair between my fingers again. When she didn't pull away, I brought my head down.

The first touch of our lips was everything I'd imagined it would be.

Between her hands on my arms and the feel of Mev's mouth pressed to mine, I could no sooner keep back a groan than I could let her go. Deepening the kiss, I touched my tongue to hers, intending to move slowly. As our mouths melded together, those intentions fled as quickly as a glintwing fitch being pursued by a hawk. We fit together perfectly, the kiss one I'd be content to last all eve.

That was... until Mev made a little sound in her throat. Of pleasure. Of need. One I understood and wanted to reciprocate. I did, for a moment. Pulling her head even closer to mine, I devoured her. Images flashed through my mind... the first time I saw her, watching Mev sleep in Estmere, seeing her eyes widen at Elydor's beauty, sitting beside me on a rock with her arms wrapped around her legs.

I didn't just want to consume her. I wanted to protect her, as if she were a Gyorian. As if she were *my* Gyorian.

She is not yours. Not Gyorian, but the daughter of King Galfrid.

Just as my free hand began to roam from Mev's back lower than it should, given that fact, I pulled away. Enough moonlight streamed into the shelter to illuminate her face clearly.

"I don't hate you, Mev."

Though I may have stopped, I found it impossible to pull away completely. Tracing her bottom lip with my thumb, I resisted the urge to taste her again.

"You kissed me."

That seemed fairly obvious, but I agreed with her just the same.

"You did tell me to prove it. Seemed the most obvious way to do so." I dropped my hand, the tightness of my chest concerning given the identity of the woman in my arms.

"Though I should not have done so."

The fire was back in her eyes. "Why?"

"You know why."

"Because we are enemies." Mev moved toward the door, giving me her back.

How could I explain to her the complications that would arise if she and I were to continue down this path? A few days ago, Mev knew nothing of our world. Centuries of history could not be easily explained, nor did I have any wish at this moment to speak of politics and hatred, especially the one that ran so deep between our people.

Mev knew nothing of our world. She would not know what lay just outside from us, and the urge to show her, to see her face, had me moving past her. Inhaling the scent that was uniquely Mev as I walked by, I encouraged her to follow me. She did, without argument. As we approached the water, her eyes widened, as they tended to do often when she took in her surroundings. Mev's mouth opened, and not kissing it was difficult now that I knew how sweet my princess tasted.

Not yours, Kael.

"It's... I have no words. I thought the skies in Aetheria were easily the most beautiful thing about Elydor, but I think that takes the cake." We stood at the water's edge. "What is it?" she asked.

"Bioluminescent algae. As the starlight reflects off the surface, algae emits that glow."

"Isn't it extraordinary?"

I wasn't looking at the lake. I'd seen it, and ones like it, many times before. Instead, I watched Mev. Perhaps there had been some part of me that knew since the moment I spotted her Mev was no ordinary human coming through the closed Aetherian Gate.

"More than you realize."

I shifted my focus to the lake.

Through the corner of my eye, I could see her looking at me. Mev didn't acknowledge my words, nor would I explain them. It was enough that I'd kissed her, that I continued down this path despite knowing it would lead to my own demise. Best to let that go, at least for tonight.

I'd set my course, but that did not mean it was necessary to crash while navigating it. One mistake did not necessitate another. With that thought in mind, I turned away.

"Stay as long as you'd like."

I meant for her to enjoy the view, as I knew she'd been doing, but could tell Mev took my words as a rejection. Best to let her think that than the alternative.

This time, the truth would simply not do.

19

MEV

So much for Kael's insistence I stay with him. He never came back.

I assumed he would return to our shelter eventually, but his bedroll was as empty now as it had been when I fell asleep last night.

Demi-immortal.

Most sane people would make that particular fact a priority, but it was the memory of Kael lowering his head to me that greeted me first when I woke up. That kiss was everything, and it seemed, nothing. By the way he reacted afterwards, it might as well have never happened. A man who looked like that, who was the son of a king, a prince, and hundreds of years old... kissing women meant nothing to him, I supposed. Especially kissing very ordinary human women.

But you're not just human, Mev. And you're not ordinary.

I fully opened my eyes and looked at my hands. Besides desperately needing a manicure, nothing else seemed to have changed about them. But the memory of putting out that fire told me otherwise. Everything had changed.

I had actually done that.

Another thing that hadn't changed was a battle between staying in bed or getting up to pee. In the end, the latter won. There was no sign of Kael or Lyra. I took care of business, fished a piece of thornroot from Kael's leather bag and chewed on it.

"You seem skeptical of something?"

Where had Lyra come from? One second, I was alone. The next, Lyra was beside me.

"This," I admitted, taking the thornroot from my mouth. "It's a far cry from the toothbrush I'm used to."

"Some humans do fashion it into a contraption that seems unnecessary. If you'd prefer, in Aetheria, many use a tooth powder for the same purpose."

Unfortunately, tooth powder wasn't the strangest thing about Elydor. "This is fine, thanks." I looked around camp.

"I haven't seen him all morn."

She said it without judgment, but Lyra was watching me carefully.

Pretending I didn't care about Kael's whereabouts, I moved to the fire and sat. Though the air wasn't cool, exactly, it wasn't warm either. Lyra handed me a piece of something that looked like a large cracker.

"Airbread," she said. "Though I'm afraid I have no honey or cheese for it."

I took a bite. "This is good."

Lyra sat on the rock beside me, her movements slow and graceful. "It is easy to carry, though as I said, preferable with a bit of cheese and honey. It is eaten by all Elydorians."

"Do they call it airbread in Gyoria?"

Lyra laughed, the delicate tinkling sound as pleasant to the ears as she was to the eyes. "No, they do not."

I had so many questions, it was hard to pick one to start with. "What will happen now? With my abilities?"

"They will grow, each day you are here. I can teach you many things. To create, calm, or redirect storms, use air currents to enhance your speed and agility, alter air pressure to create and amplify sound, and some things, just for fun."

With that, she looked up into the sky, so I did as well, keeping her in my peripheral vision. Lifting her hand, Lyra began to swirl it gently in a circle. At first, nothing happened. As I watched, though, a cloud above us began to shift. To anyone else looking, it would appear natural, as if the cloud had taken shape on its own. But since I knew otherwise, it was easy to spot a heart.

"Can I do that?"

"Not yet. It is more difficult," Lyra said, lowing her arm, "to manipulate air waves over long distances. But you will, before long. Shall we get started?"

I hadn't realized we would train so soon. "Now?"

Lyra jumped off the rock. "Every opportunity we have. Kael mentioned leaving at first light, so I do not believe we will have much time before he returns."

A pang of jealousy, that he'd obviously spoken to Lyra after I'd gone to bed, despite the fact that she had already retired, was a reminder that, unlike that cute heart-shaped cloud, real-life feelings were not so fluffy. They were raw, sometimes unwanted, and damned irritating.

I followed Lyra who walked toward the lake, not looking around for Kael. For someone so worried about keeping tabs on me, he was literally nowhere to be seen. At least, until I spotted him. The jerk was swimming toward us which was when I noticed his clothing.

"He's... swimming?" I asked.

"Most likely. Kael usually either runs or swims in the morning. Or when he's angry."

I tried not to care that Lyra knew that about him. "You guys spent a lot of time together, I guess? On the Council?"

I'd never seen an Olympic swimmer before, but imagined that was how smooth and fast they would swim. He was like a machine.

"We did," was all she said. "Remember what we talked about yesterday. We'll start by understanding how air interacts with water by creating ripples. There is a delicate balance between the two elements. All elements, really, but we'll start with these."

I tried to concentrate, but the closer Kael got to us, the more I thought about our kiss instead of Lyra's words. Even so, creating ripples in the water was easy enough. Until he was so close that I couldn't ignore that he'd be at the shore, and getting out, any second.

"I'm thinking now would be a good time for a break," I said, turning away.

Lyra chuckled. Was she just going to stand there and watch him? Completely naked? Had the two of them been together?

Stop it, Mev. One, he's your enemy. Two, you can't be jealous of every beautiful woman in Elydor. Isolde. Lyra. The list of his conquests, after hundreds of years, was probably a mile long.

The sound of splashing water was followed by, "Humans."

Obviously Kael directed that to me, but I didn't deem it worthy of a response.

"She is only half human, Kael. Or maybe you've forgotten."

"Trust me," he said, as briskly as usual. "I haven't."

"Please let me know when you're decent," I said, imagining Lyra looking Kael up and down.

No one said anything. I could hear Kael getting dressed, but then... silence.

Why was I so angry? Because he'd kissed me and bolted? Because Lyra was familiar enough with him to stand there and watch him dress? I could put out a fire with wind. Manipulate air. My father was a king, for God's sake. And I would finally get to meet him. Why did I give a shit about some high-handed guy? Who, if we were keeping score, had also kidnapped me.

"You can turn around now."

He was standing right behind me. I didn't move. Mostly because he made it sound like an order.

"Mev?"

"What?" I snapped.

"Are you angry?"

"No."

His voice was so close, I could feel Kael's breath on my ear.

"Lyra—"

"Is gone. She's cleaning up the camp."

My hair, which I'd combed through with my fingers, was swept to one side as Kael laid it over my shoulder. A second later, two firm hands held me in place, one on each arm. Waiting, hoping, I still jumped when his lips touched my neck like it was the most natural thing in the world. Tilting my head, to give him better access, annoyed at myself for doing so, I otherwise didn't move. That kiss was followed by another along the sensitive part of my neck. Shivering, I anticipated the third and fourth, until his lips teased my ear.

"I should not have left you last eve."

"Agreed," I said, but the edge was gone from my voice. "What if someone had come for me? Or I'd tried to escape?"

"I'd have known immediately if either of those things were to occur."

Another kiss, just below my ear.

"I almost forgot. You're 'one with the land' and all that."

His lips were gone. Kael spun me around to face him. Or more accurately, to look up at him. "And because I slept just outside the entrance."

"You did?"

"I did."

He lifted my chin up toward him.

"Why?"

I looked into his eyes, and Kael did the same. Neither of us spoke.

Did he feel it too? That sense of rightness with us being together? How was that even possible? He'd kidnapped me. His father had kidnapped my mother. I was half human. Half Aetherian. Both of which he hated.

Yet...

"Because it was easier than acknowledging this."

I knew what he meant, but asked anyway, "Acknowledging what?"

His head lowered. Not caring if we had an audience, or if he was my enemy, I closed my eyes. I'd wanted to kiss him again, in every waking moment since last night. When our lips met, slightly more familiar than yesterday, they melded together perfectly. I wrapped my arms around him as Kael deepened the kiss, and I shoved away any intruding thoughts. Fear for my future, Lyra's presence, my jealousy, Kael's identity. Each one, I filed away, and concentrated instead on enjoying the moment.

When he groaned, I tugged him closer. Wanting more. Wanting all of him.

Dear lord, that escalated quickly.

"Acknowledging that," he said, breaking us apart. At least he didn't run off this time.

"It's just a kiss," I said, lying so boldly, for the sake of saving face, that the words nearly stuck in my throat.

It was anything but.

"Is it, princess?"

No, it wasn't.

"You must have kissed hundreds of women like that. Maybe thousands."

He did smile then. "You think highly of my prowess."

"After hundreds of years..." My gaze darted from him to the camp. I didn't see Lyra but knew she was close by. When I brought it back to him, Kael was looking at me intently.

Too intently.

"You're jealous of Lyra."

"I don't get jealous." Another lie. And just one of my many faults.

"Hmm. I suppose you weren't jealous of Issa, either?"

Such a big jerk. "No, as a matter of fact, I wasn't."

Kael took my cheeks into his hands, forcing my head upwards. I had no choice but to look deep into his eyes once again. He was no longer smiling.

"Until our kiss, I'd intended to keep you by my side until I could learn how you came through the portal. You were my captive still, because my priority is to protect Gyoria and its people."

I could hardly breathe. Somehow, I knew what he was going to say. Goosebumps covered my arms. If his father burst into camp at this moment, I could not have looked away.

"Though I've not been with Issa or Lyra, I have been with many women, Mevlida. It is for that reason I could not sleep, realizing I could no sooner keep you as my captive than deny that our kiss was more than just that. Never, in all the years I have been alive, have I kissed a woman and felt the very ground beneath me settle in contentment, as if it were at peace. When I saw you on the shore, I knew."

I didn't ask what Kael knew. The answer was there already, as if it were a missing piece of a puzzle that was now whole.

"We are meant for each other." It was a statement of fact, as true as any I'd ever uttered.

He didn't bat an eye. "When did it manifest?"

I said we were meant for each other, and that was Kael's question?

"Huh?"

"Your visions of the future. When did they manifest?"

"I... I don't know what you mean."

As if to show me his words weren't meant to accuse, Kael's thumbs rubbed my chin, his hands still cupping my cheeks as if I were a precious piece of porcelain.

"I've been in the presence of mages and seers, of humans who called themselves psychics when on Earth, whose magic grew here in Elydor. You said we were meant to be together as if it were as much a fact as your true identity."

I cupped my hands over his. "I'm not sure why. Honestly."

"Think back, Mev. Since the moment you came through that portal. Has there been another instance when you felt something more strongly than just an inkling? As if you knew, deep within yourself, about something that had not yet happened?"

"Yes. When I met Lord Draven, I knew he was bad. Or at least, not to be trusted."

He nodded, as if my explanation were the most logical thing in the world.

"You have the Sight."

Jesus. As if having air magic wasn't enough.

"I do?"

"Yes. You do. As did your mother. They say she was as gifted as any human who had ever come through, so I suspect you may be as well."

We fell silent. The ramifications were enormous. Kael seemed to realize it too.

"That's why this feels so... right?"

"I assume so. This isn't an area of expertise for me."

"So is it like we're fated mates or something? That we don't have a choice to be together?"

He chuckled. "No. You are simply sensing the future. And in the future, we must be together."

We couldn't be together. Tears sprang into my eyes as my cheeks tingled. "My mother. Kael, I cannot stay here. She'll have no idea what happened to me. She'll be worried sick. It will kill her. I can't—"

"Shhh." He pulled me into his chest. "Relax. Time works differently in your realm. You could be here for years and it would be like minutes there."

I pulled back. "Truly?"

"Truly."

"Why didn't you tell me that? I've been so worried about what Clara must be going through."

"You didn't ask."

I frowned. "Seriously?"

He seemed pretty unrepentant. "We'll figure it out. In the meantime"—he tipped my chin up again—"you've no need to lie to me. Nor will I lie to you. You have my word."

"I appreciate that, but I didn't lie about anything."

Kael's brows raised. "You don't get jealous?"

Oops. "Well, not usually. Especially not like that. But Isolde and Lyra... maybe you haven't noticed, but they are both incredibly beautiful. And you seem so close to them. And—"

"*You* are incredibly beautiful," he said. "And if we seem close, it is because I share a history with both. As friends, and nothing more."

I waited for him to continue, but in true Kael fashion, it seemed he'd used his morning's allotment of words. "I cannot stay here," I said. As *right* as it felt in Kael's arms, I had a life and a mother waiting for me.

"We shall see."

I ignored that. "So what now?"

I could sense Kael's unease as he looked up to the sky and then toward camp. For the first time since we'd met, there was doubt in him where usually none existed.

"We take you to Aetheria, to meet your father. Lyra will train you along the way. Perhaps we can also uncover how you were able to come through the Gate."

So he could ensure it remained closed. "And then?"

He met my eyes once again. "And then, your fate is yours."

Earth. Job. Mother. Friends.

Elydor. Kael. Magic. Immortality.

I didn't relish the choice.

"In the meantime, you are mine, princess. In every sense of the word."

20

KAEL

"She is strong."

I agreed, having watched Lyra train with Mev that morn. Even as we began to ride north, Lyra continued to explain air magic to her. We'd stopped again, the human half of Mev necessitating it, and waited for her to return from the thicket.

"Did you doubt she would be?" I asked. Lyra knew as well as I that magical strength ran through families. All three clans, the humans notwithstanding, held a version of our Rite of Stone and Soil to determine a new leader, if any proved stronger than the current king or queen. Often, however, it was the sons and daughters of the current leader who came out victorious.

"No, but as an Uninitiated who knows little about our world, she should not be able to harness her ability so easily."

"True."

"Kael?"

We'd served on the Council together for many years. That tone meant Lyra intended to probe, but I had no wish to discuss it.

"You cannot avoid speaking to me for the entire journey."

"If you wish to discuss my father, I can." Turning my gaze from where Mev had disappeared into the bushes back to Lyra, I wondered which of the women were more stubborn. I'd have said Lyra, before meeting Mev. She was as relentless as any Gyorian warrior. Raised by one of the most prestigious families in Aetheria, her lineage tracing back to the ancient air mages who'd first harnessed the power of the Wind Crystal, Lyra was difficult to waylay when she set her mind to something.

"He will not forgive you." I gave her a look that Lyra did not heed. "What will you do, after Mev returns?"

"Is that what she told you? That she wishes to return to her realm?"

"With words? Nay."

"So you have the Sight now too?"

"Do not be cross with me. I wish only to aid her. Mevlida's choices are her own. Though it's clear you care for her."

We're meant to be together.

She emerged from the thicket, thankfully. I had a mind to ensure her safety even knowing there were none around us. We took a little-traveled path north, Lyra and I having agreed on a course. Using this route, we could avoid the contentious borderlands but it would add time to our journey.

I'd wondered if she would begin to harness her human abilities alongside her Aetherian ones. Even so, I had not been prepared for that. This morn, on my swim, the need to return to camp, ensure Mev's safety and be in her presence was as strong as any need I'd ever had. She called to me without words, that kiss one I could not put from my mind.

It was the height of folly to allow myself into Mev's orbit, but her presence on the shore beside Lyra had solidified my thinking. I could no sooner stay away from Galfrid's daughter than I could go back to Gyoria anytime soon. I loved my brother, my people, and in some ways, even my father. But Mev's presence changed everything.

Dismounting, I waited for Mev to approach. As always, the desire to touch her was difficult to ignore, even more so now. Lifting her onto my mount was not enough. Having her hold onto my waist from behind was not enough. I needed her closer.

"When you look at me that way," she said from behind me as I re-mounted, "I find it difficult not to have... thoughts."

We began to ride. "What kind of thoughts?"

"You know. Those kind."

Humans were so delicate.

"Thoughts of sex, you mean?" I asked, turning and trying not to laugh at her expression, a mix between surprise and desire. I faced back around, grateful Lyra was well ahead of us.

"It's strange to hear you say the word. And to know you guys have sex in the same way we do."

"You guys? I'd thank you not to confuse Gyorians with any others."

Her hands tightened around my waist. "Are you that different?"

"Yes."

"No," Lyra called back.

Not far enough, it seemed. "Must you listen?" I yelled to her.

"Can't help it; the wind carries your voices to me."

Mev chuckled, a sound I very much enjoyed. Since this morning, she was more relaxed. Not being held against one's will, it seemed, did much to improve one's temperament.

And if she tried to get away, with Lyra?

I pushed away the thought. Not wanting to put her in harm's way by bringing her to my father did not mean that learning how she'd gotten through the portal wasn't of utmost importance.

"Tell me more about you. About the different clans."

"I liked our previous conversation better."

She slapped my shoulder. "Is that a village?"

We'd crested a small hill. Below us, patchwork farmlands and fields of wheat and barley swayed in the wind. Further along, thatched roofs and timber-framed houses clustered together marked a farming village that had seen their share of warfare these past years.

"It is."

"Can we ride through it?"

"No."

"That's it? Just, no?"

"I'd not likely be welcomed there. Two years past my men met a contingency of human and Aetherian warriors nearby. Some of their buildings were lost to a fire."

"Not how I would describe that battle," Lyra called back. "But I agree, we cannot pass through."

"Are there many places you're not welcome?" Mev shifted in the saddle. Already acutely aware of her at my backside, I tried to ignore the fact and answer Mev's question.

"Yes."

"It's like pulling teeth with you."

"One of your many barbaric human practices."

"You don't pull teeth here? Do you have dentists?"

"No and no. We've few of the advancements you do in your realm because there is no need for them here."

"Why?"

As we skirted the village, I told Mev about Elydor's beginnings. Of the celestial event that created our world, imbuing everything with so-called magic. How we started as one people but eventually became a realm of three clans. I told her of the differences between us, which was when Lyra hung back to join the conversation.

"It is more than just our magic which differentiates us. We have different values that can make maintaining peace difficult."

"I would think not kidnapping the queen might be one way to achieve peace," Mev said, as innocently as possible. But there was an edge to her tone, one I understood.

"My mother was killed by a human disease. Since they've come, nothing has been the same," I said tightly, watching the road ahead of us. Something had shifted in the ground, and I had yet to determine if we were being followed or if riders came toward us from the north.

"Sometimes, change is good," Mev said.

"Usually," I countered, "it is not."

"He will never sway from his position," Lyra added. "In all the years I've known Kael, he's sung the same tune. Be thankful it was he, and not his brother, who found you."

"Why?" Mev asked.

"Terran is more like his father than Kael. Sometimes, unlike the other two, Kael even sees reason. Other times, not as much. There was much anger when you left the Summit, for instance," she said to me.

Of course, Lyra's accusation led to more questions from Mev. About the Summit. About the differences between our clans.

"It's true, Gyorians value loyalty and bravery," Lyra said. "But under King Balthor's reign, they remain loyal only to each other. Even before your mother was taken and the Gate closed, his hatred of humans did little to encourage peace in Elydor."

I ignored that.

"Tell me more of the other clans," Mev said.

I didn't have to wonder about her change of topic. As she said the words, one of her hands moved from my waist to my shoulder, as if to comfort me. Or perhaps calm me. Both were equally unnecessary. Lyra's complaints about my father were nothing new, and neither would I address them. Still, the gesture made me smile.

"The Thalassari value freedom and independence above all, which is why they avoid most conflicts. They were the first to break from all others in ancient times, traveling to the south to separate themselves and to see the warmer climate."

"And your clan?" she asked.

Lyra turned in her saddle and grinned. "*Our* clan. You are as much Aetherian as me. Your father is the king."

"I do not feel Aetherian."

"You will. Attune yourself to the wind currents," Lyra said. "When you feel them, amplify the sound waves carried by them."

"How do I do that?"

"By channeling your magic to the task, just as you did back at camp." Neither of them spoke for a few moments, until Lyra continued. "Now shape the air currents like a funnel, guiding them from me to you so my words remain intact and do not disperse."

More silence.

As it stretched, I began to suspect they were communicating silently. My suspicions were confirmed when Mev laughed.

"What did she say?" I asked.

"That information"—Mev adjusted herself behind me—"is for women only."

"Aetherians," I muttered. Their whispers to each other were a particularly annoying trait.

"Aetherians. Humans. Who *do* you like?" Mev asked.

I looked over my shoulder. "You," I said with an honesty that surprised me.

"Even though I'm both."

"Despite the fact that you are both."

"Hmm. Well, I like you too. Despite the fact that you are—"

Whatever Mev had been about to say, I could only guess at. The movement I'd felt earlier was more pronounced, and it was coming from behind us.

"Lyra," I called. She halted immediately. Jumping from the saddle, I yelled for Mev to take the reins and for Lyra to protect her. "There is just one," I said.

If there was ever a time, along the borders, when it was not necessary to prepare for battle when meeting another rider, I could hardly remember it. Coupled with the knowledge that Lyra would not be the only former Council member looking for Mev, I pulled out an obsidian shard. If I needed to create a shield between our newcomer and Mev, I'd ensure it was strong enough to keep her safe from any other magic.

They were getting closer. Just around the bend, if the vibrations beneath my feet could be trusted, and I was certain they could.

When the sole rider appeared, I lowered my guard.

A human.

Their brand of magic was just as dangerous; humans' ability to foretell the future or see events that happened in the past had won them battles. But one on one, they were less of a threat.

He rode atop a warhorse, a breed that marked him immediately as either a noble or a knight. Or both. Humans adored their titles and rankings, but I had no need for either.

"Prince Kael of Gyoria," he called out. "I mean you no harm."

I squinted, taking in his features. He knew me, but I did not know him. I liked it not.

"Who are you?" I demanded. "Why do you follow us?"

He stopped. Dismounted. I watched his hand carefully, the broadsword by his side a dangerous weapon, even for an immortal.

"That is not my intention. I travel north, to Aethralis."

"Alone?"

"Aye," he said, not elaborating.

"You know me, but I do not know you. What is your name?"

"Sir Rowan," Lyra said from behind me. I'd felt her approach and gave her a look of disapproval for allowing Mev to accompany her.

Sir Rowan of Estmere. I'd heard the name many times before. A respected diplomat and emissary whose lineage dated back to the humans who'd first come through the Gate. He'd negotiated as many trade agreements these past few years as generations of humans before him. Somehow, we had never crossed paths.

Bowing to the women, Sir Rowan confirmed his identity. "Sir Rowan of Estmere, at your service."

"How can you two not have met before?" Lyra asked us.

As Lyra said, I'd never met the man.

"You've spent little time at the capital," Rowan said,

addressing me, "since I've been named the royal emissary. And of course..." He grinned at Lyra, a smile that may have put others at ease, but not me. I trusted no human, not even one with this man's reputation. "I've no cause to visit Gyoria, or you, to visit the royal court of Estmere," he said to me.

Catching my retort, one Mev would have disliked, I instead asked on his purpose for traveling north, knowing his business was his own but caring little for protocol. He was, after all, a human.

At that, Rowan looked at Mev. Studied her. I stepped between the two of them.

"What is your business in Aethralis?" I asked again.

His gaze returned to me.

"The same as yours, your highness." That damn smile again. I liked it not. "To discover how she got through the Gate."

21

MEV

I didn't even have time to react before Kael closed the gap between him and the human knight. Lyra shoved me behind her as both of them demanded answers. Peeking around her shoulder, I couldn't see Kael's face, but could imagine it.

Surprisingly, this Rowan guy didn't appear at all intimidated. If he knew Kael, then he would know how strong he was.

"How do you know?"

Four words, but Kael uttered each one as if it were a deadly threat. It occurred to me just now that I'd not been as terrified as I should have been when Kael first took me.

"Surely you're aware word is spreading?" The knight's response was calm and not at all sarcastic or taunting. Just a simple question. I pushed away from Lyra, but she kept moving in front of me.

"He's not a threat," I whispered to her.

"Tell me of this 'word' that is spreading?" Kael asked, not backing down.

"You don't know that," Lyra whispered back to me.

"That a woman came through the Gate. You took her and the other former Council members have been looking for you since. None know, yet, she is the lost princess."

Kael's eyes widened.

"It was not difficult to discern. Her age." He gestured to me. "Her hair. Perhaps the Gate made an exception for King Galfrid's daughter?"

He wasn't a threat. I *knew* it. Pushing past Lyra, I joined Kael.

"Go back to Lyra," Kael said in a tone that left very little for interpretation. It was a demand but, unfortunately for him, I wasn't a fan of demands.

"He isn't a threat to us, Kael," I said.

Both men turned to me. Kael was furious. The knight, confused.

He was extremely handsome. His brown tousled hair, lighter than Kael's, and roguish smile, coupled with mischief-filled eyes, made him even more attractive up close. Though not as attractive as Kael, of course. He had that look about him that said, "Only come close if you're good at mending your broken heart when it's all said and done." Actually, more like the kind of guy that would help you mend it, give you answers and closure and all that. But he'd break it, nonetheless.

But more importantly, he would not harm me. That I knew, for certain.

"Kael," I said again, more firmly. "Trust me."

This time, it seemed to get through. He glanced from me to the newcomer and then moved to my side. When Kael grabbed my hand, I couldn't have been more surprised. Mostly, because possessive guys weren't usually my type, and despite the fact that the movement was a clear sign of possession, I was actually a little turned on by it.

No fucking way I'd ever let Kael know that, though.

"You will tell us everything you know." Kael had apparently forgotten this guy wasn't one of his men. But strangely, Rowan of Estmere didn't seem to take offense.

"Only that you are the most hunted man in Elydor at the moment. None are pleased that you took her, especially with the Summit still in session and former Council members in attendance."

"It is as I said." Lyra's version of "I told you so," directed at Kael, nearly made me laugh. But I didn't dare. Kael was not a happy camper at the moment.

"Was Lord Draven on the old Council?" I whispered, thinking of something suddenly.

All three of them stared at me. Kael, apparently satisfied he'd staked his claim, let go of my hand. "Why do you ask?"

I belatedly realized the knight, Sir Rowan, was human. He very well might know Isolde's commander, so speaking openly about him wasn't a great idea. But I had a difficult time forgetting the feeling of foreboding I'd had when he was near.

"For... reasons."

Not surprisingly, Kael didn't seem amused.

"No." It was Sir Rowan who answered. "No humans served on the Council. We are not recognized as one of the clans of Elydor."

Oh yeah. I'd forgotten about that.

He said it so matter-of-factly, and without bitterness, that I didn't know what to say. Wasn't he angry? Or resentful?

"We ride at once." Kael was apparently done with his interrogation.

No one moved. I studied the human, knowing Kael would be pissed. But if these feelings were truly glimpses into the future that I could not see, I should begin embracing them.

What that meant for Kael and me, for me leaving Elydor, I wasn't sure. But those were problems for another day.

"Sir Rowan," I said. "You travel to Aethralis. Come with us."

"Rowan only, if it pleases you, princess."

Only one man would call me that. "Mev," I said. "And you can ignore his glare."

"You'd do well not to take her advice," Kael grumbled. "On either point."

"Be nice," I said, earning a smile from Lyra who seemed to be enjoying the whole exchange. Realizing she might be an ally in this, I recruited her. "Lyra, do you not think a man as capable as Rowan clearly is, would be best served to join us? We're going to the same place, and he's not a threat to us."

"You have the Sight?" Rowan asked me, before Lyra could answer.

"Maybe," I said. "This is all new to me. Back home, I had as much psychic abilities as a piece of chocolate. Wait, do you guys have chocolate?"

Rowan grinned. "We do, but it is more common in the south."

"Do you have the Sight too?"

"A form of it."

"Kael," I said, pretending he wasn't about to explode. "Rowan can help me learn about my human abilities, just like Lyra is doing with my magic. Great idea, right?"

"No. It is not."

"Good. It's settled. You will come with us. I mean, if you want. I'm not in the business of making people do something they don't want to do."

That last bit was for Kael, specifically.

Lyra outright laughed and headed back toward her horse.

The more time we spent together, the less I remembered to be intimidated by her and liked her a lot.

"I would be glad to accompany you."

"I do not think—"

Shoving Kael toward Stormbreaker, I whispered, "You're being ridiculous."

"I am being anything but ridiculous," he responded, but walked in the right direction nonetheless. "We know little of his intentions."

"That's where the 'trust me' part kicks in."

"You believe he is not a threat?"

We'd stopped just beside Stormbreaker. Kael reached out a hand to pet him, likely without realizing it. That gentleness was one of the things I liked best about him. It was so at odds with the man he was, prince of all things hard and immovable.

"It's more than just a belief," I admitted, unsure how to put it into words. "My mother always said gut instincts were just your body remembering something your brain did not. That the body has a longer memory. I had no idea what she meant, but I think I do now. These are more than just feelings. It's like a certainty that courses through my body even before I'm aware of it. With you—and Lyra and now Rowan—there's a rightness there. Like the opposite of a threat."

Somehow, I made him even angrier. "You had the same feeling of him as you did me?"

Oh shit.

"No, not like that. Not at all." He didn't believe me. "Are you telling me, an actual prince, an immortal who can do all kinds of Thor-like magic is threatened by a mere human?"

In response, Kael grabbed me around the waist and lifted me with two hands onto his enormous warhorse. With a grunt, he mounted in front of me just as Rowan caught up with us.

Though I couldn't see Kael's face, he must have given Rowan quite a look because the corner of our knight's lips raised just before he rode ahead of us to join Lyra.

"First of all, I am not threatened."

Thankfully Kael couldn't see me roll my eyes.

"Second of all, I do not have Thor-like magic. Mine is rooted in the ground, tied to the land. It works through connection, not force."

Oddly, I understood what he meant. All of Lyra's teachings were tied to harnessing the air in some way. Without it, there would be nothing.

"Kael?" I asked quietly, needing a real answer.

"Princess?"

Ignoring what that did to my insides, at least for now, I forged ahead. "Why do you hate humans so much? I understand their coming here led to your mother's death, but... except for the whole magic and immortality thing—you don't seem all that different from us."

I thought maybe he didn't hear me, Kael was so quiet. Waiting for his response, I rested my cheek on his back, scooting closer and hanging onto him more tightly. We'd passed the village and were back to traveling in a dense forest, the dirt road below only wide enough for riders in one direction. Aside from a quiet, otherworldly energy and the distant calls of unfamiliar creatures, I could still be on Earth.

Maybe, I thought as I listened, waiting for him to answer, there was one more difference. Lyra's words rang through my ears. *Listen to the whisper of the wind through the branches, feel the air flow past you.*

"My father hates them," Kael said finally. "My brother and I have watched that hate consume him over the years, and neither of us wishes to become that man. I... do not hate them as much as I fear them. Humans are not native to Elydor, and I've witnessed firsthand the implications of their integrating into our world."

A part of me knew Kael admitting fear of anything was unusual. "Thank you for your honesty," I said, wondering how to respond to the rest of it. I could only go by my own experiences which were admittedly much more limited than Kael's. Who was I to give him advice?

Limited, but different. Just speak from your heart.

"I was terrified of dogs," I said, lifting my cheek from his back. "When I was four, a dog knocked me down, just being playful. No big deal, except it must have been. My mother said that little fear grew into something that paralyzed me anytime a dog was nearby. She stopped visiting friends who had dogs, put me into therapy. When I was in high school, I still had the same therapist, but we didn't talk much about dogs anymore. Somehow, I got past what was a debilitating fear. So I asked her once how she'd done it. I couldn't remember a single instance where I'd begun to feel more comfortable around dogs, but just knew by that point I was no longer afraid of them."

I paused, remembering that conversation. Over the years, whether it was my fear of dogs or worry about failing a test, my therapist had been an amazing resource. One of the best things my mother had ever done for me, and she did a lot of amazing things, especially as a single mom.

"What did she say?"

Brought back to our conversation, I quoted her exactly. "That most people fear what they don't know. She said, 'I haven't treated a single patient who fears grass or trees. But planes? Plenty. Animals? You aren't the only one. When we aren't exposed to something, we can make up stories in our mind about that thing.' My story was that dogs were scary and could hurt me. I don't remember all of it, but she said my mother took me to a neighbor's house with a dog, and we sat in the car while she brought her dog onto the porch. We went every week, apparently, eventually moving from the car, to the lawn, until I worked up the courage to pet it. Just being exposed to a dog, and not having anything bad happen, eventually changed the narrative in my mind about dogs. I stopped crossing the street when a dog would pass or hightailing it in the opposite direction when one came toward me in the park. I love dogs now and can't imagine a time when I was that afraid of them."

While he took that in, I shifted to the side, looking past Kael. Rowan rode ahead of Lyra, each of us still single file. Kael said Elydor had no need of human innovation and that mostly seemed true. But a quick plane ride to Aethralis would have been nice.

"I do not fear humans in that way. They cannot easily kill an Elydorian," Kael said finally.

"But you are afraid of how they might change Elydor. And fear clouds our judgment." He went quiet again, so I asked, "How much time have you spent with humans or in Estmere?"

"As little as possible, and only when it's unavoidable."

As expected. "Exactly. You need a new narrative. Obviously you like Isolde, and she's human. There must be a few others."

"There's not."

He was quick to answer, and his tone was still curt, as it always was when he spoke of humans. But I didn't believe him. Instead of probing, I focused on something else.

"You like me. And I'm half human."

He didn't say anything.

Attempting to pull the man from the Gyorian was proving

a monumental task. He knew how little I cared for silence. But I refused to need validation from a man who'd kidnapped me.

Don't ask, Mev. Do. Not. Ask.

And now I was at war with myself. Independent "doesn't give a shit" me, meet the "don't want anyone to dislike me, people pleasing" me. It was a constant battle.

"You *do* like me, don't you?" I asked.

He smiled, shaking his head and turning back around.

"I like you very much, princess."

22

KAEL

"Absolutely not. No."

Lyra's calmness was a trait I'd always admired about her. In all the years I'd known her, not once had I seen her lose her temper. So it wasn't a surprise that her response to me was a serene smile.

"You are being unreasonable."

The path had widened allowing Lyra to ride beside us. Although I hadn't spoken to Rowan all day, not as we rode or when we had stopped, that did not seem to bother him as he sat ahead of us, watching and waiting. Apparently, he was still intent on staying with us.

"Zephros is a border town, and in case you've forgotten, our borders have been in conflict for a long time."

"The last battle here was more than five years ago," Rowan added from in front of us, slowing as we had. "And if rumor is true, you prevented it from escalating. You may be surprised at your reception here."

I was about to tell Rowan his opinion on the matter was not welcome, but held my tongue instead. Earlier, as we'd begun to circle the village, Lyra had suggested our party take refuge in the border town. Built on gently rolling hills, its moss and vine-covered stone houses having stood for centuries, Zephros was known for being a refuge for Aetherian sages and scholars looking to further study the mysteries of the air.

The thought of laying my head on Aetherian soil did not appeal to me, though the one of sharing a bed with Mev did. I was not trained to make decisions in such a manner, however.

"She will be safe here," Lyra said quietly.

Rowan watched me, the human knight saying nothing. I could see him measuring my reaction, no doubt wondering where my true loyalties lay. I'd run each and every member of the former Council through my mind many times.

I did not believe either Caelum or Nerys of Thalassaria would be a threat to Mev. Both fiercely loyal to their clan, they prioritized Thalassaria's sovereignty above all else and both welcomed the Gate.

Lord Valdric, however, was likely tracking us as well. As my father's chief advisor with a deep mistrust of outsiders and belief in Gyoria's isolationist policies, Valdric would not hesitate to take Mev to my father. When we were young, my brother and I called him uncle.

And then there was Eirion of Aetheria. He would be the least worrisome in terms of a threat to Mev. A seasoned warrior and former general of the Aetherian forces, Eirion was the Council's enforcer, ensuring that any threats to the portal were dealt with swiftly and decisively. Most importantly, he was a friend and mentor to the king and therefore an ally to Mev.

Of course, word would have spread beyond the Council members. Like Rowan, others would know by now of Mev's presence in Elydor, and it would not be long before her true identity was also known by all. Including my brother and father.

My pride held little value compared to Mev's safety.

"Very well. Though you may be confident they can keep our secret, I am not. She needs a cloak," I said of Mev, reaching down into my saddlebag.

"Keep yours," Rowan said. "You will want to use it to hide yourself." He dismounted, removed his own hooded cloak and lifted it toward us. I took it. The damned man grinned when I reached for it, as if my taking it symbolized my acceptance of him.

It didn't.

I simply wished to keep Mev safe, and speaking my mind to Rowan would upset her. So I kept my opinions of the human to myself as we set off in the direction of the village.

"I've never seen anything so pretty," Mev said as we headed toward Zephros. "I mean, except for everything else in Elydor. Kael," she said suddenly, "do you have poverty here?"

"Not as you do. Even those with only a basic mastery of their abilities in Gyoria can summon plants and grow food. Thalassari can easily catch fish as Aetherians can harness their air magic to manipulate air currents for crops or control airflow to reduce spoilage."

"And the humans?"

It was the hope in her voice that crushed me.

Hope that her people escaped the same fate as their counterparts on Earth who lacked resources. I was about to shatter Mev's vision of Elydor as a utopia, as it was anything but. Border towns experienced many hardships, especially in these last thirty years. Though we'd avoided all-out war, one was coming, and all of Elydor knew it.

"They are not insulated from the kind of poverty you know

on Earth. Tradition has kept them a feudal society, and though some benefit from an alliance with Aetheria, and to a lesser extent, an uneasy peace with Thalassaria, others do suffer for lack of resources."

"That is... shameful."

I was spared having to respond when two riders approached. I couldn't hear what Lyra said to them, but almost immediately they both looked our way. Mev and I had pulled up the hoods on our cloaks, and the simple disguise appeared to work as the riders did not look twice at us. By the time we caught up with them, the riders had turned back toward the village, and we followed.

"The air," Mev said. "It feels lighter here. Or something."

She was Aetherian, for certain. Not that I doubted it, given her emerging abilities. For further confirmation, each passing day Mev's hair lightened, its white color almost as if it was woven from the stars themselves.

"You'll notice, Mev"—Lyra had hung back and rode beside us now—"the buildings here are designed to be in harmony with the natural flow of air. The open courtyards, wind chimes and terraces catch the breeze. This is a special place even Gyorians rarely touch, despite the fact that it sits along the border."

"It sounds almost religious."

"Of sorts," Lyra replied. "We have temples, to our gods and goddesses, as do the other clans. This place is different, though."

"What did they say?" I asked Lyra of the riders.

"That we are welcome. We'll head directly to Wind Haven Inn where I will secure rooms. Thankfully, it lies on the outskirts of the village."

I liked it not. If we'd remained on the road, Mev and I

would not be forced to hide ourselves. On the other hand, if Lord Valdric was looking for us, he would not likely enter Zephros.

"I will scout the area tomorrow before we leave," Rowan said, as if he were reading my thoughts. If he were one of my men, I'd have praised his foresight.

I kept my head down as we approached the outer edge of the village. Mev tightened her grip around my waist, but said nothing, I reached for her hand and squeezed it.

She would be safe here.

I repeated the phrase, shrugging off my discomfort. I'd spent many years surrounded by Aetherians, especially when travelers through the Gate were more common. As the years wore on and humans without psychic abilities died attempting to pass through, news of their deaths spread. Less made the attempt, allowing me to return to Gyoria for more extended periods.

"The letters on that sign. Are they Elydorian?"

"They are," I said, as our party slowed to a stop. Dismounting, careful to keep my head down, I reached a hand up for Mev. She was swimming under Rowan's cloak.

"I will stable the horses," Rowan said as Mev dismounted. "Stay scarce until Lyra secures rooms."

"Thank you," Mev said from beneath his cloak. As Rowan walked away, she elbowed me and nodded to the human. I mumbled my thanks and moved toward the side of the inn with Mev in tow to wait for Lyra's return.

"Be nice," she said.

In response, with Mev's back against the stone wall of the inn, I lowered my head and claimed her lips, giving into that particular temptation which had been growing inside me since our first kiss.

A dangerous temptation with many reasons to resist. Pulling back, I conjured my brother, Adren, my men... all those who counted on me to keep them safe.

"I should not have done that." Not the words I'd planned, but I could not take them back.

"Should you not? You'll notice I did not stop you."

"But perhaps you should have."

"Given you literally kidnapped me and have admitted we are still enemies? Aye, I should have. But sometimes our heart tells us to do things our head advises against."

When I said nothing to that, Mev reached up and touched her fingertips to my cheek. That simple touch almost had me considering her words might be true.

"I do have a question." The sudden shyness in her tone as she pulled her hand back piqued my curiosity.

"What is it?"

"So," she hedged. "What does birth control look like in Elydor?"

"I sometimes forget you are an Uninitiated."

"That my backside nearly constantly hurts from riding and my million questions aren't clues?"

I refrained from commenting on her backside and took her hand instead. Moving us to the front corner of the inn, I bid her to watch as the residents of Zephros walked past.

"What do you see? Or not see, I should say."

Keeping to the shadows, we stood hand in hand, watching.

"There are no children," she said, picking up on the fact more quickly than I'd have expected. "Wait. Why are there no children?"

"It has always been the way of things. Babies are rare in Elydor. When they are conceived, it is cause for great celebration."

"Why?" she asked.

"Elydor has always sought balance. It is the reason your human technology is not welcome. Why those who come through the Gate are unable to bring anything with them which would threaten that natural balance. Too many children in a world of immortals would soon see our land overpopulated."

"You can be killed, though."

"True. But imagine if as many babies were born here as in your world."

"Hmm. So birth control is not necessary?"

"Nor desired."

"Lyra has secured our rooms." Rowan came from nowhere. I did not like how easily he approached without my sensing it. When we were alone in the woods, it was easy enough to feel the land's vibrations. But here, with so much activity, individual vibrations were more difficult to detect.

"There is a back entrance," he said, pointing in the direction from which Mev and I had just come. "This way."

I let go of Mev's hand as she followed Rowan. It seemed the human was intent on keeping her safe, and though I was grateful for it, I also wondered at the reason. Was it only because he hoped she would be the key to reopening the Gate? Some humans had been particularly distraught when it had closed, never having intended to remain here permanently. My father had, essentially, trapped many in a world they'd thought they'd be visiting temporarily.

I'd have asked him that very question if all hell hadn't suddenly broken loose.

23

MEV

One second, we were following Rowan to the inn's back entrance. The next, I was shoved behind Kael, my back against the wall. I had no idea what was happening. Rowan moved to stand beside him, so I was essentially blocked by two behemoth men and couldn't see a thing. Aside from a gust of wind and Lyra shouting for someone to stop, I had no idea what was happening.

But I could sense an energy all around me, like a tempest. I peeked around Kael's right arm. A woman stood there, glaring at Kael but speaking to Lyra. Her dark hair, streaked with silver, whipped around her as if the wind gust hadn't gone away already.

But it had.

"What is the Prince of Gyoria doing here?" she asked Lyra.

"Lower your voice, lest we be discovered," Lyra argued. "He is a friend—"

"Prince Kael is no friend to Aetheria," the woman cut in.

"In this, he is. Please," Lyra begged, her normally calm

tone tinged with urgency, "I can explain, but do not wish for them to be discovered."

"Them?" The woman's sharp gaze turned to us. I pushed against Kael who did not budge. "She is not an enemy to me," I said to both men. "And I do not wish to hide."

This time when I pushed, Kael stepped aside.

The woman's eyes narrowed. "So the rumors are true?"

"I knew this was a bad idea," Kael muttered.

"They are," Lyra confirmed. In response, the woman bowed her head, as if in deference, to me.

"I meant no disrespect, Princess Mevlida."

I definitely would never get used to that. "None is taken," I responded as the woman lifted her head. "Though Prince Kael is friend and not foe."

I was starting to sound like the rest of them. Friend and not foe? It was like being plonked into the middle of a Renaissance Faire and, by the end of the day, you find yourself saying things like "Greetings" and "Fare-thee-well."

This is no Ren Faire, Mev.

"Come inside," Lyra urged. "Please."

With that, the woman followed Lyra into the Wind Haven Inn. I was not sure what I expected as we walked through the door, but it probably wasn't something similar to a medieval tavern in York. Had this place been influenced by the humans, or vice versa?

There were differences, of course. The air was filled with a subtle hum of magic and the tables and chairs were elegantly carved with intricate patterns that swirled and shifted, almost like living symbols of the wind. Soft, ethereal lights floated in the air, illuminating the space with a calming glow, casting long shadows that danced across the room.

Lyra took us to a private room. In the center was a round

table, but it was the hearth that held my gaze. The large stone structure at the far end of the room wasn't particularly remarkable, but the fire itself was. There was no wood, as far as I could tell. Instead, the fire seemed to be fed by the very air itself.

Remarkable.

As we sat, the scent of fresh bread and roasting meat filled the air. There was an underlying tension in the air, and it was Lyra who spoke first after trays of food and pitchers of ale were brought in and dispensed by two young women and one male, all with shades of light blonde or silver hair.

When they closed the doors on their way out, Lyra spoke first, directly to me.

"Salvia's rare ability to read winds told her of our arrival, though I've taken care to ensure no others will know of this visit," Lyra said. "Rooms are being prepared as we speak, and there is a back entrance to those as well."

Kael looked skeptical. Rowan, thoughtful.

For her part, this Salvia alternated between glaring at Kael and watching me closely.

"Thank you, Lyra," I said. Then to Salvia, "Why did it appear as if you arrived in a windstorm? And please forgive my forwardness. I am, as they say, an Uninitiated."

Salvia glanced between Lyra and me. "You are truly the lost princess?"

"Apparently," I answered, taking a bite of meat. The others ate heartily as if it were their first meal for days.

"How did you—"

"Unknown," I interrupted her, knowing the question already. I had a feeling it was one I would be asked a lot. "I knew nothing about this world until ten minutes before I put my hand on the portal and... boom."

She blinked, watching me. "I can control many aspects of the air around me," she replied. "But I've never been good at tempering it when I am riled. That is why it swirled around me."

I was about to say I'd never seen such a thing before, but I didn't exactly have a lot of exposure to her kind. I knew precisely two other Aetherians, myself and Lyra.

"I've begun to train her," Lyra said. "Her abilities are innate, though."

"To be expected," Salvia said. "She is King Galfrid's daughter."

I wanted to ask about him. And about a hundred other questions, until I noticed Kael's expression. He looked cautious and uncomfortable, and especially grumpy. He didn't want to be here, and who could blame him? Salvia didn't help, the sharp woman's gaze when it landed on him one of open contempt.

For good reason. His father banished your mother. Closed the portal. It did not help that Kael kidnapped you.

Lyra was right, of course.

All of the questions I wanted to ask Salvia were forgotten as Kael met my gaze. It was the first time I saw a vulnerability there, and it bothered me. Made me want to protect him, which was ridiculous.

I didn't care that we sat at a round table and everyone could see everything. I reached out, for his hand, and Kael let me take it. Then turning back to the others, I ate with one hand and caught up with the conversation.

Salvia noticed. I had a feeling the woman didn't miss a thing. But if our being together upset her, she hid it well.

"How prevalent are the rumors?" Rowan asked Salvia.

"I would expect all of Aetheria to know of her return by now," she said. "Whispers on the wind."

What did that mean?

The same way I can speak to you now, Lyra responded.

Remembering our lessons, though having little air to manipulate, I attempted to respond.

How far can these whispers travel?

For some, no farther than us now. But the most skilled Aetherians can send whispers carried on the wind to the farthest reaches of Elydor. Of course, the recipient must be just as skilled to receive it.

My eyes widened.

So that means... all of Aetheria will know I am here.

Lyra nodded, which was when I realized everyone was staring at us. I pulled my hand from Kael's and took a sip of ale to cover my face. They knew what we were doing.

"Part of your training," Lyra said aloud, "will be to learn to conceal the kind of discussion we had just now."

"Wait," I asked, sitting forward. "Could you hear us, Salvia?"

"I could hear you," she confirmed. "But not Lyra."

Now I was properly confused.

"When two Aetherians whisper as you did," Salvia said. "They aim to create a channel of wind tightly controlled and directed only toward each other. Think of it as a private, invisible tunnel that carries their words to the other person's ears without dispersing into the surrounding air. The magic binds the sound waves to a narrow path, ensuring that no one else can intercept or overhear the conversation."

"I haven't gotten that far with you yet," Lyra confirmed. "But I don't expect it will take long. By rights, you should not be able to hear me so clearly, or respond so easily, with so little training."

Interesting.

As conversation veered back to the portal, I finished my meal and leaned toward Kael to whisper the old-fashioned way. "I am finished."

"Are you now?" he teased.

"Yes. But if you want to stay—"

He stood before I could get the rest of my sentence out. "If you would point us to our rooms, Lyra? We wish to retire."

No one questioned him.

"Apologies for the Irish goodbye. I mean, not exactly, since we're announcing it." As I blabbered, it quickly occurred to me not one person in the room understood.

Right. Not Earth. Elydor.

"What I mean to say is, thank you all for everything, but it's been a day, so..."

They waited.

"A day?" Rowan asked.

I was batting a thousand. "It's just an expression we use back home. Kinda hard to explain. Anyway..."

I noticed Lyra hand Kael a key, whispering something to him. Waving awkwardly, I pulled my hood up and followed him out of the same door we entered through. Kael quickly turned a corner before I could get a good look at the main room and climbed a set of stairs.

Which was when it occurred to me... Lyra had handed him one key. Assuming Kael and I would be sleeping together in the same room because he was clearly still in control of me, despite the others' presence, and actually walking up a set of stairs behind him were two different things.

The million and one questions I had about the whispers and my abilities and Elydor suddenly didn't matter. Kael strode to the top of the stairs and headed down a long hallway without saying a word. When he finally turned toward me, I froze at his look.

"What?" I asked, not able to get a good read on him.

"Have I told you of Adren?"

The change of topic threw me. "No, I don't believe so."

"He was hand-picked by my father to train me. Over the years, he's become my right-hand man, as the humans would say. Adren is a hardened warrior, fiercely loyal but also pragmatic. I could not ask for a better man to stand by my side."

If there was a reason he was telling me this now, I couldn't decipher it.

"I would like nothing more than to continue that kiss," he said, Kael's eyes darting toward our room.

"It feels like there's a big fat 'but' in there somewhere." I smiled at my own sort-of joke.

Kael raised his brows in a way that made me want to laugh. But I didn't. He was being too serious.

"I have responsibilities to people who count on me."

In other words, people who mattered more than I did. "Got it." Though it went against my nature not to talk it out more, this was "hard Kael" and there wasn't a lot more to say. Except, "Let's get inside."

Though he paused, for the briefest of seconds, Kael moved toward the door, put in the key, and turned it.

This was gonna be a long night.

24

KAEL

The frustrated look she'd given me outside seemed long forgotten as she rushed to the tub. The room was well appointed, but the tub was its crowning glory. It was made of crystal fibers, and the light reflected from the hearth and candles throughout the room made the water appear iridescent. Having seen human equivalents, I had no doubt Mev would be enchanted by its unique design, and she was.

"How? I mean, what the heck is this made of? It's beautiful. Oh my God, I never thought I'd be so excited about a hot bath in my life."

"Aetherians, you should know, very often make bathing a ritual."

"I would think that was a Thalassari thing?"

"I believe," I said, approaching her, "the custom originated from them and spread."

"But skipped Gyoria?"

Instead of answering, attempting to mitigate my speech in the hall and being unable to resist touching her, I lifted Mev's chin. "Thank you."

I expected Mev to ask why I'd thanked her, but she already knew. We could never communicate the way she and Lyra had, but there was something between us that was just as strong.

A knock at the door interrupted us, which was probably a good thing. "This best be urgent."

"Kael." Lyra's tone penetrated. I quickly unlocked and pulled open the door. "We need to talk. Immediately."

I refused to take this night away from Mev. She might be angry at me for not including her—Mev's continued insistence on not being shielded hadn't gone unnoticed—but I would make it up to her.

I turned from Lyra. "Enjoy your bath. I will just be a moment."

"Is everything okay?" she asked, peering around me and asking both Lyra and me the question.

"Yes. Go on, while it's hot. I won't be long."

Mev was torn, clearly, but the hot bath won out. Stepping into the hall, I closed the door behind me.

"She will want to hear this."

"I'll tell her. What?"

Lyra made the same frowning face she had whenever a newcomer had come through the Gate and we'd disagreed on whether they should be allowed to enter Elydor fully. Which was to say, often.

"Salvia knows Elydorian artifacts better than anyone. She said something that concerned me."

I crossed my arms and waited for Lyra to continue.

"We were speaking of Mev, and she made a comment. That it felt, to her, the Wind Crystal stirred in a way it hasn't ever before."

"She can sense it from here?"

Lyra nodded. That was quite a skill, and not one any Gyorian could claim.

"Why is that concerning? Likely it's due to Mev's presence."

"No, I don't think so. The Wind Crystal's disturbances are often a sign of turbulence in the realm. The air carries whispers of unrest, and when the balance is threatened, it can be a harbinger of darker forces at play. It's not just the Crystal—it's what it's trying to tell us. I think Mev's presence would cause just the opposite."

"What are you thinking?" I asked, not able to completely follow Lyra's logic.

"Salvia said she first felt it around the same time Mev came through the portal, but that the stirring dissipated, as if there was no longer a threat. But then, as we sat around the table, I could sense a shift in her demeanor. She admitted the same stirring had once again begun."

This time, I understood more clearly. "You believe I was the original threat to Mev, and now there is a new one?"

She nodded. "I do."

This was not welcome news.

"Rowan is going to lead a contingency of Salvia's choosing to scout the area. If all is clear, we should leave when he returns in a few hours. Perhaps allow Mev to rest until then. She will be the only one unused to the pace we will need to set."

A good plan, except... "Do you trust him?"

"Rowan? I do. His reputation as a royal emissary and a man of honor precedes him. If I did not trust the man, he'd not already be traveling with us," she added.

I hated all of it. Mev being in danger. Having to rely on an Aetherian and human to help protect her. If we were in

Gyoria, I would be the one to scout. But here, my presence would do nothing but hinder the efforts.

"Very well. Keep us apprised on the situation."

"We will. Have her rest in the meantime, Kael." As I headed back into the room, Lyra called out, "Rest, in case you are uncertain, means sleep."

One look at Mev in that tub, and I knew why Lyra had called out that particular piece of advice.

"What is it?" she asked.

"I'll explain later."

Though she was hidden from view, the top of Mev's breasts were visible, and it was enough to have me re-thinking asking to join her in that tub.

Instead, summoning what little self-control I had remaining, I reached for a stool and sat on it beside the tub.

"You're planning to watch me bathe?" she asked, Mev's earlier modesty seeming to have dissipated, though not completely disappearing as she lowered into the bubbles that hid her from my view.

"I'm planning to discuss this thing between us."

"Thing?" she asked, the picture of innocence. "That was Lyra, at the door?"

"Us first."

"Oh look. High-handed Kael is back. Or more likely, he never left."

Ignoring the sarcasm, and re-thinking my decision to talk to Mev while she lay in the tub, I made it quick.

"I may be high-handed—"

"*May* be?"

"But I am not one to toy with others' emotions. The urge to kiss you, to do a hell of a lot more than that, is strong."

"I told you once and will say it again. Prove it."

Ohhh. This woman. I could not, would not, be baited into doing something I would regret. "I could do that, but it would not end well."

"How, exactly, would it end?" she pushed.

Time to be blunt. "With broken hearts when I am forced to choose between you and my clan."

I thought that would enrage her. Or shut Mev down so she would stop looking at me that way, with the same longing in her eyes as I probably had for her. Instead, she seemed to take my words as a challenge.

"Hearts? Plural? Yours included? You'd have to have one first."

I felt a tug on the corner of my lips but tamped it down. "I do have one. It is just buried very, very deep inside my chest."

"Good to know."

What the hell did that mean?

"Are we done discussing us? Because I'd love to wash without worrying about my boobs popping out of the water."

She had such a way with words. Also, the thought of said "boobs" just beneath the bubbles was too much for me to take.

"Finish your bath," I said, standing. "I will be just outside the door. Let me know when you are done."

With that, I stalked to the door, recognizing the ease with which Mev could enflame my otherwise even-keeled emotions, and closed it behind me. Leaning against it, I wasn't certain, but it seemed as if the sound of moving water was laced with laughter.

Well done, Mev.

My princess had won that round.

I was determined to win the next one.

25

MEV

My mother was standing at the entrance of the Aetherian Gate. I could see right through it to the other side. Clara was next to her, nodding. When my mother held out her hand, I hesitated. But Mom didn't seem upset by that. Instead, she just waited for me. I wanted to tell her to come to me, but for some reason, I couldn't speak.

Something hit me from behind, but when I turned, no one was there. This time, I was jostled from the left side. Blinking, the portal was gone. Mom was gone.

"Go back to sleep," a deep male voice said.

I was so tired, I listened. But soon there were other voices.

"I'd like to speak to her."

The woman's voice was vaguely familiar. This time, I did open my eyes. Instead of being in front of the portal, or in bed with Kael, I was cradled in his arms like a baby surrounded by people and horses, apparently all ready to leave even though it was still dark.

"How did I sleep through you carrying me down here?" I asked.

In response, Kael let me down. We were in the same alleyway beside the inn where he'd kissed me yesterday. Lyra, Rowan, Salvia, and three others who appeared to be Aetherian guards were all mounted. When I looked their way, each inclined their head, as if in deference. I smiled sleepily and adjusted the cloak I didn't remember putting on.

"Quickly, Salvia. We must be off," Lyra said.

"There's no one following us?" I asked Rowan.

"We found no evidence of being followed here, but they will escort us out of town to be certain."

Kael, predictably, didn't seem pleased about that fact.

"Princess Mevlida?" Salvia stepped forward. "A quick word, if you please?"

"Of course," I said, scurrying to the side where she'd separated herself from the others.

"I trust you were told of the disturbance in the Wind Crystal?"

"I was, but have to admit, I don't know anything about this Wind Crystal."

"Relics are an important part of our magic. Each of the clans have many of them, some more powerful than others. My role was once as Keeper of the Artifacts."

"Back home, I was a museum curator specializing in ancient artifacts."

That seemed to surprise her. "I suppose," she said finally, "that is not a coincidence."

Unsure what that meant, I waited for her to continue.

"Listen to me closely," she said, her tone serious enough for me to lean closer and mark her words. "It is not well known precisely how your father opened the human portal or how Kael's father closed it. There are very few with that knowledge, but I'm certain your father will explain soon enough."

"I don't understand," I admitted. Her words were like a puzzle to me.

"The Wind Crystal is Aetheria's most powerful relic. It has been many years since I've felt a disturbance such as this one, which I believe is significant. You can ask Lyra more about it, and Kael can tell you of the Gyorian equivalent, the Stone of Mor'Vallis. The most powerful Thalassari relic is the Tidal Pearl, but I doubt your companions will know much of it beyond rumor and conjecture."

"We are ready to leave," Kael said, coming to my side.

I implored Salvia to finish, but she was either reluctant to speak in front of him, or had nothing else to tell me, because she stepped back and bowed her head, as if ending our conversation.

I could not leave it at that. Her words made no sense. What was it about these relics that she wanted to tell me?

"I still do not understand," I said, aware the remainder of our riding party was mounted.

"If I knew more, I would share it with you. Be aware of their existence and know I am here if you have any need of me." Her slight smile was full of confidence. "None are more well-versed on the subject of Elydor's relics than me. Not even your father."

"Mev." Kael was getting more impatient by the second. "We have to go."

"Thank you," I said to Salvia, not having any clue what I thanked her for, besides an offer of aid. I would try to work it all out later. For now, Kael was tugging me toward the others. I raised a hand to wave to Salvia, but she was gone.

"Where the heck did she go?" I asked, peering down the alleyway.

"Aetherians can be slippery," Kael said.

"You make it sound like a slight."

"It is."

Frowning at him, fully awake now, I approached Storm-breaker.

"They offered an extra mount for you," Lyra said. "But Kael declined it."

I shot him an accusatory glare. "What if I wanted to ride by myself?"

"You are not skilled enough. Not at the pace we will be riding. Besides, Stormbreaker can bear the extra weight, so there is no reason for it."

We would talk about agency later. In the meantime, I mounted with Kael's assistance and was surprised when he climbed up behind me. Reaching around my waist, Kael took the reins and said, "Lean back and get some rest."

As one would expect, the village of Zephros was empty at this time of night, whatever time it was. As we set off, I couldn't move as freely in front, but had to admit, the feeling of security, being wrapped in Kael's arms, wasn't at all unpleasant.

I would tell him about my dream. Ask about the stone. Tell Kael he really needed to let me make decisions. Later. For now, I just wanted to close my eyes for another second or two.

"Mev!" Kael's voice jarred me awake. "I need you to duck."

Not the way I wanted to be woken up, but I did what he asked. As I lowered my head, a dark shape swooped past, barely missing me. My heart raced as I glanced up to see a shadowwing, its black feathers glinting in the early light. It flew low, its wings nearly brushing the ground before it ascended again, disappearing into the canopy of trees above us.

"I thought you said they were harmless?"

"Mostly, they are."

Mostly. Fabulous.

"Shadowwings are seen as omens and guardians of the night by Aetherians," he said.

Interesting. That reminded me...

"Bad news," I said, turning my head. Kael was right there. The way he looked at me reminded me of my dream. Leaving him seemed... unthinkable. Almost as unthinkable as staying here and not going home.

"You have to pee?"

I pursed my lips together to keep from laughing. He sounded so non-Kael. So human. Even though I knew he was repeating my words, it brought him down a peg from the powerful magic-wielding prince to a regular guy.

Kind of. Kael could never actually be regular. And that was the problem. He was starting to feel like more of a friend than enemy, my growing feelings for him as undeniable as the chemistry between us.

"I can hold it a little bit." Although dense forest surrounded us, it was clear we rode uphill. "What do you know about the Stone of Mor'Vallis?"

At that moment, Lyra looked back at us. The other riders were gone. Only she and Rowan remained.

Are you well? she whispered to me.

I am surprisingly comfortable. Ask me again in a few hours, and I'll probably have a different answer.

"Why do you ask?"

Ask?

Oh. The stone. I paused for the briefest of moments.

This was King Balthor's son. But it was also the one who risked his father's wrath not taking me to Gyoria. And the one who looked at me with the kind of adoration a woman only dreams about. I either trusted him, or I didn't.

"It was what Salvia wanted to talk to me about. She said the Wind Crystal's disturbance was unusual and then told me of all the relics in Elydor, and that each clan has one equally as powerful. She mentioned the Stone of Mor'Vallis and some Thalassari pearl."

"The Tidal Pearl. Like the Wind Crystal, none truly know its full power, only that each is a very valuable relic. Rumors about each of them have served as conversational fuel for as many years as I've been alive."

"The Stone too?"

When Kael didn't immediately answer, I knew he was measuring his words, just as I'd done. Holding my breath, I waited. It did little good to fully trust him if Kael did not reciprocate.

"For many, yes. But not for me. I am one of a very few who know much about the Stone of Mor'Vallis's powers."

Would that be it? I sat up in his arms, as much as I was able.

Trust me, Kael. Please.

I wish I could whisper to him, too.

"For most," he said, navigating Stormbreaker around an animal that looked very much like a raccoon, though God knew what mystical properties it had as the thing scurried away rather quickly. "The Stone of Mor'Vallis does nothing more than intensify the holder's abilities. Legend would have us believe it was responsible for all of the streams and rivers in Elydor. Some say each was the result of its holder separating the ground, either on purpose or accidentally, but I doubt that is true."

Before he could continue, Rowan and Lyra slowed. When they navigated off our path, the pine-scented air alive around us, I hoped against hope it was to rest and water the horses. Because I really did need to pee now. But instead of following them, Kael stopped and called for our companions to go ahead.

"This is for your ears alone, Mevlida."

I couldn't remember the last time, if ever, he'd called me that. His tone, the softness to it, was unlike him. Kael's glimpses of gentleness, from a man that was hard in every other way, nearly brought tears to my eyes. He claimed we were still enemies, but times like this made me doubt it was still true.

"The Stone of Mor'Vallis was molded by the ancients who first harnessed magic in Elydor. It was initially used to balance the overwhelming power of its early users by draining their magical energy when in prolonged contact with the skin."

"Wow. I could see why that's kept on the DL." At his expression, I added, "The down-low. It just means, kept quiet. Seems like it could be pretty dangerous in the wrong hands."

"Extremely. Especially since that magical energy includes immortality."

"Wait, what?"

"Precisely. The stone is capable of stripping away immortality, but eventually, if used incorrectly or for too extended a period, it will kill you. Only the most skilled Gyorians can wield it. There are legends of Elydorians who became mortal. My father says they are not tales but true stories of the Stone of Mor'Vallis being used in such a way."

Elydorians who became mortal. Holy shit.

"How could something like that be kept a secret?"

"It's not a secret among kings and queens and their families. But none who know the truth have thus far parted with the knowledge."

"So like, a handful of people know about this?"

"Of Gyorians, yes. And only one Aetherian, that we know of."

"Me?" As soon as I said it, I realized Kael's use of "we" probably meant someone else.

"Two, including you."

Somehow, he didn't have to tell me.

"My father."

"Aye. Your father. He used it to open the portal. I suspect Salvia and others like her, who make ancient relics their life's work, might know as well, but I cannot confirm it."

None are more well-versed on the subject of Elydor's relics than me. Not even your father.

"She knows. I'm certain of it," I said, offhandedly. "Thank you for sharing that information with me," I said, deciding to push him, "but you hold back still. Why?"

"Hold back how, princess?"

As if he didn't know the answer. "Don't play coy with me." At his confused expression, I re-phrased it. "You know exactly how. Must I challenge you for every kiss?"

"My clan—"

"Yeah, I know. They depend on you. Got it."

His eyes narrowed. "I am already risking much, not bringing you to my father."

"Try falling through a wall into a world you didn't know existed," I said, becoming irritated. "Only to be kidnapped before learning you aren't actually fully human, and demi-immortal, with the power to read others' minds and, oh yeah, wield air." I finished my speech with a swish of my hand, the movement blowing said air between us like a light breeze. It really was getting easier and easier to do that.

"I have lived for hundreds of years, Mev. And never have I wanted to kiss a woman more than I do you. Surely you realize that? Last eve, when you were in that tub…"

"What? Say it, Kael. What did you want? And why didn't you take it?"

I wasn't sure about pushing someone like him to the limit, but I knew I wanted to. Push him there, and over it. If only he would relinquish control for three seconds.

Without warning, he reached up and grabbed my head, as if about to pull me toward him.

"We have company," Lyra called out in front of us.

Just like that, the moment was over. Kael spurred Storm-breaker forward. As we came upon a small riding party, I was less concerned with any potential danger, and more interested in replaying in my mind everything Kael had shared with me. Obviously, his loyalties were still torn. Part of me was disappointed, but part of me understood. Family dynamics were complicated.

No one knew the fact better than me.

26

KAEL

Of all the riders we'd come across, none had been a threat to Mev. Staying on back roads had done us well. But the closer we got to Aethralis, the fewer options we had. Last night we slept among the stars, our party exhausted by the hard pace.

"Have you ever been married?"

Mev had asked that question as I'd begun to stir this morning, intending to get up and check on Stormbreaker and ready our party to leave camp. Instead, I'd answered her question.

"We call your marriage a union. There are no officiants involved, but most unions are celebrated with an offering to the gods, though each clan has their own tradition. But no, I have not been."

"In all the years you've been alive? Why not?"

"There's not been one person I've wanted to spend an eternity with."

"Not one?"

"Not one," I'd affirmed. "Have you ever thought to marry?"

Her pause should not have made me feel anything more

than a mild curiosity. Instead, I'd imagined the man she was thinking of now, wondered what he looked like. Why they hadn't married.

Jealous of a human? Impossible.

"Once."

I'd waited. And waited. Eventually, I realized the silence she so despised was, in fact, unbearable. "Are you going to continue?"

There was no guile, only curiosity, in her expression. "Do you want me to?"

Good question. "Aye," I'd said, despite myself.

"I met him my first day at the museum. We bonded over our love of artifacts."

"He sounds fascinating," I'd said with more than a measure of sarcasm, earning a hard look from Mev. "Apologies. Do continue."

"We dated for almost a year. I did think maybe we'd get engaged. Married. House with a picket fence and all that. But we broke up instead."

"Why?" I'd asked, catching myself memorizing every feature of Mev's face. The outline of her smooth cheeks. Her delicate nose and eyes that were so Aetherian I still could not believe I'd overlooked the fact.

"Something about that life just didn't appeal to me. Not the being married part, and he was a great guy." She'd taken a deep breath, so deep that I had almost seen the sense of calm that claimed her. "I wonder if maybe... I was meant to be here."

As we rode now, I considered Mev's earlier question and her response, as well as my reaction to the faceless man that had claimed her heart, at least for a time. To say my future with Mev was uncertain would be a wild understatement. Yet nothing had felt more right than waking up beside her. Talking to her. Connecting to a woman that was my enemy.

Or at least, should be my enemy. Of course, if I were honest with myself, she'd become anything but that.

Sensing a slight shift in the ground, I pulled on the reins. We were less than a day's ride from the capital if we kept this pace. Had I cursed us in thinking prematurely we'd gotten Mev to safety?

"What is it?"

I handed Mev the reins and dismounted. Kneeling, I closed my eyes and concentrated. They were far off still, but my initial suspicions held true.

"Someone is coming?" Lyra asked.

I stood. Both she and Rowan had ridden back to us.

"More than one."

"How many?" Rowan asked.

"Sensing a disturbance in the ground is not as precise as that."

"Now is not the time to be difficult," Lyra said.

Being difficult to Rowan came so easily though. I'd admit, his aid had been welcome, but he was human. And had a good rapport with Mev. Which was fine, but the man could charm a tree to bloom in the dead of winter.

I smiled. Except, he couldn't do that because Rowan didn't possess such magic.

"I'm glad you are in good humor about our company, Kael," Mev said. "But perhaps we should devise a plan?"

Lyra and I exchanged a glance. "Do we run or stay?" she asked.

Precisely the question I pondered. If Mev was an experienced rider, I would be inclined to outrun them. I disliked their numbers—at least ten riders.

"Mev," Rowan said. "Listen to me. You have the Sight. My own abilities are not like yours and are of no use here. You've worked with Lyra to harness air magic. Do the same now with your mother's abilities."

At mention of her mother, Mev sat up straighter. "What do you know of my mother's abilities?"

I'd been about to ask the same.

"We can discuss that later. For now, just close your eyes and try."

Though Mev eyed the human suspiciously, she listened. He seemed to know a lot, even for a royal emissary.

"Quiet your mind," he said to her.

I reached up to steady Stormbreaker, smoothing his mane.

"Feel the energy around you. Focus on the riders. Try to sense their intent."

Mev closed her eyes and breathed deeply, in and out. She looked so fragile and beautiful.

"Let your intuition guide you. Can you feel their purpose? Are they friend or foe?"

She continued to breathe even as the riders came closer. I would not interrupt them, but we needed to make a decision. And soon.

"Think of it like reaching out with an invisible thread," he prompted, Rowan's voice calm and soothing. This was not the first time he'd instructed someone on how to tap into their subconscious mind.

My own abilities are not like yours and are of no use here.

What were his abilities, precisely?

Mev's eyes popped open.

No, not fragile at all. Her blue eyes were wide with determination. Sitting atop Stormbreaker that way, back straight and expression full of purpose, she looked so very different than the woman who'd come through the Gate. And it wasn't just because of her hair.

"They are foe. I am certain of it."

"Well done," Rowan said, smiling at her.

Mev looked down to me and dismounted. Knowing what I had to do didn't make it any easier. I was about to tell her the plan when Mev's earlier words rang through my ears.

What if I wanted to ride by myself?

"In my opinion," I said to her and not Lyra or Rowan. "Based on the number of riders and your assertion of their intent, you should ride ahead with Lyra while I stay to slow them."

"No." Her response was swift and sure. "I will not leave you."

"Mevlida?" Lyra never used her full name but did so now. Mev gave the Aetherian noblewoman her attention. "Prince Kael is the strongest of all Gyorians, save his father and brother. If he wished to best me, he could do so easily. It would take more than a few men to overcome him, nor would they even attempt to do so unless they courted a war."

I was grateful for Lyra's words, but was unsure if they swayed Mev. Her panic at leaving me was apparent. The vibrations below me were getting closer.

Knowing she wanted me with her, even as my intentions had been duplicitous... something inside me simply snapped.

"I will join you in Aethralis, Mev. If not before then. You have my vow."

"Promise me you will not be killed."

"I am immortal, princess. Lest you forget." Also, I would not promise something I could not guarantee. It was unlikely, aye. But I'd witnessed with my own eyes the death of seemingly indestructible warriors, though I had no intention on today being my last.

"But—"

"I will stay with him," Rowan said. "And give my life for him, if needed."

Everyone turned to Rowan then, no one more surprised than me.

"She is the key to opening the Gate," he explained. "Mev must get to Aethralis safely, something we cannot guarantee if we remain here and debate for much longer."

"Kael." That one word, from Mev, broke open my heart. She said it as if we'd not see each other ever again. I held her, allowing our hearts to beat as one for as long as I dared and then kissed her deeply.

"I will re-join you soon."

Wiping away a single tear that escaped onto her cheek, I nearly pulled her back to me as Mev walked away, toward Lyra. I'd have helped her mount, but between Lyra's outstretched arm and Mev's agility, she was sitting atop the white steed before I could take a step.

I love you.

Without warning, the two rode away.

If she'd stayed just a moment longer, I might have said the words. They were true, after all. I'd known it the moment I'd decided not to take Mev to my father.

Maybe sooner.

"We need to talk," I said to Rowan. I intended to find out how he knew about Mev's mother's abilities, a closely guarded secret even in Aetheria. But first, we needed to prepare. If Mev and Lyra hadn't fled behind us, I'd simply have crossed my arms and waited for the riding party. But they needed to be stalled. Now.

"Glad we're at the talking stage," Rowan replied. "Tell me what to do."

"Stay behind me and don't hurt yourself," I said in response, lifting my arms and surveying our surroundings, ready to get started.

27

MEV

It was completely different, riding with Lyra. For starters, hers was not a warhorse capable of carrying both our weight as easily, so the pace was slower. I also couldn't rest my head on her back, or wrap my arms around her in the same way. It felt like I would fall at any moment. Somehow, though, I'd managed to stay astride all day.

We only stopped once, for me, but immediately got back onto the road. As we continued uphill, the steepest section of the day, Lyra let go of the reins and extended her right hand. She swirled it backward and forward a few times. I suspected she was manipulating the wind, so I wasn't surprised when it picked up from behind us. With the wind at our backs, we climbed and climbed.

Had I really descended these mountains with Kael such a short time ago?

"How did you do that, exactly?"

"It's no different than the way you put out the fire. We will practice more when we're not being chased."

"Who do you think it is?" I asked. The question had been on my mind all day, but part of me was afraid to know.

"It could be anyone. Another Council member. Or any number of Gyorians, having learned about your presence. Or even humans who, like Rowan, are invested in reopening the Gate."

I'd read *The Most Dangerous Game* in high school but never thought I'd be acting it out. Being hunted by humans was one thing, but immortal beings with powerful magic? It was a whole new level.

"The trees are thinning out," I said, looking up.

"We are getting closer. If we do not stop again, it's possible we can reach Aethralis by nightfall, even at this pace."

Attempting to keep my mind from worry over Kael, I remembered Salvia and her artifacts.

"Can you tell me about the Wind Crystal?" I asked, adjusting myself and vowing, if I could not immediately go back home, to make learning to ride a horse my main priority.

Go back home.

The thought of it made my stomach turn. I would take things day by day. First, I had to get safely to my father.

"Certainly. It is said to have been created by the first king of Elydor."

"Elydor? Not Aetheria?"

"Before there was an Aetheria. Although it's just a story, so no one knows for certain. But it has remained in the hands of the kings and queens of Aetheria since, with the exception of the time it was stolen."

"Stolen? By whom?"

Her shoulders tightened.

Oh. "Kael's dad?"

"Precisely. Which is why some believe it was needed to

close the Gate. Either way, stealing one of our most precious relics was as horrific, to some, as closing the Gate. It nearly began an all-out war between us and Gyoria."

"What does it do?"

"Like other powerful relics, it enhances the user's manipulation of magic. True flight, and not simply gliding through air currents, becomes possible. Storms like the ones Thalassari can call up become easier to summon. It's said the Wind Crystal was used in the Great Storm of Arathia, where fleets were scattered across the seas and an entire Gyoria village was flooded."

"No wonder they don't like us."

"Long before your mother was taken, Aetheria and Gyoria were enemies. Our way of life—embracing change, just as air shifts and makes things possible—is unthinkable to them."

"Salvia said she sensed a disturbance in the Wind Crystal? What did that mean?"

"Some, like Salvia, are so attuned to its power that they can read it, much like a human reads an orb. It's not the same, of course, because she's using air currents and humans' abilities come from within, but it's the best way I can describe it. Very few have that power, though."

I hadn't heard anything beyond "orb." At that word, a sense of... foreboding? No. Awareness? Something washed over me, like the time I'd met Lord Draven. But this wasn't as defined and made even less sense than meeting Isolde's general had. I pushed the thought aside and got back to the Wind Crystal.

"Can anyone use it?"

"No. Most could not harness its power and would disrupt the natural air currents and wreak havoc on weather systems, causing a great imbalance. It is kept locked away in the king's palace with layers of protection around it. Very few are able to wield such a relic properly."

My father could, though.

I hadn't noticed Lyra slowing until we came to a complete stop. I looked behind us.

"Is someone coming?"

"I don't believe so. But we are close enough now that I should be able to whisper all the way to Aethralis. I must listen carefully, though."

In other words, be quiet. Lyra had such a diplomacy and gentleness about her. She was like one of those women who could insult a man without him even realizing he was being insulted.

I tried to see through the trees, but they were still too dense. This didn't seem to be the same path we'd taken south, but I hadn't exactly been in a state of mind to remember at the time. As Lyra remained still, I breathed in the air, realizing something. That buzz of energy I'd felt was gone. It was replaced by a sort of... peace in my surroundings. Maybe getting used to being here, or something of the sort?

As quickly as we stopped, Lyra spurred us forward. "Hold on," came a bit late but I did as instructed. We were riding faster than we had all day.

"I was able to reach a friend in the capital. Apparently, all know of your arrival now and rumor is that you were in Estmere but are now coming north."

"How do they know that?"

"Between whispers and humans' abilities, word travels swiftly in Elydor, especially in the north and east."

It was the last we spoke, Lyra concentrating on navigating us up the steep path, and me attempting to hang on. Eventually, as the trees began to thin even more, Lyra took a path that opened wider than any we'd taken since leaving Zephros. I sat up straighter, looking into the distance.

"Is that—"

"Aethralis. We're almost there."

It was difficult not to be excited by the prospect, despite the fact that Kael hadn't caught up with us. I tried not to let my mind go down the rabbit hole of wondering what was happening. He would be fine. He *had* to be fine.

I'd seen Aethralis in the distance with Kael not knowing what I was looking at. Now, as we got closer, I knew so much more. This was the capital of Aetheria. The place where my mother had lived with me inside her.

My father's home.

Built into the mountains, some buildings were on floating plateaus connected by bridges of what looked like white stone. Spires and towers stretched upwards, as if they were trying to touch the sky.

"The buildings almost look as if they're shimmering."

Lyra looked behind us, as she did often. I did as well.

Nothing.

"They're crafted from a blend of lightweight stone and crystalline materials. At this time of day, when the sun sets, they are the most spectacular. Though some argue their soft glow in the moonlight is even more so."

As we got closer, I could see open terraces, large windows, and so many balconies. Courtyards and gardens filled with wind-swept trees and streams that spilled water to plateaus below them. It was as if the entire city hovered above the mountainous landscape, defying gravity.

In short, it was the most beautiful place I'd ever seen.

It settled into my chest almost as if... I was home. Without warning, the insides of my cheeks stung and tears sprang to my eyes. No doubt I'd have broken into tears, but they were staved off by riders approaching us. Six of them, all dressed in a similar fashion as Lyra. Shades of whites and blues and silvers were everywhere, but these were obviously warriors by their dress.

That was when I saw him.

As they rode closer, one man stood out easily from the rest. He was in front, his hair white and his beard neatly trimmed, and sitting taller than the rest. In human years, he might have been in his late forties. It wasn't that I looked like him—or maybe I did a little—but that the man's gaze told me this was my father.

"That's him, isn't it?"

"It is."

I'd thought about this moment so many times, but the reality of it was so unlike the fantasy. Instead of running into his arms, I felt like I was about to stand up in front of a crowd and give a speech. Actually, I think facing a crowd might have been easier than this. What if he didn't believe I was his daughter? What if he wanted nothing to do with me? What if he was mean and awful?

I remembered the first thing Lyra had said about him.

He will be very glad to see you, Mev. Your father has been searching for a way to reopen the Gate since the moment your mother left.

Looked like I would find out if her words were true sooner rather than later.

28

KAEL

By splitting the ground open horizontally across the road, careful not to sever any roots or disturb the ancient trees lining the path, after building a wall on the other side of it, certain no human, Aetherian or Thalassari could pass, Rowan and I waited.

But not for long.

With Mev safely away, I'd intended to question the human further but our opponents had other plans. When the wall shattered with a rumble that could only have been created by a Gyorian, I focused on creating a new one. Again, and again, the rubble piled up.

Now, dirt rumbled beneath my feet, the soil cracking and shifting. Gritting my teeth, I concentrated on the balance required to maintain control—too much force and I risked collapsing the ground beneath all of us. Too little and the pursuers would cross easily.

My breath came in short, sharp bursts, but I refused to allow myself to tire. Whoever was on the other side of the new wall I'd constructed was undoubtedly after Mev. I assumed at first it was Lord Valdric and his men, but although the former Council member was highly skilled, he lacked the precision necessary to wreak havoc on the land but also leave it so unmarred. Despite the fact that we were in Aetheria, and no Gyorian cared about preserving this particular land, it was intricately tied to our own, Elydor's natural balance necessary as it affected all of us.

"They are tiring," Rowan called from behind me.

"Stay. Back." The damned man refused to listen, and though I would not mourn his loss, Mev would. For that reason, I attempted to keep him safe.

Emphasis on "attempt."

Nothing worked to keep my opponents away. Rock spires. Land tremors. Walls. Who the hell was over there? If I didn't know better, I might think it was my father. But he was as unlikely to step foot on Aetherian soil as anyone.

Terran.

That it hadn't occurred to me sooner, I'd blame on the certainty that, if whoever was on the other side of that wall came through, Mev would be in danger. It had been hours, however, and knowing Lyra's riding capabilities, and Mev's determination, they were more than halfway to Aethralis.

So I stopped. Stood back, and waited.

"What are you doing?"

Of course, Rowan was right behind me.

"They are safe," I said, assured of it now. If that was my brother currently dismantling my new wall, I could convince him to turn around.

Rowan's hand moved to the hilt of his sword, but I stopped him with a glance, shaking my head. "There are few who have the skill and stamina for this." I waved a hand toward the path where the wall was coming down. "My brother is one of them."

Rowan's hand stayed. "Not a comforting thought."

Of course he knew my brother, or at least his reputation. Rowan of Estmere seemed to know everything about Elydor, and I would discover why.

Later.

As I suspected, the sight that greeted us consisted of all Gyorian warriors. Also not surprising, my brother stood side by side with Lord Valdric. I stepped forward, spotting Adren. I'd not seen my friend at first, but he clearly had not been fighting.

"Why has no one been wielding?" I asked nobody in particular as the group eyed Rowan suspiciously.

"Terran knew 'twas you and refused to allow it," Adren said, his gaze steady. Questioning. Unlike the others, Adren had moved past the battered path toward me. If a battle re-ignited, I had no doubt he would stand by my side. Unfortunately, the same could not be said for Terran. He was too much my father's lapdog these past years.

"Honorable," I said to my brother who finally crossed our battleground. I met him halfway, the man that was as much my twin as he was a stranger. Though his hair was shorter and a thin scar ran down Terran's left cheek, we appeared nearly identical.

"Where is she?" he asked as we embraced.

"You won't find her."

Terran's nose flared, his expression one that would terrify most others. But I'd been on the receiving end of it too many times. I didn't know a more disciplined, unyielding man, except our father. But unlike our namesake, Terran was also pragmatic and protective of me.

"Why?"

As the others looked on, and listened, I had little choice but to declare myself. There was one reason alone that I'd not brought Mev to our father, which I knew was Terran's question. And it was not one that my brother would understand. Unlike me, he had never been in love. Terran once admitted he didn't know if he was capable of it, though I knew better.

"I am in love with her."

My admission had the precise effect I'd imagined it would. Terran appeared disgusted. Adren, shocked. Rowan, for his part, seemed more amused than anything, which my brother did not take kindly to.

"Who is this human you travel with that smiles at such foolery?"

Answering his question would not endear myself to him or the other men. Admitting I did, indeed, travel with a human was unnecessary. The proof stood, chuckling, beside me.

"Rowan of Estmere," he said, in a bow that Terran would take as mocking. But I knew otherwise. Rowan was, if nothing else, savvy enough to respect Elydor's chain of command, even his enemy's.

By his expression, Terran knew of him already. My brother turned his attention to me.

"Father will care little for your feelings for the human woman," he began.

I corrected him. "Half human. She is, if you will recall, half Aetherian as well."

One of Terran's men cleared his throat, earning a stern look from my brother. By now, Adren stood directly at my side.

"How did she come through?"

Hell if I knew, but I'd not let Terran tell that to our father.

"The more important question is... what do we do now? I will not allow you to pass, brother."

Terran's eyes widened. I did not often directly challenge him, or my father, but when I did, there was little question of whether or not I'd follow through. Terran stared at me, thinking. He was as strategic as any and was currently assessing the consequences of every possible action. I'd make it easy on him.

"You can fight me, but she'll have reached her father before we're through." By now, Terran knew precisely where Mev was heading, so there was little reason to be coy about the fact. "Or you can turn around and tell Father she is lost to him."

"Another possibility, Kael." He looked at his men. It was true, I was not strong enough to battle my brother and all of the others. But I would put up one hell of a fight.

We locked eyes.

He pleaded with me, but I would not back down. Lest he not fully understand, I gave Terran the only remaining information necessary for him to make a decision.

"I will die for her, brother."

Adren gasped. Rowan stopped smiling. Terran said nothing. His expression did not change. But I knew him better than anyone, which was why it did not surprise me when he closed his eyes, took a deep breath and expelled it.

Opening his eyes, Terran said, "Father will not be pleased."

"No. I don't expect he will be." It was an understatement, and we both knew it well. I'd already considered the consequences of my stance many times these past days. "Thank you, brother."

He had no need to respond. Terran was not the sort to

explain his reasons or even show any sort of emotion. Instead, he held my gaze. "This will not be the end, Kael."

Nay, it would not.

With that, he turned and motioned for his men to do the same. "Take care of my brother," he called, presumably to Rowan and Adren who'd not moved to return with the others. "He will need it."

Terran would not take kindly to my next words, but given the circumstances, they needed to be said, even if my brother would not reciprocate. "I love you, Terran."

I'd expected no acknowledgment, but Terran managed to surprise me by raising his arm just before he mounted. I could not worry what the future held, but there was little doubt my life would ever be the same again. For a Gyorian, there was peace in stability. Change brought only chaos. But what choice did I have?

"So... my prince." Adren crossed his arms, his expression one of resignation. "What now?"

29

MEV

Before I could ruminate any further, my father dismounted.

"Come," Lyra said. "Let us get you down from here."

Scrambling off Lyra's mount, I wished the clothing Isolde had given me was not so travel weary. That thought intensified as the King of Aetheria strode toward me. His cape flowed gracefully behind him, as if it were commanded to do so. A tunic of fine cream peeked out from under a polished silver breastplate, wind patterns emblazoned in the center. He appeared as if ready for battle, but could just as easily be sitting on a throne in such attire. If I knew nothing of this world, looking at him, I could have easily guessed this was the King of Aetheria.

I had little time for nerves as he marched up to me, and without warning, tossed his arms around me. I was engulfed in a hug unlike any I'd felt before. It was not a mother's warm embrace or Kael's protective one. This was the embrace of a father who had lost his daughter many years ago. Before I could stop them, tears flowed down my cheeks as I held onto a man I'd wondered about my entire life.

When he released me, I was surprised to see his ice-blue eyes glistening with unshed tears. He cupped my cheeks, staring into my face.

"You are her mirror image."

I'd heard as much many times before, but this time was different. "I take that as a compliment."

"As you should." He released me and stepped back. I'd been about to wipe my face when a light breeze swept across it, accomplishing the task. I stared down at his hands. They'd barely moved. "How did you do that?"

"I will show you. But first, tell me. Is she well?"

By his expression, I realized my father had no notion of whether my mother was even alive. I quickly reassured him. "Very well. But she will worry about me when she learns about my disappearance, if she hasn't already."

His visible relief told me all I needed to know of his feelings for her. "We have much to discuss." He looked to Lyra then. "Thank you." And then before she could respond, "Are you being followed?"

"Aye, I believe so."

He looked past me, toward the path we'd just traveled, and addressed Lyra again. "Take her to the palace. We will remain here."

Oh boy.

"Father?"

Lyra shook her head, but I ignored her warning. This wasn't a conversation that could wait.

"May I call you that?" I asked when our eyes met.

"I would not have you call me anything but. What is wrong, Mevlida?"

"Naught that cannot wait until we reach safety." Lyra had

made her way to my side. She tugged on my hand. "Come. We will speak to him shortly."

"Speak to me of what?" he demanded in a tone that was impatient, though not harsh.

Lyra didn't flinch. "I will whisper to you when we reach the palace." The way she said whisper made me realize Lyra was telling me to open my ears to her.

You cannot tell him now, in front of the others. Let us reach the safety of the palace first. Kael will not come before then. Trust me.

Without giving either of us an opportunity to respond, Lyra pulled me back toward her mount, and I allowed it. I did trust her, and Lyra knew much more than I did about the men that had accompanied my father.

I hadn't noticed, when my father and I were speaking, that the road ahead had begun to line with Aetherians. And lots of them.

As we climbed, at times navigating across bridges of polished white stone and gleaming crystals, I tried not to look down. Though I'd never been afraid of heights, this was something else entirely. Everywhere we went, claps and cheers greeted us. I didn't know where to look first.

The waterfalls, which seemed to glow, courtesy of silk-spore or lumina moss or who knew what else? The masses of white and silvery hair and flowing capes? Some stood on plateaus waving, others on each side of the bridges we crossed. I waved back, all the while urging Lyra to hurry. The sooner we reached the palace, the sooner she could tell my father to return and I could warn him about Kael.

"There it is," Lyra said, my attention turning ahead rather than behind us.

Built from what looked like pale, iridescent stone, its

towers spiraled gracefully toward the sky above us. It had large, arching windows with so many balconies overlooking what looked like floating gardens. I'd wonder how such a thing was possible, but there was no time as Lyra spoke to the guards that stood on both sides of a pathway that ascended upward toward the palace.

After the guards greeted me, we were riding once again.

"This is the Skyway," Lyra said. "From the guards below to more magical wards than you can imagine, your father's palace is more secure than any place in Aetheria, maybe even Elydor."

So that explained why Lyra waved her hand periodically, to get through the wards.

When we reached the top, the stairs of the palace were lined with people, all smiling and waving to me.

It was all too much.

"Are you okay?"

I wasn't. For the third time in my life, twice here in Elydor, I was going to faint. I tried to warn Lyra, but the words didn't come out before I felt consciousness slipping away.

"Unused to the air."

"So many people."

"Take the salts away."

The softest bed I'd ever been in cushioned me, its bedding like lying on clouds. The ceiling above me was painted with constellations that appeared to be alive, just like the ones in the portal in The Crooked Key. As I turned my head toward Lyra's voice, it was a man who grabbed my attention first. He sat beside me, smiling.

Perhaps as old as my father, though it was hard to tell since Elydorians aged differently, his long silver hair was pulled back into a low ponytail. His eyes, unusual for an Aetherian, were a shade of light brown and not blue.

"Your eyes?" I blurted.

"My mother was Gyorian, before such a name even existed."

"Galindre is valieth," Lyra said. "He has lived here since before the clans emerged."

"Wow." I tried to sit up, but he stopped me.

"Rest. Your father will be along soon. I've asked for food to be brought to you. Lyra, it seems, forgot how often humans need sustenance."

Lyra gave the man a look. "Perhaps I should have arranged a picnic when she fainted?"

It was clear by their camaraderie the two were close.

"Where is she?"

I hadn't even heard him come in. A moment later, my father sat beside Galindre. He took my hand, a kind and loving gesture. My mother's love language had always been touch. She told me once that a hug needed to last ten seconds to count, even though thirty was preferable, and that human beings needed at least ten hugs a day. I still had no idea if this were true.

"She is well," Galindre said. "The air and lack of food and water—"

"As well as the entire palace coming out to greet her," Lyra added.

"The palace?" I asked, remembering. "All of Aethralis, it seemed."

"Word has spread," my father confirmed. "It is a day many thought would never happen. That *I* thought would never happen." He squeezed my hand. The bed shifted. Galindre had risen and was leaving the enormous bedroom, with Lyra by his side, through an equally enormous double door.

"He seems nice," I said, rather lamely.

"Galindre is the palace's high steward. He tends to it, and the people of Aethralis, and has been doing so for longer than I've been king. There is no better man, or healer, in all of Elydor."

A steward and healer. Made sense. And was also my opening. "He said his mother is Gyorian?"

My father shrugged. "She has long passed, but aye. She would be called so today. Back then, the clans were just beginning to form."

"So it's possible for an Aetherian and Gyorian to be together?"

His expression revealed nothing.

"Lyra has been teaching you of our ways?"

I nodded, but waited for my own answer before responding.

King Galfrid, my mother's partner and my father, sighed so heavily that I knew what came from his mouth next wasn't something I'd want to hear.

"It was possible, once. Now however..."

He didn't seem inclined to continue. And if I wasn't so worried about Kael being turned away, or worse, attacked, I'd have waited to give him the news. But this had to be said.

"Father." I sat up, still holding his hand. "I don't know how much Lyra told you."

"She whispered to me that you'd arrived at the palace safely, but said nothing else."

The coward part of me wished Lyra had broken the news to him, but it wasn't her duty. That fell squarely on my shoulders.

I'd survived falling through a portal into an immortal world. I could survive this too.

"It was not only Lyra who escorted me here."

His eyes narrowed. "I know well who intercepted you from the Gate and am sorry for it. By the time we learned someone had come through—"

"He did not harm me," I rushed out. "Kael kept me safe and allowed Lyra to find us and train me. He escorted us until we realized we were being followed and stayed at the base of the mountain to slow them down while Lyra brought me here."

His eyes darkened with each word. I could not stop now, though. It was true. Kael might have claimed we were enemies, but his actions proved the exact opposite. By not taking me to his father, he'd made a choice that, until now, had not truly hit home. I might not have been able to break down all of his walls, but thinking back to the way he looked at me, held me, kissed me... how could I have been so blind?

"I am in love with him."

There. Now I was done.

Everything I knew about my father, including the way he'd treated me since I arrived, told me not to panic. He would listen. Understand. Talk this through. Together, he and Kael and I, with Lyra's and Rowan's help, would figure out how I'd come through the Gate, how to get back, maybe even how I could get my mother and bring her here, if that was something she wanted.

"I would give you"—my father's words were calm and measured—"anything. I would learn to harness the very stars themselves for you. Every day since your mother was taken from me, with you growing inside her, I prayed to the gods for her return. Worried for your safety, and hers. I thought of what you might look like. Wondered if you had her curiosity and determination. I would give you anything, daughter."

My heart soared.

"But that."

30

KAEL

By the time we reached the Skyway, none in Aethralis stirred, except the guards.

"Prince Kael of—"

"I know who you are. You may not pass. You know the custom."

Had I really thought this would be easy? Adren had asked me as much, but I'd refused to consider the possibility that I'd not be allowed to see Mev. No one, except those residing at the palace, would be allowed entry once the sun set.

"Did the princess reach the palace?" Rowan asked.

The guards' sharp gazes even extended to Rowan. They didn't appear inclined to respond.

She had to be in there. "We only wish to ensure she is safe," I said. If I had to wait until morn to get in to see her, I'd gladly do so. Besides, there was no way up the Skyway without an Aetherian due to the wards, even if I could overpower the guards. Traditionally, it was a station reserved for some of the most powerful in their clan, though I did not know either of these men.

"We are not leaving until we know she is safe," Rowan said. Silence.

"Will you send for Lyra, at least?"

The guards exchanged a look.

"You may not pass." The second guard spoke for the first time.

"And Aetherians are supposed to have better hearing than most," Adren muttered, earning him a sharp look from both guards.

"If you will simply send for Lyra," I said, knowing they would not let us through, or give us any information about Mev. It was the best hope we had. "She will tell you that we escorted the princess here and wish only to ensure her safety." I wished for much more, of course, but that would have to wait.

"If you simply tell Lyra we are here—" Rowan tried again.

The guards ignored us both.

I could wreak havoc, awaken half of Aethralis and gain the king's attention. And was close to doing just that when Rowan stayed my hand.

"I have seen what he can do and have no wish to be embroiled in another battle," Rowan said. "We will leave, straight away, if you simply tell us if the princess is safe. Alternatively, we can awaken everyone in the village so we might question them, but since I assume you'd prefer to avoid—"

"She has returned and is safe," the one I'd decided to attack first said. "We will say no more."

I hated when Rowan forced me to be impressed by his diplomacy.

"You refuse to summon Lyra?" I asked.

"If she, or the princess, wish to see you, they will do so."

She was safe. Nothing else mattered. I wanted to see her,

but it was clear we'd not be allowed to do so this eve. "I will take you at your word," I said, knowing we'd be forced back downhill to the borders of the city to find respite and rest. "But I will return in the morn to speak to her myself."

Before waiting for a response, I spurred Stormbreaker back down the mountain. There was nothing more to be gained at this time of eve here, and mostly importantly, we had the information we needed.

"He's coming with us?"

I turned at Adren's question, watching as Rowan expertly mounted his horse. He said nothing, and the human still had questions to answer.

"Aye," I said, grudgingly. "He comes with us."

Adren mumbled under his breath. Rowan laughed.

For my part, I cared little about anything other than seeing Mev. And telling her what I should have earlier that day.

* * *

By now, all of Aethralis, and half of Aetheria, it seemed, knew we were here. Before the sun had risen, we made our way back up to the Skyway only to be stopped by the same guards. I'd hoped new ones would be on duty.

"She's not coming, Kael," Adren said.

I would forever be grateful for his loyalty, Adren knowing full well the implications of standing against Terran and with me, but at this moment, I wished only for him to cease talking.

"You've said as much all morn," I mumbled.

The guards refused to speak to us. Rowan had left, saying he would return, but thus far had not. Every so often we would glimpse a rider behind us, as if seeing for themselves that I were indeed sitting at the palace gates.

She would come.

The sun had risen already, but still no Mev.

"Your human returns."

Rowan rode toward us. I was as uncertain of him as I was the situation with Mev. Speaking to him last eve, the knight revealed nothing. Since he'd been too young when Mev's mother was taken, if he'd met her, Rowan himself had been just a babe. How he knew of her magic with such certainty was still a mystery, and I liked it not.

On the other hand, he'd proven loyal to Mev and a worthy companion thus far.

"Princess Mevlida is within, though I'm uncertain why she's not sent for you," Rowan said. "None have seen Lyra since she returned."

"How do you know such things?" Adren asked before I could.

Before Rowan answered, a rider in the distance caught our collective attention. Our party of three made our way back to the guardhouse.

Lyra.

"When did you arrive?" she asked us.

"Last eve," I said. Before the words even left my mouth, Lyra was glaring at the guards.

"Why were we not informed?" she said. Her anger was not feigned. "You were asked to fetch me when our guests arrived."

"Guests," one of the guards muttered.

"King Galfrid was," the other said. Apparently, that was to be his entire explanation. Neither of them looked in my direction. I had a mind to grow a thorned rosebush at both of their feet. I imagined it entwining their bodies and crawling upwards, the men screaming as it circled around their necks.

Mev would not be pleased if I tortured her guards.

"Where is she?" I asked Lyra. And why has she not sent for us or come to the Gate? Had Galfrid turned her against me? I had no doubt he would attempt to do as much. Neither did I blame him.

"In the palace," Lyra said, as if I didn't know that already. "They are coming back with me." When one of the guards opened his mouth to argue, Lyra did not let him speak. "You will not deny these men entry. If it were not for them, your princess would not have been returned to you. Either admit them, or you will both find yourselves at the mercy of my winds. Tell the king we are coming."

Apparently they were strong, but Lyra was stronger. I didn't doubt it. She'd been trained by the best.

"Kael, Rowan, Adren... mount up and follow."

So she did remember him. Though Adren had remained in Gyoria when I'd served on the Council, he'd come periodically to bring news from home or at the behest of my father who had no notion that Adren was more loyal to me than him.

I'd expected one, or both guards, to stop us, but it seemed they were already whispering with the king. By the time Lyra removed the wards and we reached the palace steps, a dozen or so more guards greeted us.

"Your king," I said to Lyra, "has forgotten how many years I served in Aetheria without incident."

As we dismounted, Lyra motioned for our mounts to be taken away.

"Even then, you rarely visited the palace. And never with the princess in attendance."

Still no sign of Mev.

"Rowan. Adren. I will escort Kael to the throne room. Galindre will see you are fed."

I hadn't seen the royal steward appear at the top of the white marble steps. Knowing Adren would refuse, I stepped in.

"Go," I said. "One Gyorian in the king's presence is enough for today. I will be safe."

Uncertain, as we reached the top of the steps, Adren paused. "Go," I repeated, this time as a command. He did not hesitate. As he and Rowan were led away by the steward, I followed Lyra inside.

"Why did she not come?" I asked as the guards followed.

"I have not seen her since last eve. She took a meal privately with her father, and I was told she slept still this morn. I've been busy, in the interim, speaking with Eirion, who is most anxious to talk to her."

He was not the only one.

Leaving the soaring ceilings and arched windows of the grand entrance hall, we walked through wide and spacious corridors. Lined with tall columns of white marble that stretched upwards toward the sky, each was subtly carved with motifs of wind and flight. Rich tapestries depicting the history and legends of Aetheria hung on the walls, their vibrant colors and fine threads shimmering in the morning light.

Reaching the throne room, I was reminded of the last time I'd stood inside with my brother. We'd come to return the Wind Crystal, a gesture that might have moved Aetheria and Gyoria toward peace, but did not. King Galfrid would never forgive our father for his actions against his wife and unborn child and for closing the Gate.

The throne room, located at the heart of the palace, was a vast, open space with a domed ceiling painted with a mural of a swirling vortex of clouds and stars, capturing the essence of the Aetherian skies. The throne itself, atop a raised dais, was crafted from polished silver and set with sapphires and aqua-marines. Flanked by statues of past Aetherian rulers, each carved from a single block of white marble, even I had to admit it was an impressive sight.

As was the figure seated at it.

But still, no sign of Mev.

"You may go," Galfrid said to Lyra who bowed and left us. "As may you all," he said to the four guards who followed us into the throne room. They hesitated, but obeyed.

Neither of us spoke at first. For me, there was just one question.

"Where is she?"

The king raised his eyes. Before he could respond, I realized Mev had joined us, doing so as quietly as any skilled Aetherian.

I turned, seeing neither Mia nor even Mev.

Standing before me was Princess Mevlida, daughter of King Galdrid of Aetheria. Her hair had never shone so brightly as it hung in waves around her shoulders. She was dressed in an elegant gown of soft, flowing gossamer, a hue of pale blue that matched the color of the Aetherian skies at dawn. Silver embroidery along the edges of her dress caught the light, reflecting it like a thousand tiny stars. Her presence was commanding yet serene, embodying both her royal heritage and the newfound confidence that had grown every day we'd been together.

She had not sent for me. Or come to me. Because this was not my princess, but *the* princess.

Not my love, but my enemy.

31

MEV

My relief at seeing Kael in the throne room almost had me running to him, tossing my arms around him and refusing to let go. He appeared tired but otherwise healthy, if not extremely confused.

"You look well," I said, giving him a wide berth since I didn't trust myself not to break down completely. It was one thing to hear my father's story and learn about Kael's part in my mother's abduction, but it was quite another to see him standing before me.

I stood beside my father, folded my hands in front of me, and waited, though I didn't know for what, exactly. There was nothing he could say to excuse the facts he'd left out. Kael must have known my father would tell me. He could have explained. Should have explained.

"I arrived last eve," he said, reminding me of the emotionless and reticent man I'd first met.

I looked sharply at my father. He'd promised to send for me the moment Kael arrived.

"Why are you here, Prince Kael?"

My father's tone was the opposite of how he'd spoken to me. Each word was harder, more unforgiving, than the one before it.

"Because I love your daughter."

My knees nearly buckled. I'd hardly slept, worry and anger warring inside me.

"You do not love me," I countered. "If you had, I'd have known before my father told me that it was you who stole the Wind Crystal, enabling your father to close the portal. I'd have known you were the one to allow your father entry to the Temple." My anger rose with each word. "Were you the one to bind her hands? Push her through?"

His jaw ticked, but otherwise Kael offered no reaction to my words.

"I wanted to tell you."

"*Wanted* to tell me? You spoke of trust and yet kept that from me? You are a hypocrite, Kael of Gyoria. Do you have that word here? If not, I am happy to tell you what it means."

Every word that came from my mouth was more venomous than the last. I had no excuse except a broken heart. When my father told me how he'd opened the Gate, and how Kael's father had closed it—by imprisoning an Aetherian mage and forcing secrets from her—I had been properly mortified. Even more so to learn his role in it all.

Say something, Kael. Say something that will fix it. Show me you are the man I thought you were.

Silence.

"I would thank you for returning my daughter to me," my father said. "But since you were the one who took her, you'll understand why my thanks will not be forthcoming."

Still nothing.

Had I been that naive? So much for my powers of intuition. To think we were meant for each other...

Kael stepped forward, his eyes locked on mine, a flicker of vulnerability showing through. His voice was steady, but it carried an edge I hadn't heard before.

"I understand your anger, Mev. I deserve it. My actions, misguided as they were, were never meant to harm you or your mother. They were to protect my people. In my blindness, I believed there was no other way. The longer we were together, my resolve to keep my past from you strengthened, for fear you'd never forgive me."

I opened my mouth to respond, but he raised a hand, stopping me.

"I'm not asking for your forgiveness, not yet. Instead, I will earn your trust again if you'll allow it."

I was not certain I'd remain long enough in Elydor for that to happen.

"Mev, Mia." His voice was shaky, barely a whisper. It was not a tone I'd ever heard from him before. "I've spent my life following my father's orders, doing what I thought was right for my people. You've showed me there is another way. A better way."

Tears stung my eyes. His words were not an excuse, but they were honest.

Could he earn back my trust? I wasn't sure. Either way, this would not be resolved here, with my father as witness. He had made it clear he would never forgive Kael or his father, and I couldn't say I blamed him.

"Thank you," I said, willing my tears back as my resolve strengthened. "For returning me safely."

He waited, but I had no more to say. Not now. Not yet.

Bowing, to me and not my father, Kael stood up straight,

raised his head and squared his shoulders. "I love you and will do whatever it takes to atone for the mistakes I've made. Good day, princess." Then to my father. "Your majesty."

With that, he turned to leave.

Princess.

If I were going to call him back, it would be as he uttered that one word. I waited until Kael left before looking at my father. When he shot up from his throne and wrapped his arms around me, tears fell immediately from my eyes, and I apologized for them.

"Never tell me you are sorry for showing emotion. Feel it. Welcome it. But never, ever apologize for it."

No wonder my mother loved him. When I was finally able to regain some measure of composure, he stood back and sighed. "Of all the men you could have loved, it had to be that one."

It wasn't a question, so I didn't answer. Neither did I refute his words. It was clear to him, and to myself, I did love Kael, very much.

But sometimes, love simply wasn't enough.

32

KAEL

"Every one of them is staring at us."

I stared into my ale, the taste far inferior to Gyoria's more hearty brews, and ignored Adren. Of course they stared at us. We sat at a tavern on the outskirts of Aethralis where I did not expect them to welcome us. Rowan stared out of the open window beside us, Aetherians as fond of their cool breezes as they were of their secret whispers. He'd said little since leaving the palace.

"What is everyone eating that smells so good?"

Adren would not give up on attempting to get me to talk. "A honey-glazed pastry."

"Too sweet for him," Adren said to Rowan. "In case you haven't noticed, there's nothing sweet about Kael."

With that, Adren got up to brave the stares and, apparently, fetch some pastries for himself.

"Adren is more accepting of me than you were." Rowan took a swig of ale.

"Were?"

In truth, my animosity toward him had weakened, but I wouldn't let Rowan know as much.

"Not all Gyorians feel as your family does about humans. Adren is a testament to that. We do not need to be at war."

"My father—"

"Is a bitter old thaloran whose views are a blight to Elydor."

How could I disagree with him when I'd thought the same, many times?

"All humans know what you did for Isolde's parents. They do not hate you, but will, if you continue to allow hate to guide you. As he does."

"A fine speech from a man with more secrets than truths."

"The two are not related."

I was in the mood to fight, and it seemed Rowan would indulge me. "Are they not? You wish to lecture me on tolerance, when in truth, I know nothing of you. Of what sort of man you are, truly. Your opinion would hold more value if you ever deemed to answer a question in a straight manner."

"Do you wish to know me, Kael? If so, this is the first I've been made aware of it."

"Your bickering is not endearing us to the Skylark's other patrons," Adren said, sitting and placing a tray of pastries in front of us. Rowan immediately reached out and popped one into his mouth. He and Adren made sounds that should not come from grown men, and while the two of them bonded over the Aetherian delicacies, I sat back and tried to put Mev from my mind.

Of course, it did not work.

"It's been said, since Mev's arrival, that the king authorized an Aetherian and a human to pass through the Gate to ascertain if it is now open."

Rowan's statement pulled me from my reverie.

"What happened?" Adren asked, before I could.

"Nothing. It is as inaccessible now as it always was." He gave me a pointed look. "At least, since your father closed it."

I didn't flinch. Rowan was not the first, nor would he be the last, to implicate me for the Gate's closing. In truth, I'd tried to dissuade my father. Despite my distaste for humans and the changes they wrought in Elydor, cutting them off from their families and disabling any Elydorian to ever pass through again... had not been ideal.

"He did not know his father kidnapped the queen," Adren said.

The look of confusion on Rowan's face was understandable. I'd told them both all that had transpired in the throne room.

Rowan grabbed another pastry. "You said Mev's anger was because of the role you played?"

"In stealing the Wind Crystal, aye. But also that I'd asked her to trust me but failed to do the same."

"How is it possible you did not know? You were the one who opened the Temple doors for your father. And if you did not know, why would you let Mev believe you were complicit?"

A fair question. "I deserve her anger. As to how it's possible, that is not a story I wish to recount."

After his third pastry, Rowan licked his fingers clean, lifted his mug, and sat back in his seat, watching me.

"I can read emotion."

It took me a moment to fully absorb his words.

"I cannot do it at a distance, nor can I discern precise intent. But I do know, for instance, that your antagonism toward me has lessened, despite the glare you're giving me now. I've felt calm when you've claimed anger toward me."

"That skill is not common," Adren said, reaching for another pastry. "Or perhaps it is? I've spent little time with humans these past years."

"No, it is not common but was a skill both my parents possessed. It is one of many attributes they share, along with their good humor and intellect."

"You can sense emotion," I repeated.

"Aye."

"A handy skill, one would think."

"Quite handy."

Which was why Rowan had stuck around, despite my treatment of him. I might have disliked the man, but I never wished him ill, and he'd known it from the start.

"That is similar to Mev's skill, is it not?" I mused.

"Hers is more powerful. She not only senses emotion but intent as well. She can also glimpse visions of the future where my skill is wholly focused on the present."

"By the stones," Adren whistled.

"I appreciate you sharing your skill with me," I said, the words less like gravel coming from me than I would have expected. "But the story of what happened that day is not mine to tell."

Adren frowned. "Maybe not all of it. But your part, perhaps."

I thought on my friend's words. Rowan waited, but did not press. I looked around the tavern, noticing fewer seemed to be staring at us now. Sharing some form of an explanation would do little harm.

"I knew nothing of the queen's capture. Just after I allowed my father entry to the Temple, I sensed a rockslide from the mountains behind us. I ran to it and stopped it from destroying the Temple. By the time I returned," I said, regret nearly choking me, "the Gate was closed."

Rowan did not ask questions, and I respected him for it. But he was an intelligent man and could deduce some of the details. Namely, of my father's deceit.

"Did you tell Mev this?"

"No."

"She needs to hear of it."

I disagreed. "There are no excuses for my role in the Gate's closing. And though I cared little for his methods, I never mourned the humans' inability to continue to inhabit Elydor. Mev's anger is justified."

"She loves you, Kael. And will forgive you," Rowan said, despite the tick in his jaw. His words were softly spoken, and I did not ask if they were his opinion or if he'd felt her emotions toward me.

"Just one question, and I will drop the matter."

I looked to Adren who simply shrugged his shoulders as if to say, "He's human. What can I say?" "What question?"

"Would Mev wish for you to decide for her, whether or not her forgiveness is warranted? Or would she prefer to make that decision herself?"

He knew the answer to that as well I did. "I need more ale."

33

MEV

"Perhaps you should wait a few days."

That, from Lyra.

I turned from the Aetherian Gate to look at my father. He agreed. I knew because he'd spent the day attempting to dissuade me. Comforting him, and myself, with the knowledge that, if it did work, I could likely return, I finally asked him point blank to take me here.

I had to know.

Was I stuck in Elydor or did the fact that others had attempted to pass through since my arrival have no bearing on my own journey? After all, I shouldn't have gotten through in the first place. It stood to reason that there was something unique about me that had enabled the portal to open, despite the fact that Kael's father had closed it.

Kael.

There was a chance this did work, and I could not return. Could I really live with that? Never seeing him again? And on such bad terms? It was like the ultimate "no contact" after a breakup, but this time, there would be no temptation to check their social media profile or send that text.

There was a part of me that wanted to go back for that very reason. If there was ever a complicated relationship, it was mine and Kael's. I was as angry as when my father told me about Kael's role in my mother's abduction, but still... his intentions toward me were pure. He had helped safely reunite me with my father and, even in the throne room, had sought to protect me.

He loved me, and I loved him. That should be enough, but this wasn't Earth. Our fathers were enemies for good reason. And worse, Kael had asked me to trust him knowing he wasn't giving me that same trust back.

"Mevlida?"

I had no words. My desire to stay, to see him again. Talk to him. Kiss him. Make love to him. It was almost as strong as the urge I had to step through and be surrounded by familiar sights and sounds. I imagined wrapping Clara in my arms and thanking her for being such a good friend. Going home and telling my mother everything. She'd think I was crazy, of course, but she had to know.

"I will bring her back," I said, not for the first time.

That was the plan, if the Gate was open for me. I'd step through, go home and tell Mom. We'd make our way back to York and come through again. My parents could reunite. By then, I wouldn't be so angry at Kael because I'd miss him so much. It was a perfect plan, except for all the things that could go wrong. Namely, my inability to come back.

I only had to reach my hand up, as I'd done on the other side, and watch the symbols of Elydor come alive. I looked at each now, understanding them. Winds for Aetheria. Stones for Gyoria. Waves for Thalassaria.

"Where are the carvings for Estmere?"

Neither my father nor Lyra spoke. There was no need. As soon as I asked the question, I knew the answer. No humans had sat on the Council. They may have been able to pass through, but only because their right to do so was closely monitored and controlled. For all intents and purposes, the humans were not a legitimate clan in Elydor.

And that was the reason there were no symbols of Estmere carved into the marble. How could they be so advanced in some ways but have such little foresight when it came to the damage such divisiveness would wreak?

I had said my goodbyes. All that was left to do was place my hand up and either watch the energy of the Gate come alive or be crushed with the knowledge that it was as closed to me as it had been for the others.

Heart pounding, I approached it as the familiar sting of tears forming clouded my vision. If I looked back now, I would run into my father's arms. I would call Kael's name, mourning the loss of a love I couldn't explain even if I tried. More of me wanted to stay than return home, but the people who loved me there needed answers. And there was a comfort in the familiar, too.

Do something each day that scares you.

It was one of my favorite quotes, but deliberately staying in a place where people wanted you killed was a hell of a lot different to getting up to speak in front of a crowd. What if I stayed? Talked to Kael? Spent some time with my father.

This wasn't just about me though. It might not happen for a long while, thanks to the passing of time here versus on Earth, but eventually the day would come where Clara had to step into my mother's house and tell her I'd disappeared. I could not let that happen.

Wiping my face, I reached up.

I pressed my hand onto the etchings, waiting for the hum and their illumination. Waiting for the blue glow. But nothing happened. I pressed a second hand, my father's instructions still ringing in my ear.

"That illumination, as you call it, is the Gate coming alive. When it was open, it remained that way at all times until King Balthor closed it. Simply walk through, as you did the first time, and keep your eyes closed. It's easier, that way."

But I couldn't walk through a wall. It didn't take an expert to realize nothing was happening. The Gate was, for all intents and purposes, still closed.

Pulling my hands back, I turned. Even through my tears I could see there were more people in the room than there had been when I'd approached the Gate. One of those people was Kael.

It was him I ran to.

Kael opened his arms to me as I soaked his tunic. He held onto me as if he'd never let go. I had no idea when he'd come in. Or what my father thought of this display. Or how to make sense of the fact that, even though I'd come through the portal in York, it seemed to be closed to me going back. The only thing I knew was that I never, ever wanted to let go.

"You were going to let me pass through," I said finally, through sobs and as many tears as that first time I'd broken down.

"It was your choice to try. I'd not take that from you."

This wasn't the same Kael I met. But I supposed I wasn't the same Mev either.

"I can't go back." That fact was beginning to crystallize, the implications washing over me in waves of nausea. When we did finally separate, my father was right there. Wiping away my tears, in his unique air-king way, glaring at Kael, but saying nothing.

"We will open it again. I vow to you, daughter, we will find a way."

I went from one man's arms into another's. "My mother—"

"We will reopen the Gate," he said, letting me go. That was when I noticed Kael's companions.

"Rowan." I went to him, nearly smiling at Kael's expression as I hugged the human.

"That's enough," Kael said, his voice familiarly gruff.

"He has something to tell you," Rowan said, pulling away and looking at my father. "To tell you both."

If Kael wasn't pleased with Rowan before, he definitely wasn't now.

"That can wait."

"No," a man next to Rowan said. "It cannot."

Who was he?

Kael reached for my hand, and I took it. He addressed my father.

"I knew nothing of your wife's abduction. It is true, I stole the Crystal. It is also true I gained entry into the Temple for my father and... another. The moment I did so, before my father joined me, a rockslide called my attention. By the time I returned, it was done. I do not tell you this to excuse my actions but only so you can know... I never would have allowed it. At least, not in that way."

Before my father could react, I stared incredulously at Kael. "Why did you let me believe otherwise?"

"Because he is a hard-headed fool who thought he deserved to be punished for lying to you," the newcomer said.

"Mev, this is Adren. My right-hand man. And best friend."

Adren bowed. "I am pleased to meet you, Princess Mevlida."

"Mev," I said, absentmindedly. "How did you come to be here?"

"I will tell you later," Kael said. "Are you okay?"

Was I?

I looked around the room. It was filled with people who loved me, and who I loved in turn. People who had risked their lives for me. Family. Friends.

Kael.

He would have let me go. Not because he wanted to, but to honor my choice.

"I will be," I said, "if we can find a way to reopen this thing before my mother learns of my disappearance."

"I will make that happen," my father said, resolute. And clearly unhappy with Kael's presence, evidenced by the way he glared at our joined hands.

"*We* will make that happen." Kael let go of my hand, moved to stand before my father, and bent down on one knee. Before I could stop him, he bowed his head.

"As recompense for my involvement in closing the Aetherian Gate, I offer myself into your service and vow to reopen it."

Kael on his knees, before my father, was a sight I couldn't really reconcile. I wasn't sure who looked more surprised. Lyra, Rowan, Adren... or the King of Aetheria.

Probably, the latter.

He recovered quickly. "I cannot accept the word of King Balthor's son."

Kael and I had a lot to talk about, but remembering the sleepless night when I'd thought he might be in danger, and the torture of turning him away this morning knowing how much I loved him, firmed my resolve.

My father had asked Lyra how much I'd learned under her tutelage. It was time to show him. I knew the precise moment when he felt the channel between us open. My father looked directly at me, ignoring Kael.

He is also the man who brought me safely to you. We've heard the rumors. Ask him if they are true.

My father's smile when I began whispering to him made me feel like a young child who'd just received praise from a parent they adored.

"Is it true you battled your brother to allow Lyra and Mevlida to escape?" my father asked Kael.

"It is."

My heart lurched at his admission. Kael loved his brother above all. Why did it have to be Terran, of all people, to come after me?

We only talked about my Aetherian abilities but not about the ones passed down from my mother. I didn't know until coming here that I had any, but those have manifested too. I can sense intent, and sometimes, future intent too.

My father's kind eyes widened.

Why did you not tell me?

I didn't trust myself with these newfound abilities, until now. But I can tell you for certain, Kael and I are meant to be together. If you're not able to trust him, which I totally get, trust me instead.

Kael hadn't moved or uttered another word. Instead, he remained, knee bent and head lowered, at the mercy of my father.

Do you love him?

As much as he loves me.

It was more powerful, to my thinking, than a simple yes. A

Gyorian prince simply did not bow to the Aetherian king without very good cause.

With a final glance at me, my father looked down at the kneeling prince and hovered a hand above his head. For a second, I thought he'd change his mind. Instead, he placed his hand on Kael's head as my shoulders sagged in relief.

When he stood back a few seconds later and Kael rose, the two stared at one another. Neither smiled. Nor did they shake hands. Instead, Kael bowed, as if my father was his king, and backed away.

"It seems we have much to do then," my father said, turning his attention to the Gate.

Kael took my hand.

"An understatement," I said with a resolve that could only come from being separated from the one person that had loved you unconditionally your entire life. "But we *will* open it. Together."

34

KAEL

It was the same round table I'd walked away from on that fateful day. I was not fully prepared to be here as a sworn man of King Galfrid.

Since yesterday, everything and nothing had happened.

I was installed in a bedchamber as far away from Mev as possible, and when I'd sought her out last eve, the king had stopped me.

"She is asleep."

I had been inclined not to care. Nothing would keep me from her.

"Also, I wish to speak with you."

Except that.

Mev had searched for answers about her father her whole life, living without him, and I would not force a choice between us. That meant the only way forward was a truce between me and the Aetherian king.

So I went with him. We'd talked about Mev, the current state of affairs in Elydor, and the reason I'd left the Summit. We spoke into the morning, reminding me of the years I'd served on the Council. None, even my own father, doubted King Galfrid's character, but our opposing views on the impact of humans on Elydor had never seen us on the same side. Until now.

"Is it not strange to be sitting here?" Adren whispered after Galfrid welcomed everyone.

We'd both been surprised my friend was invited. "Strange is one word I might use."

"Father is looking at you," Mev whispered to my right. In response, I reached below the table and rested my hand on her leg. If the king was looking, which he indeed seemed to be, I'd give him a reason to do so.

Instead of moving my hand, Mev laid hers atop mine.

I dragged my attention away from Mev. From having served on the Council, I knew everyone around the table. In addition to our crew—Mev, Lyra, Rowan and now Adren—the king had brought Eirion and two of his other close advisors. All were briefed on Mev's failed attempt to open the Gate, a vision of which I needed no reminder.

It would haunt all my days to come.

Seeing her lift a hand, saying nothing but wanting to bring down the entire Temple to prevent her from leaving me, had been one of the hardest things I'd ever done.

"Our shared goal," the king said, "is reopening the Aetherian Gate, allowing Princess Mevlida to pass through at will. To bring back the Queen of Aetheria and reunite the humans in Elydor who wish to return."

"The same goal we've had for many years," Eirion pointed out.

He was not wrong.

"There is a difference now." Mev spoke up, her voice strong and clear. "I might not have been able to return, but the fact is, that portal did open for me at The Crooked Key." Mev's chin raised as she looked squarely at Eirion who was, in turn, glaring at me. "I would reiterate my father's wishes for the past to remain as such when it comes to Kael and his companion. He brought me safely here, and I will not accept animosity toward him."

I smartly resisted smiling.

All three looked to the king.

"While she remains in Elydor, the princess speaks with my authority."

After that, there were fewer glares my way. And because of her words, I kept my own at bay as the king spoke once again.

"I would ask for your vow, on the spirit of Elydor, to reveal none of which I am able to tell you."

Silence.

To Mev's confused expression, I whispered, "The spirit of Elydor is our land's essence. Breaking such a vow could disrupt the balance necessary for the magic we wield. Only a king or queen can ask for such a vow. It is rarely requested, or given."

One by one, each of those present offered their vow. Returning Mev to Aethralis, battling Terran, kneeling to the Aetherian king, and now... this. I would be dead to my father when he learned of it.

When it came to me, I paused, sensing Adren's unease. He knew the stakes as well as I. But the die had been cast the moment I'd decided to bring Mev here instead of to my father.

"I vow it," I said. Unsurprisingly, Adren did the same.

"More than eight hundred years ago," the king continued, "I opened the Gate to the human world using the most powerful relics from each of our three clans. After years of studying the ancient texts, it became clear we could only connect to the human realm with the support of all three clans. It took many years to determine the use of the Wind Crystal, the Stone of Mor'Vallis, and the Tidal Pearl were the embodiment of that support. I was not the first to attempt to open a portal to the human realm, but I was the first to wield all three relics without forfeiting my life doing so."

His explanation came as a surprise only to Mev and Lyra. It was clear the king's advisors knew how the Gate had been opened already, the same knowledge my father spent hundreds of years trying to learn himself. He'd told both Terran and me, of course, as we'd helped him accomplish the Gate's closing. We, in turn, told only those who'd accompanied us on that fateful day.

Most interestingly, however, the news did not appear to surprise Rowan. Though Galfrid had asked if I trusted him, the king had revealed little of his own relationship with the royal emissary. It was clear the two knew each other, but that the king had asked him here, asked for his vow and now revealed the biggest secret in Elydor's history to him? I'd always known there was more to Rowan, and this solidified my belief.

"King Balthor devoted his life, those many years, to gaining the same knowledge I once had. He gathered the relics—"

I winced.

"And closed it."

Mev squeezed my hand when, in truth, it was I who should be comforting her. It was clearly a painful memory for the king, and I could never properly atone for the role I'd played. I would try, though, by helping to reopen it.

"I will retrieve the Stone of Mor'Vallis," I said.

A bold claim as it resided, as all knew, in plain sight.

Embedded in my father's crown which he wore at all times, one which was locked inside his bedchamber at night.

"Unfortunately," Galfrid said. "Even with the Stone of Mor'Vallis, the Gate cannot be reopened."

"I am confident," Rowan said, "Queen Lirael will cooperate and offer the Tidal Pearl for such a use."

He knew the inner workings of the Thalassari too? My eyes narrowed, but Rowan ignored me.

"I am not as confident," one of the king's advisors disputed. "She may not hate humans, as Balthor does, but neither has she mourned the Gate's closing."

"I know as well as anyone." Rowan sat back in his seat, the epitome of calm. "How little the queen has aided my people these past years. But neither has she been hostile to us, as you said. And there is a faction within the Thalassari, a growing one, pushing for a closer alliance with us. I believe the tides have been changing for some time."

"Tides." Mev smiled. "Well spoken, Rowan."

"It was unintentional," he teased her back.

Damn human. "How is it you know the queen's thinking?" I asked.

"It matters little," the king interrupted. "Even with the Tidal Pearl, we cannot open the Gate."

Every head in the room turned toward him.

"We also need the Wind Crystal."

I was not the only one confused. Even the all-knowing Rowan appeared perplexed at the king's words, as did his own advisors.

Galfrid sighed heavily, looking in my direction.

"Your father still has it."

Everyone began talking at once, but my eyes never left the king's.

"Impossible. I handed it to you myself."

"Which is how I knew, despite your part in the Gate's closing, you were not complicit in your father's deception in the Wind Crystal's negotiation."

His hand went up for silence. All others quieted.

The king waited, apparently for me to unpuzzle his words. I thought back to that day. After many months of negotiations, my father had sent me north to return the Wind Crystal. In exchange, King Galfrid once again allowed the free exchange of goods across our borders which had been cut off when the Gate had closed.

Adren had accompanied me, but he'd not been allowed into the throne room when I handed the encased Wind Crystal back to Galfrid. The king took it, I remembered now, looked at me and said nothing. I turned and left, the deed completed.

"There was a human with you that day," I said, remembering.

"Indeed. One with similar abilities to my daughter. He is now deceased, but at the time, served as an ally to me and Aetheria."

Similar abilities to my daughter.

Mev sensed intent. Could see pieces of the future. If the king's human advisor sensed intent, but mine was solely to return the Crystal... a knot began to slowly unfurl in my stomach. One of disbelief. And yet, when it came to thwarting King Galfrid, was it surprising? My father had kidnapped a woman with child, separating her for eternity, or so he believed, from her husband.

"It was fake."

King Galfrid nodded. "I know not how he created such a replica, but I could immediately sense its lack of power."

I ignored the collective gasp around the room.

"A power I would have no knowledge of." The Wind Crystal was nothing more than a pretty gem to a Gyorian.

"How could we not have known?" Lyra asked. "There have been instances, these past years, when the Wind Crystal was used."

King Galfrid's smile was a sly one. "Some of those instances, merely rumors of its use. Other times, I did indeed rely on other relics to intensify my magic. But it was never the Wind Crystal, as it's been lost to use for many years."

Stunned silence.

"There is only one who knows of its disappearance," Galfrid said. "And she ensures me that it still resides within Elydor and has not been destroyed."

"Salvia," Mev blurted. "The old keeper of artifacts."

"Aye. Even the new keeper does not know of its disappearance. Which"—he shrugged—"convinces me she is not as capable a keeper as Salvia."

I thought back to Salvia's insistence that there was a disturbance in the Wind Crystal. None knew, at the time, it was not with King Galfrid. But the Aetherian woman had known. What did it mean, that there had been a disturbance? And where was the Crystal now?

"My father knows of its location," I said. "We will find it."

"He will no sooner reveal that location than offer up the Stone of Mor'Vallis," the king said. "I've been searching for it for many years."

The king had obviously not been in Gyoria these past years searching for the Wind Crystal himself. There were few Aetherians who roamed freely in Gyoria. So who had been doing the searching for him?

Rowan.

His expression revealed nothing, as always.

Mev let go of my hand and put both of hers on the table in front of us. "So we recover the Wind Crystal, get the Stone of Mor'Vallis, and reopen the Gate. How shall we begin?"

My father's treachery did not matter. Rowan's secrecy did not matter. That I was now King Galfrid's man did not matter. Only one thing mattered at this moment, and it was the woman beside me. The beautiful, determined Princess of Aetheria.

My princess.

35

MEV

I stood by the window of my bedroom wondering how I'd possibly explain this moment to anyone. Clara. My friends. My mother. It wasn't just the sheer number of stars or the fact that they were brighter, appeared closer, or that some glowed blue, reminding me of the way the etchings came alive in The Crooked Key. There was something else different about this night sky. Maybe that I knew what lay between it and the palace where I stood?

Aetheria didn't just look different from Earth. It felt different too.

I turned at the click, watching the door from across a room that I'd learned was designed for me, the lost princess. Arched windows were draped with deep blue curtains, their embroidered, silver threads depicting wind patterns. Soft, muted shades of cream and sky blue adorned the walls. A grand four-poster bed with a sheer canopy and silk bedding wasn't even the most striking feature of the room. That honor went to a marble fireplace with intricate celestial carvings reaching all the way up to the raised ceiling.

I wasn't chancing a repeat of last night. Giving Kael the key, my father insisting I lock my door even with all of the protections around the palace, I'd prepared for him. Chalk having a lady's maid up to the things I never thought to experience in my lifetime. After a bath that put the huge one in the Wind Haven Inn to shame, she'd given me more clothing than the first day. I had no idea where they came from or how it was possible they fit so well, but tonight was no exception. I could see from Kael's expression he appreciated the nightgown as much as I did. Made from lightweight silk, the fabric a soft, pale blue that shimmered like the early morning sky, it was easily the most beautiful, delicate, thing I'd ever worn.

"Mev..."

He strode to me, Kael's arms open before he'd reached me. I fell into them easily and willingly, our lips meeting and melding. It was a kiss I hoped would never end. When he reached down and lifted my nightgown, I wrapped my legs around him. As purposefully as he'd strode to me, Kael did the same as he climbed the steps to my raised bed.

Placing me on it, he began to undress as I watched.

"I'm going to make love to you. Again, and again, and again."

With every article of clothing he tossed aside, my heart raced. "We don't know what will happen," I blurted, not wanting to have this conversation now after waiting so long for this. But I'd said it anyway.

Since he'd removed his boots and tunic, only Kael's leather breeches remained. He sat next to me on the bed. Reaching up, he began to twist strands of hair through his fingers.

"When you've lived as long as I," Kael began, "you learn to do so with uncertainty. I am unsure how humans can fully grasp such a lesson in one lifetime. But there is one thing you can be certain of, if it brings you comfort."

When he released my hair, Kael's fingers tracing my cheek and jaw, then lower still down my neck, I guessed, "Your love?"

Kael smiled. "That too. But something far greater.",

When I didn't immediately guess, he leaned down and whispered into my ear, "Your ability to choose your own destiny."

Kael sat up.

"As you've done."

"As I've done. And I do not regret it, Mev. Nor did I make any decision lightly."

"But your father. Your clan—"

"My brother will see to our clan. And to my men."

He left out his father. Kael's feelings for him were complicated and always would be.

"How can you be certain you've chosen the right path?"

"The alternative, to be without you, is not acceptable." His answer was swift and assured.

"Because I foresaw it?"

"No. Because I've never felt this way before. We will open the Gate, Mev. And you will choose a path. Here, in Elydor. Or in your realm. Just know, princess"—his lips curved upwards —"whichever path you choose, it will be with me by your side."

Surely he did not mean...

I didn't have the chance to ask him. Kael had leaned down, and this time, the kiss wasn't soft or light. It was one filled with need and promise. He lifted my nightgown, and I shifted under him to allow it. With his hands everywhere at once, I reached between us and began to unbutton his breeches. In seconds, we'd gone from serious discussion to serious about being together.

"I need you," I said as he helped me undo the buttons.

Pushing down his breeches, Kael moved between my legs. Without warning, he spread them. The last thing I saw before his head lowered was Kael's wicked smile.

At the first touch of his tongue, my ass lifted from the bed. I reached down, grasping his hair even though he didn't need any encouragement. Like everything Kael did, he excelled here too, and I wouldn't think too hard on the reason.

My breath came quicker as he plunged in and out with an expertise that could only come from many lifetimes.

Because I've never felt this way before.

The words meant more from him than they would have from any other man. I believed him. Loved him. Never wanted this to end.

His thumbs pressed into my thighs, the pressure, and flick of his tongue, bringing me so close to release. "Please, Kael..." Thankfully, I didn't need to say any more, because I couldn't. But he sensed my meaning anyway, plunging in and out, licking me with such wild abandon, as if he enjoyed it immensely, that my ass squeezed... my muscles tightened... my heart raced and threatened to explode out of my chest as I called his name.

Aware he'd stopped, it wasn't until my eyes popped open that I saw him between my legs, smiling. "That's my princess."

Oh dear lord. That was all it took. At the next flick of his tongue, everything tightened and then released. Letting go so completely, I forgot to breathe. By the time he stopped and scooted up to me, I'd not only recovered but was more than ready to have him inside me. "I need you, Kael."

He positioned himself above me. "I need you too, princess."

With that, he moved slowly, at first. The man was all muscle and hard lines, a glorious sight and even more glorious feeling as he filled me, little by little. I'd imagined this so many times, but the reality was so much better than the fantasy. I tried to grab him by the arms, but it was like holding onto tree trunks. Thrusting my hips up, into him, worked well though. Just like that, he was buried inside me.

"I cannot wait to learn precisely how you like me," he said, moving more quickly. "What gets you off," Kael said, reaching a hand between us. "What makes you moan."

Guess that discussion Clara and I had had not long ago about not being able to orgasm without a vibrator was useless now. Hopefully I'd have a chance to tell her. Some guys really did know how to make it happen.

"That," I said. "That does."

"This?" he asked innocently, burying himself full hilt as his thumb circled my clit. "I wonder what would happen if I flipped you over and did this from behind? Would my princess like that too?"

His words. The feel of him. Watching Kael watch me, his expression as intent as when he used magic. "You are unbelievable," I said, meaning it.

"No." His voice was as silken as the gowns I'd been given. "You are."

It was the guttural tone to his voice, the knowledge of what Kael could do, that nearly sent me over the edge. Again. But I wanted to give him as much pleasure as he was giving me.

"I wonder what my prince likes. If I wrapped my lips around him—"

"Mev," he warned. "You will come first."

I could literally do it any time. He was that good. "Come with me, Kael."

Pulling away his hand, Kael drove hard. I met his every thrust, his lips claiming mine as we climbed together. I clawed at his back, trying to pull him closer, deeper. As if that was possible.

"Kael." I couldn't hold on any longer. Didn't want to.

With a roar of pleasure, Kael thrusted one last time, remaining there as my entire body tensed, my core throbbed and all thought fled for the briefest of luxurious moments. Though he collapsed on me, it wasn't a crushing weight at all. I actually tried to get closer, but there was nothing between us. No shame. No judgment. No space. Just pure bliss and joy and love.

"I love you, princess," he said, before I could say the same.

Kael propped himself up then, and I was glad for it, to be able to look into his eyes. "I love you, Prince Kael of Gyoria."

As soon as the words left my mouth, I regretted them. Would he be welcome home ever again? Certainly not by his father.

Kael kissed my nose.

"Tonight, there is no regret or remorse. There is only the two of us, in this bedchamber, loving each other and making promises to each other that will withstand anything that is to come."

"Then I'll start. I promise you will always have a home with me."

"Careful, princess. In Elydor, a vow such as that, freely given, can constitute a union."

Was he serious? "You don't need someone to marry you? Or witnesses? Or anything?"

"Just a few words."

I didn't need to think. To contemplate. We were meant to be together.

"What are they?" I asked.

He didn't hesitate.

"By the earth beneath us and the stars above us, I vow to stand by your side, honoring the bond we share. With this promise, I bind my heart and soul to yours, now and always."

I'd never felt more sure about a decision in my life. "Prince Kael of Gyoria, by the earth beneath us and the stars above us, I vow to stand by your side, honoring the bond we share. With this promise, I bind my heart and soul to yours, now and always."

He didn't say anything.

"Are you going to repeat them?"

Kael's slow smile hinted at his answer. "I don't need to. I said them already."

My eyes widened. "Are we married?"

"We have entered into a union. So... yes."

"No fucking way."

He laughed, spinning us around so I was on top of him. "There's the Mia I first met."

"A lot has changed since then."

Kael reached up, kissed me, and lay down once again.

"Aye, princess. Everything has changed."

36

KAEL

"You are certain?"

Adren rarely lost his temper, but I'd asked him so many times, my friend appeared almost ready to do so.

"I am certain," he said, though it was clear Adren wished to say something more. We stood in the palace courtyard, his horse readied, waiting for Mev. The others had bid their good-byes earlier but Mev had been in training, as she was each morning. Lyra had returned to her duties so Mev received training from some of the most skilled of all Aetherians, including, at times, her father. The sessions had already begun to pay off. It would not take years, as it did for some, for Mev to see her full capabilities realized.

Adren studied the palace over my shoulder.

"Could you ever have imagined?"

"Never. To have pledged myself to a woman, both human and Aetherian? To live in Aethralis, in the palace, no less? Nay. Never."

"And yet, I've not seen you happier in all my days."

That I was. Mev and I reveled in learning more about each other as I watched her continue to flourish.

"I like it not."

"Being happy?" he teased, deliberately misunderstanding.

"Adren—"

"We've discussed this, many times. There is no better way."

"Tell no one," I reiterated. "Not even Terran."

On this, Adren and I disagreed. He thought my brother could be trusted, and I believed so as well. To a point. Or more accurately, until my father was involved. He clung to the man our father was rather than the one that had been consumed by hate.

"Not even Terran," he agreed. "Do not look so worried. They will believe me."

I was not so certain. The bond between Adren and me was well known, especially by my brother. If he suspected Adren was anything but disgusted by my union with Mev—if he had any inkling Adren's purpose in returning to Gyoria was as a spy—his life would be in danger. It would not matter that he was a celebrated warrior. His ties to me, a known traitor as my father will have labeled me, would be Adren's downfall.

"I cannot say how much time it might take to learn the Crystal's location without raising suspicion."

More time than Mev would be comfortable with, do doubt.

"Apologies," Mev said, running up to us. I'd felt her coming and grabbed her by the waist as she tried to pass. Kissing her head before she broke free and went to Adren, I watched the two embrace.

"I do not want you to do this," she said, squeezing him. My chest tightened at the sight of them. Adren's loyalty to me had been unwavering. It was I who had fallen in love with Mev, forcing this situation. But Adren had said repeatedly, it had been his choice to follow me here as it was his choice to spy for us now. My father closing the Gate had never sat well with him, and Adren claimed there were many Gyorians who felt the same but were too loyal to the king to admit as much. It would be a delicate balance, aligning himself with such people while searching for the Wind Crystal.

At least we knew where the Stone of Mor'Vallis was located. When it was time, I would return to claim it and already had a plan to do so. But first, we needed the other artifacts.

"I will find it," he said, releasing Mev. "You have my word."

"We do not deserve you," she said, tears falling onto her cheeks. I'd become accustomed to Mev's show of emotion and loved that part of her. I loved every part of her, actually.

"There are no need for tears. It is a joyous day."

"How so?" she asked as my arm slipped around Mev's waist.

Adren turned, pointing to a spot far down the mountain. "Rowan," he said, "is well on his way. The wheels have been set in motion and that Gate will be reopened."

"Thank you," I said. There were no other words to offer such a man as Adren.

He bowed, unnecessarily. "It is my honor to serve you both."

With that, he left. Mounted and rode away, following Rowan's path. They'd decided the two should not be seen together.

Mev sighed. "I feel useless, sitting here while they put themselves in danger."

"I understand well. Sending Adren back alone does not sit right with me, but neither of us are likely to discover the Crystal's location in Gyoria."

"We'd be more likely put in a dungeon instead."

I wished I could disagree with her. "As to Rowan, he will be safe enough. The man is clearly a skilled negotiator."

"I wish I could go with him. From all I've heard, Thalassaria sounds amazing."

"It is beautiful. You will see it, someday."

Mev frowned. "You're still mad at him?"

I sighed, weighing my words. Mev disliked any tension among us. Was I still angry with Rowan? "He could have told us sooner."

"True. But you can understand why he did not?"

Perhaps. And Mev was right, that Rowan had proven a loyal member of our group and clearly his goals were aligned with our own. That he was traveling to Thalassaria to negotiate with Queen Lirael for use of the Tidal Pearl, when such a time became necessary, was proof of it.

"You are so stubborn."

I leaned down to kiss her, lingering long enough to earn a whistle from a passerby. So many damn Aetherians in Aetheria.

"You love me despite it."

"I do."

"We will open it, Mev. I promise."

"I know we will," she said, her arms tightening around me. "And maybe, that's what I'm afraid of."

EPILOGUE
ROWAN

"Greetings, friend."

Unfortunately, these were not my friends at all. I smiled at the travelers anyway, glad at least they were human. Against my own kind, I had no worries. Against magic, I was always at a disadvantage.

"Greetings," I said, wishing now I'd stopped at the inn. What had I been thinking to push on, when no good was to be found riding this road in the dark? Getting as quickly as possible to the queen was important, but remaining alive in the meantime was just as so.

"Alone on an abandoned road in Southern Aetheria, friend?"

There were three of them. The kind of humans that gave us a bad name. Mercenaries, most likely. All three carried swords, but their armor was old, consisting of padded gambesons and helms, but not much else.

"Heading home," I said, when in truth my home was north of here.

"That is a fine-looking horse." Their leader rode toward me.

My father once said I could charm my way out of any predicament, and it was true, my inclination was usually to do so. To make friends, as these men called me, and not enemies. But I also knew the type of men I was dealing with. They were intent on robbing me, and nothing would stop them.

Nothing short of force.

Sighing, I tried to head off the inevitable.

"He is a fine horse, but also mine. Attempting to claim him, or any other of my possessions, will see this night as your last. So if you would allow me to pass—"

The first man who had spoken laughed, a cruel and overly loud sound. I didn't need to be close enough to him to sense his emotions. He was scared. Rightly so.

"Get off the horse."

The leader was, not surprisingly, the largest of the three men. By the way the others looked to him, it was clear he would have to be my first target.

I had no wish to spill blood this night and tried one last time.

"I have no quarrel with you. But if you do not allow me to pass, none in your party will be left alive to follow me and slit my throat in my sleep." The man closest to me gave pause for the first time, glancing nervously behind him.

The leader shook his head.

Dammit to hell. I hadn't been lying. The first time I'd shown mercy in a similar situation, the men who'd attempted to rob us later followed my mentor and me. If not for his keen senses, we may have indeed died in that roadside camp. Instead, it had been a hard lesson. Honor was indeed a virtue, but not as coveted as remaining alive. When the two could not be balanced, the latter took priority.

When the man closest to me reached for his sword, a flick of my wrist sent my dagger slicing across the throat of their leader. Clutching his neck, blood spilling between his fingers, he fell from his mount.

The second man was slower to react, fumbling for his sword. I dismounted and was at him in two steps, pulling him down and, aware the third man had also dismounted, dispensing him with one thrust. He crumpled at my feet as my new attacker tried to send me to my maker from behind.

I swerved my body out of the way, side-stepping his swing and driving my knee into his gut. He gasped, doubling over, and I brought my fist down hard on the back of his neck, having no wish to clean more blood than was necessary from my tunic.

He dropped.

All three were dead. An unfortunate circumstance, but an unavoidable one.

Wiping my blade clean, I muttered, "Should have let me pass."

Burying the men, without the aid of a Gyorian or even a shovel, stole precious time from my journey. By the time I did so, and rode off-course to send the men's horses into a small village for safe-keeping, it was nearly dawn.

Finding a place to clean and rest was now my new goal. Reminding myself it would likely take Adren weeks, if not longer, to learn the location of the Wind Crystal, I vowed to rest at dusk and travel only by day even though a pit-stop was necessary before I headed to Thalassaria. One that would give Adren an advantage in his quest.

I needed to see my mentor.

I needed to speak with the Keeper.

ACKNOWLEDGMENTS

A heartfelt thank you to my family and friends for your unwavering support and encouragement.

To my editor, Megan Haslam, for your invaluable guidance, and to Andrea Hurst and Katie Reed for helping bring this book to life. And to my readers—thank you for joining me on this otherworldly adventure.

ABOUT THE AUTHOR

C.L. Mecca is the author of historical romance and also writes contemporary small town romance as Bella Michaels.

Sign up to C.L. Mecca's mailing list for news, competitions and updates on future books.

Follow **C.L. Mecca** on social media here:

facebook.com/MeccaRomance

instagram.com/meccaromance

tiktok.com/@clmeccaauthor

Printed in Dunstable, United Kingdom